A COTSWOLD MYSTERY

Despite the catastrophic outcomes of her three previous house-sitting commissions, Thea Osborne is convinced nothing can go wrong on her next assignment. The Montgomerys have asked her to look after their house and elderly mother, Granny Gardner, while they take a holiday. The arrival of Jessica, Thea's daughter, is a welcome surprise, and while Granny's behaviour is peculiar, so too are the Montgomerys' instructions to keep her trapped in the house. When a body is discovered next door it isn't long before Thea and Jessica find themselves involved and the quiet village turns out to have very sinister undertones.

A COTSWOLD MYSTERY

A COTSWOLD MYSTERY

by

Rebecca Tope

Magna Large Print Books
Long Preston, North Yorkshire,
BD23 4ND, England.

British Library Cataloguing in Publication Data.

Tope, Rebecca
    A Cotswold mystery.

    A catalogue record of this book is
    available from the British Library

    ISBN   978-0-7505-2825-2

First published in Great Britain 2007 by Allison & Busby Ltd.

Copyright © 2007 by Rebecca Tope

Published in Large Print 2008 by arrangement with
Allison & Busby Ltd.

Magna Large Print is an imprint of Library Magna Books Ltd.

Printed and bound in Great Britain by
T.J. (International) Ltd., Cornwall, PL28 8RW

*For some of my oldest friends
Dot, Margot, Sally and Willow*

Author's Note

The house at the centre of this story is in Blockley High Street. I don't know which one it is, and neither does anybody else. Details of walls, alleys and gardens have wantonly deviated from reality.

CHAPTER ONE

Thea had been warned, but she couldn't help feeling the warning was inadequate when it came to the point. Mr and Mrs Montgomery – Ron and Yvette as they insisted on being addressed – had instructed her to use the street door to the 'cottage', and not the one connecting the two dwellings from the inside. 'Granny would probably die of shock if you just walked in on her,' laughed Yvette. 'And we don't want that, do we?'

Ron's flickering left eyebrow had seemed to say *Don't we?* but both women ignored him.

So Thea had to stand for four interminable minutes at the door, knocking, ringing and calling 'Mrs Gardner?' repeatedly. Feeling embarrassingly conspicuous, she considered giving up and trying again later. There was no urgent need to meet her new charge, in any case. It was mainly out of curiosity that she had headed straight for the cottage even before unloading her bag and settling into the main house. Despite the emptiness of the street, she could feel eyes on her from surrounding windows, and her dog was whining in the car nearby.

She had ample time to get to know Blockley High Street in all its charming particulars. The deep orangey-yellow of the stone; the raised pavement, keeping pedestrians well away from the almost non-existent traffic; the individualism of each house. On the opposite side from where Thea stood, the ground fell away so that the houses were considerably lower than the street. Behind them the land rose again, displaying fields and woods to the south.

Eventually her wait was rewarded when a tiny woman began to jingle keys and locks on the other side, muttering quite audibly, 'Now who can this be, just when I'm having my nap?' Thea could see her head and shoulders through the stained glass that filled the upper part of the door.

'Hello?' she said, the moment the white head was visible through the slender crack between door and frame. 'Mrs Gardner? I'm Thea Osborne. Your daughter has asked me to stay here while they're away. I'm sure they told you I was coming.' She tried to sound warm but unpatronising, loud but not strident. Nobody had mentioned that Granny was deaf.

'My daughter's gone,' came the firm reply. 'No use looking for her.' The door did not open any further, and all Thea could see was a small face looking suspiciously up at her.

'Yes, I know. I'm here instead. Can I come in for a minute?'

The door remained firmly where it was, giving Thea no further sight of the person inside. 'What for? I was having my nap. I always have it at three o'clock sharp.'

Thea refrained from advising the old woman that it was actually half past eleven. 'All right,' she said. 'I'll come back later, shall I? I'm staying in the main house while Yvette's away with her husband.'

'Oh, *Yvette*,' came the dismissive response. 'Don't talk to me about Yvette. Much she cares about her poor old mother. Selfish hussy she is.'

Thea made no attempt to defend her temporary employer with protestations about expense and trouble devoted to ensuring Granny's welfare. Instead, she withdrew and made her way along the pavement to another door in the same deep-yellow building in the historic Georgian centre of Blockley. This time she did have a key, given to her by the Montgomerys earlier in the month, which she quickly used. Directly in front of her was a small cupboard, containing the burglar alarm. She had to tap in 8442 before sirens yowled and klaxons clanged, or whatever ghastly noise had been primed to go off if the aborting numbers were not employed. Her hand shook with the sense of urgency. 'Bloody thing,' she muttered.

Out in the street, her spaniel waited impatiently for release from the car. With a rapid glance around the large hall, Thea retraced her steps, carefully leaving the door on the latch.

Despite the almost total absence of traffic in the quiet centre of the little town, she held tightly to the dog's collar, clipping a lead to it before letting her jump out of the car. A cry of delight filled the air a few seconds later.

Granny Gardner was now standing in her wide-open doorway, wearing an orange dressing gown and green fluffy slippers, her hands clasped together under her chin. 'A spaniel!' she crowed. 'The lovely little *darling!*'

Accustomed to adoration, Hepzibah strained to approach her admirer. Thea permitted herself to be dragged along, and watched resignedly as the friendship was rapidly cemented between the ancient woman and the exuberant dog. Neither paid Thea the slightest attention, until at last Granny glanced up at her. 'What's her name?' she asked.

'Hepzibah,' said Thea, feeling the usual shiver of regret at the rashness of her choice. 'Hepzie for short.'

'And a long tail! You don't see that very often. Doesn't it make a difference to the shape!'

14

It was true that Hepzie had a different outline to most cocker spaniels, truncated at the buttocks as they almost always were. Thea nodded, recognising that her initial assessment of old Mrs Gardner might have been hasty. She certainly knew a bit about dogs and Hepzie clearly judged her to be a highly acceptable example of humankind.

'Who are you, dear? I haven't seen you in Blockley before, have I? You're not one of these celebrity people, are you?'

Thea laughed. 'No, no. I'm staying in the house here – your daughter's house. She's asked me to be on hand if you need anything. She's gone away, you see.'

Mrs Gardner frowned. 'Went away a long time ago, didn't she?' She was now sitting on her doorstep, with the dog between her knees. The over-long ears and huge liquid eyes were doing their irresistible spaniel thing, the old lady's hands gripping the soft neck affectionately. 'Is she coming back?'

'Next week, yes. She's gone for ten days. To India. I'm staying in the house.' Thea heard herself shouting. Already she had lost count of the times she'd repeated herself. There had to be a better way to get the facts across.

'They cut the tails off for a reason, you know,' said Granny, fingering Hepzie's plumy appendage. 'I could do it now for you, if you like. I've got a good knife.'

15

This abrupt change of tack sent Thea's heart thumping. She took a step back, still holding the dog lead, jerking the animal. 'No!' she choked. 'Absolutely not.' She was disturbed to find how seriously she took the threat. Hepzie jumped away from her new friend and stood on the pavement watching and wagging.

The old woman smiled, showing unnaturally perfect dentures. 'Only joking, lovey,' she chuckled. 'But if you ask me, it spoils the line. And see how she wags – it's all in the hips, not really the tail at all.'

Thea looked at her squirming pet and the way her entire spine curved with the effort of expressing pleasure. 'Well, she's keeping it,' she said. 'It wouldn't be legal to cut it off now, anyway.'

With a sudden movement, Mrs Gardner stood up. She seemed remarkably supple for her years, which surely had to be at least eighty, since her daughter was sixty or more. 'Well, mustn't keep you,' she said. 'Julian's going to be here soon, and look at me – not even dressed yet! Do you happen to know what time it is, dear?' She squinted up at the bright March sky. 'Looks like dinner time. I thought I was due for my nap, but that's wrong, isn't it?'

'It's just about twelve o'clock,' said Thea. 'Would you like me to help you get your lunch ready? Mrs Montgomery did say you

16

might need a bit of a hand.'

'Who *are* you, anyway?'

Here we go again thought Thea with a sense of helpless irritation. 'My name's Thea, Thea Osborne. I'm here to keep an eye on things while your daughter's away. Your daughter Yvette. She must have told you.'

The gaps in Granny's memory were almost visible. Her small brown eyes seemed to sink further into her head, flickering from side to side in an effort to capture missing facts. 'I forget things,' she admitted. 'I can't tell you how frightening it can be.'

The lucid confession startled Thea yet again. It was like being in the presence of a growing group of people, all inhabiting one body. With a surge of hope, she rushed to engage this new one while it lasted. 'It must be awful,' she sympathised. 'Does it help to write things down?'

'A bit. Except I can't always find the note-pad. Julian says I should tie it onto myself. He's probably right. You'd better come in, hadn't you? I'm making a spectacle of myself out here like this. Though I don't suppose it's the first time.'

Blockley's streets were as near-deserted as those of most Cotswold villages, in Thea's recent experience. The Montgomery house was halfway along a street that seemed to go nowhere, with a church at one end and a dense-looking patch of woodland at the

17

other. Thea had almost despaired of finding it, when she had paid a visit a month previously to take her instructions from the absent couple. Blockley was much larger than the villages she had worked in up to now. It had a Post Office inside a general foodstore and a coffee-shop-cum-deli, public lavatories and a children's playground. There was a hotel called The Crown Inn taking up a considerable section of the High Street, only a little way along from the house Thea was minding. More undulating streets snaked out from the centre in all directions, causing Thea considerable confusion. The buildings were all in a natural bowl, surrounded by sheltering hills, but the bowl had lumps in it, making for sudden steep drops and strange levels.

Two young mothers with toddlers in pushchairs approached, making rather a production of navigating around Thea, Granny and Hepzibah. They manifested no reaction to Granny's dressing gown.

'Thanks,' Thea accepted the offer. 'Is it all right to bring the dog?'

'Of course.'

Only when standing inside Mrs Gardner's living room did Thea remember she had left the door to the main part of the building unlocked and undefended. Surely, she decided, it couldn't hurt for a few minutes. There were so few people about, and the door looked just as usual. If a very improbable opportunistic burglar did happen to try it, how was he going to make his escape, carrying an armful of the Montgomerys' possessions? The idea was ridiculous and she relaxed.

'I understand there's a connecting door between you and the main house?' The building must originally have been a fine family mansion erected for a well-to-do wool merchant or something of the sort. Granny's cottage comprised a one-bedroomed annexe at one end, with its own street door, which had doubtless once been the tradesmen's entrance.

'She locks me out,' said the old woman with a scowl. 'Thinks I'll steal her silver, I suppose.'

'I think she does it to make you feel safe and independent,' said Thea, inventing quickly. It had seemed peculiar when it had first been explained to her, but then families *were* peculiar a lot of the time.

'Julian usually comes to see me about now,' said Granny with a frown.

Learning fast, Thea accorded this statement some scepticism. Whoever Julian might be, any theories concerning his routine could easily be a decade out of date. Or he could have told her that today would be different. Nothing the old woman said could be taken at face value. It was both

19

unsettling and oddly liberating. Granny herself seemed to have a similar feeling.

'Never mind,' she said. 'I expect I forgot something they told me. If I could find my notepad, it might enlighten us.'

Thea liked the 'us'. It suggested that she had managed to cross some threshold and was now at least for the moment accepted. 'Can I help you with your lunch?' she asked.

But things were already slipping. 'Lunch? No, no dear. I ought to wait for Julian. Anyway, it isn't time. Look – I'm not even dressed yet. Off you go, there's a good woman. Leave me to get on. *Who* did you say you were?' The eyes were searching Thea's face for clues, the mouth rigid with suspicion.

Thea saw no sense in persisting. She caught the spaniel's eye and together they went to the door. 'I'll come and see you later on,' she said, wondering whether she would ever again gain admission to the slice of the building that was Granny's cottage.

Back in the larger section that was home to the Montgomerys, she tried to remember everything she had been told a month previously. The connecting door to Granny's quarters was off the hallway. 'We keep it locked, actually,' Yvette had said. 'It sounds awful, I know, but Granny needs her boundaries kept very firm. You do need to trust us on that point. She would get confused if she could make free with our part of the house as well as her own. I strongly recommend that you keep the door locked, for your own sake. If you need to get to her quickly, the key's up here, look.' She indicated a hook on the wall from which hung a three-inch silver-coloured key.

'Does your mother have a key as well?' Thea asked.

'No she doesn't. Not now. We gave her one originally, but she lost it within a week. Now we're rather pleased about that. We realised that letting her have a key would defeat the object, if you see what I mean.'

'So how does she communicate with you if she wants something?'

Yvette blinked a little at this. 'Well – I suppose she waits until *I* go to *her*. She could bang on the door if it was really urgent.'

'She could telephone us,' Ron said with a grin. 'Except she hates the phone. Never uses it if she can help it.'

'And it would be strange to telephone somebody just the other side of the door,' Thea said, well aware that she was trespassing on sensitive ground. The Montgomerys let the remark fall unanswered.

For all the oddness of the arrangements, Thea liked Yvette. She was a quietly spoken, soft-faced woman, who seemed to have worries lurking perpetually at the back of her mind. Ron was big and fleshy, well versed in social banter. He had clasped Thea's hand between his great hams and assured her that she was about to save their sanity. 'We thought we'd never get away again,' he laughed.

Thea's pulse had quickened with apprehension. Was Granny Gardner such a burden as all that? Yvette hurried to correct the impression Ron had given her. 'It's not as bad as it sounds,' she said. 'My mother's quite capable of looking after herself. We often go whole days without seeing her at all. It's just – well, she does need to have somebody here, to keep an eye ... just in case ... I mean ... well.' Her face crumpled with the difficulty of it all.

Ron gave his wife's arm a quick squeeze. 'No more to be said,' he supplied. 'No need to think Granny's going to misbehave herself.'

But Thea had learnt from past experience that it was vital to extract full details from the house owners before it was too late. 'Could you explain exactly how much she can manage for herself?' she persisted. 'I don't have any nursing qualifications, you know.'

'She's perfectly fit physically,' Yvette said, with an obvious effort to be lucid. 'She can cook and clean and cope with her clothes. She has a few friends in the village and they drop in on her fairly often. But she does get confused. *Lost* might be a better word for it. She forgets where she is and what she's supposed to be doing.'

'And she never seems to know what time of day it is,' added Ron.

'We try to discourage her from going out,' summarised Yvette. 'It's much easier that way.'

Thea tilted her head. 'You don't lock her in, do you?'

Ron snorted. 'Believe me, we're tempted.'

'No, no,' Yvette says quickly. 'But we do try to keep an eye out, and if we see her in the street, we steer her home again.'

Thea had looked out of the street window. 'You can't see her door from here,' she noted.

'Aha!' said Ron. 'But you can *hear* it.' He drew her attention to a small box attached to the wall in the hallway at the foot of the stairs. 'Every time Granny's front door opens, this goes off. It makes a loud buzzing sound – you can't miss it. We only really use it at night, actually, and we'll switch it off before we go, so you can go to her front door and make yourself known to her on your first day. Clever little gadget, though, eh? A chap from Bourton fixed it up for us.' He gave Thea careful instructions on the application of two switches connected to the buzzer. One turned it off when it was sounding – 'You'll need that one,' he grinned. 'It's quite a racket.' The other one was the main activator.

'I see,' said Thea dubiously. The switches were high on the wall, well beyond her reach. Ron, at six feet one, could just touch it, standing on tiptoe. 'I'll need to climb on a chair to switch it on and off, won't I?'

He grinned again. 'You're going to quote health and safety, aren't you,' he said. 'If you fall off the chair, you'll sue us – right?'

Yvette interposed. 'We had to put it high, to prevent Granny from fiddling with it,' she explained.

'So she knows it's there? But I thought she didn't come into this part of the house?'

Yvette and Ron exchanged a glance. 'In theory she doesn't,' said Ron. 'The thing is – when we first had the buzzer installed, she was acting up rather. It's much better now. As to whether she realises it's there – well, who knows what the old dear knows?'

This piece of sophistry felt deeply un-helpful to Thea. She tried to sum up her situation. 'So you want me to stay indoors pretty well the whole time, making sure she stays put?'

Yvette grimaced, showing small regular teeth. 'We realise that's a bit unreasonable – but if you could keep outings to a mini-mum, we'd be grateful. We've tried to supply lots of entertainment for you. About fifty thousand TV channels, for a start. Books. DVDs. Jigsaws. You can use the garden, of course, if the weather's nice. It's very sheltered, with walls on all sides. And it's only for ten days,' she finished brightly. 'We'd have liked to go for longer, to be honest, but–'

'India, you said?'

'That's right. We've always wanted to go. Ron's grandfather was there, and we want to see the places he used to talk about.'

'Will I be able to contact you?' Another crucial question that Thea had learnt to place high on the list.

'Not really,' Yvette's face crumpled again. 'We did wonder about setting up email and using internet cafes, but we decided against it. It would take up so much precious time, you see.'

'So who–?'

Yvette produced a sheet of paper. 'My younger sister, Frances. We don't have much to do with her, but in an emergency, she *is* the next of kin. She's in Cambridge. And our son, Alex. He would come if there was a real crisis. He's fond of Granny and is terribly good with her. Ideally, he'd have stayed here while we were away, but he can never get time from his work. And they've got three little children, so you can imagine how busy they always are.'

'Where does he live?'

Yvette flashed her teeth in another grimace. 'Aberdeen,' she admitted. 'It's a long way to come.'

The message was loud and clear. *Thea, old pal, you're on your own* was about it. Except that she'd already taken precautions against having to endure too much solitude.

'Would it be all right if I had somebody here with me?' She had saved this little bombshell, hoping for an opportune moment to introduce it. This seemed to be it.

Yvette's eyebrows rose. 'Well – we've only set one room aside for you. Do you mean – well, is it somebody you're in a *relationship* with?'

Thea laughed lightly. 'Well, yes. My daughter. She's twenty-one, and a police probationer. We'd be happy to share a room. She has some leave that week, and I thought it would be nice for her to see some of the Cotswolds. Especially in the spring, when it looks so fabulous.'

Ron gave a shrug. 'There are twin beds in the spare room,' he said. 'It wouldn't matter to us, would it, Vetty?'

It had been readily agreed to, although Thea could see the Montgomerys were worried that showing Jessica the local attractions would necessitate an uncomfortable level of absence from the house. 'I can send her off on her own,' she'd assured them. 'With the dog. I mentioned the dog, didn't I?'

Ron had inhaled slowly and deeply. Then he looked at her down his nose. 'We're trusting you on that,' he said sonorously. 'One small well-behaved dog isn't a worry to us. So long as it keeps off the furniture and never *ever* goes upstairs.'

'No problem,' Thea had assured him.

There followed a quick tour of the lovely Georgian house, wonderfully elegant in its proportions, with large high rooms and a lot of very nice furniture. Despite the hi-tech burglar alarm, they seemed relaxed about the possibility of crime. 'It's the confounded Neighbourhood Watch crowd,' Ron grumbled. 'They nagged us into having the thing. But–' he grinned conspiratorially, 'I disconnected it from the back door. There's no point at all having that Fort Knoxified when nobody can get in anyway.'

'They could,' Yvette argued mildly. 'If they came across the two gardens on our right, over Julian's little wall.'

Ron snorted. 'The point is, you don't have to lock it to activate the alarm. If you want to, you can bolt it. It's up to you. As far as I'm concerned, you only need worry about the front.'

Yvette was already moving to other considerations. 'Would you mind doing a bit of dusting?' she asked. 'Is that part of your job description?'

In the absence of cats, guinea pigs, sheep or ponies, this seemed a very reasonable request. 'No problem at all,' Thea had said. 'It sounds as if I'll have plenty of time.'

'Don't be too sure,' Ron had chuckled. 'Granny can be a full-time job, when she's in one of her moods.' Yvette's quick glance of reproach at his tactlessness went blithely unheeded.

Now Hepzie was defiantly curled up in one corner of the luxurious leather sofa, one eye half open, watching her mistress. If there was a way of preventing a spaniel from sleeping on furniture, Thea didn't know what it was. Simpler, then, just to ensure that every hair and fleck was brushed away before the Montgomerys came home. They had settled in easily, after a leisurely tour of the back garden, which sloped gently upwards away from the house. It was a generous size and a peculiar shape. A confusing jumble of houses showed their backs or sides, with small gates and narrow pathways between them. The property to the east was apparently much narrower and extended further back than the Montgomery house, so its side wall blocked the morning light from part of the garden. Where it stopped there was a low stone wall dividing the two gardens, and the neighbouring side was screened with a row of vigorous-looking bamboo. To the west,

Granny's back door opened onto a small area that had been created for her own private use. A rather ugly chain link fence had been erected to enclose it, giving it the appearance of a cage. Three or four plant tubs sat forlornly on a paved patio and a wooden bench was placed in a corner which looked as if it got some afternoon sun, at least. There was no way out of the cage into the main garden.

How mean, thought Thea. And how strange to bar your own mother from using your lawn and perhaps taking part in some small garden tasks. She entertained a distressing image of the old woman peering through the fence, fingers hooked into the links, watching Ron and Yvette strolling amongst the hollyhocks and flowering shrubs, forever prevented from joining them.

But perhaps they had their reasons. Perhaps in certain phases, Granny was prone to chopping down the annuals or digging in the borders. Sometimes, she supposed, you had to be cruel to be kind.

Jessica was due to arrive early on Monday: day three of the assignment. By then, Thea hoped to have got the measure of Granny and her jangled memory, and perhaps have an idea of when it might be safe to venture out for an hour or two, into the classic beauty that was the village of Blockley.

CHAPTER TWO

A thorough tour of the house revealed expensive contemporary tastes unexpected in a retired couple of late middle age. A small study behind the main living room boasted a new computer and all the peripherals. Ron, it seemed, was keen on digital photography, with a state-of-the-art colour printer and laminator to prove it. Evidence of his work was everywhere – strewn over a desk and taped to one of the walls. He obviously favoured textures and subtle gradations of colour, with pictures of stone walls and furrowed fields among his favourite subjects. Yvette's interests lay more in the direction of music, as far as Thea could tell. A picture of her playing the flute was the first clue, framed and hung in the study among the more temporary displays. There was a neat collection of sheet music on a music stand, and a number of books about classic compositions on a shelf in the living room.

It was two in the afternoon, and there were no sounds emanating from Granny's quarters. Probably the person named Julian had arrived, and an intimate lunch was in progress. Outside it was a fairytale spring day. From one of the large windows over-looking the steep slope of one of Blockley's surrounding hills, she could see young lambs leaping and racing, their vivid white legs flashing in the sunlight. Cotswolds, Thea observed – a local breed of sheep boasting thick fleece and eccentric frizzy fringes flopping over their eyes. In the past year, since house-sitting a succession of properties in the area, she had learnt quite a lot about Cotswold sheep.

The assignment she had been given this time was worrying in its contradictions. Watch over Granny, but don't let her into the main house. Listen for her door opening and get her back indoors if she steps into the street. Don't believe a word she says. Let her be as independent as you can, while keeping her safe. Thea's experience so far had suggested a physically fit woman betrayed by her deteriorating mind. Truly appropriate caring would surely include letting her benefit from exercise and fresh air beyond what she could get from her miserable prison of a back garden.

The idea bloomed slowly, one of those obvious links that has to smack you in the face before you see it. Instead of them both suffering unreasonable confinement in-doors, why not go outside together? So simple, and yet so subversive. Granny clearly liked Hepzie – the three of them could walk together through the countryside, or ride to more distant spots in Thea's car. It was so liberating a notion that she clapped her hands like an excited child. The spaniel, still dozing on the sofa, jumped up as if whipped. 'We're going out,' Thea told her. 'For a lovely walk.'

Again she stood on the doorstep of the cottage for several minutes, waiting for Mrs Gardner to respond to her knocks. 'I'm not going to keep on doing this,' she muttered to herself. 'Next time I'm going through that connecting door, whether or not it scares the old bat. This is just ridiculous.'

'Julian?' came a quavering voice that had changed dramatically from that of the morning. 'Is that you?'

'No,' Thea shouted. 'It's me again. Please let me in.' The strategy of convincing the woman that she was a familiar visitor seemed worth a try.

The door opened a few inches. 'The spaniel woman?' Granny said doubtfully, looking at Thea's legs as if searching for Hepzie.

Thea almost cheered. 'That's right! She's waiting for us next door. Now listen. We're going for a walk, and I wondered whether you'd like to come as well. Just to the end of the village and back – unless we feel like going a bit further. What do you think?'

Granny looked down at herself. She was now wearing dark blue trousers and a polo-necked jumper in a colour that echoed the ubiquitous Cotswold stone. She looked completely respectable, except for the bare feet. 'Shoes,' she said. 'I need shoes.'

'You do,' Thea agreed. 'And some socks. Can you go and find them? I'll wait for you.'

It was a gamble, but it worked. Almost instantly, the old woman was back wearing sensible black shoes with elasticated sides, the door thrown wide and a smile on her face. 'What a treat!' she said. 'Melanie used to take me for walks. A great walker, Melanie was. I wonder where she is now.'

A key had been hanging on a hook on the back of the door, and Thea used it to secure the cottage behind them. Granny was still enthusing about going for a walk, her eyes wide and bright.

Thea led the way along the pavement to the next door. She opened it and out jumped Hepzie. Carefully, Thea locked up, deliberately deciding to forget the burglar alarm.

'Can I hold the lead?' Granny asked, as they set out towards the centre of Blockley. 'I won't let her go.'

Thea handed it over unhesitatingly, in spite of the old woman's small stature. She had a birdlike energy, her movements sharp and crisp. 'It won't matter much if you do,' she said. 'She won't run off, and she's fairly

33

sensible with traffic. Not that there is any to speak of.'

It was Saturday afternoon. There were sounds of lawnmowers and smells of garden bonfires. Children shrieked from somewhere some distance away. Glimpses of bright daffodils in gardens came and went as they passed several beautiful old houses. 'Have you lived here long?' Thea asked her companion.

'I believe I was sixty when I came here. Quite long ago, yes.'

'When you retired?'

'Retired,' Granny repeated the word thoughtfully. 'In a way. But Julian was here, you see. Then Yvette wanted to have the house and Julian said I should let her. I can remember all that quite well today.' She looked at Thea, who realised with a slight shock that Granny was in fact much the same height as she was herself, which was only slightly more than five feet. And yet there was a shrunken look to the old woman. Heavens, thought Thea worriedly. If I shrink when I'm old, there'll be nothing of me left. 'I can remember the important things, usually,' Granny prattled on. 'Like how to make a pot of tea and where I keep my clean pants. But I'm very bad with people. They tell me things and expect me to carry every word in my head. Words — that's where the problem lies, you see. I'm not so good with *words*.'

Thea tried to grasp this, with little success. Surely words were crucial to *everything*. How did you find clean pants without an inner voice naming them? Maybe pictures took their place. An image of the drawer containing the garments that worked just as effectively. 'That's very interesting,' she said, meaning it sincerely. 'But you're using words now, quite normally.'

'Yes, I am *now*. But often I don't. Or I say the wrong thing.' There was a disarming tone to this apparent self-knowledge. The soft old face was the picture of blameless innocence, openly presenting her shortcomings for better or for worse. 'People are generally very kind,' she added. 'Very patient.' She smiled trustingly, and Thea was moved. She reproached herself for her own lack of patience. How could anybody fail to be affected by the poor old thing?

'So you remember coming to live here?' she said. 'When the whole house was yours? Where did you live before that?'

'Oh, it's too complicated.' The tone had changed completely to one of irritation. 'My father died, and Yvette had that baby boy and they all told me what to do. It's the doctor that was to blame, you know. I was all right before then.'

Thea tried a mental cut-and-paste exercise, rearranging these remarks in an effort to form a coherent story. The result was something very incomplete, but potentially interesting. She risked another question, already aware that it could prove worse than useless. 'Have you known Julian a long time?'

The old woman smiled at her, something impish in her expression. 'He always comes to me, even now. We watch out for each other. The work, you know. There's still the work to be done.'

'Oh?'

A gloom seemed to fall. 'Trouble. There's some trouble about the site. I forget what it is.'

'Site?' Thea wondered whether the word was actually *sight*, and if so did that mean Julian had eye trouble?

But the flow of confidences had dried up. Hepzie had relaxed into a better rhythm, matching her pace to the old woman's, as they came to a junction.

'Shall we go down here?' Thea suggested, indicating a steep downward-sloping lane to their right. 'I imagine we can find a circular route back past the church, then.' She scanned the area in question, hoping there wouldn't be quite so steep a climb back up again. She was expecting to find the re-nowned Blockley silk mills, down by the river, if not today then sometime during the week.

'Oh, no,' Granny shook her head. 'The big road is down there – the dog would get killed.'

Well, she should know, thought Thea, and amended their course, aiming for the church. Before they reached it, another downward-sloping road forked to their left, and before she could do anything, the old woman had started down it. The shop and Post Office stood at the bottom of the short hill.

'Ooh,' shrilled Granny, as the dog dragged her quickly down the slope. 'I need roller skates for this.'

Thea laughed, and grasped her companion's arm. 'Slow down,' she ordered. 'You'll fall.'

They were quickly on more level ground, with the Bowling Club and children's playground coming up on the right. Looking around, Thea could see houses of all eras, some with informative historical detail carved into stone plaques. Just over a low wall she found a memorial to the Coronation of Queen Victoria. But there were also a number of very new houses, made of the same yellow stone as the others, but starkly clean, with machine-cut edges. It was hard to believe they would ever mellow and settle to blend in with their centuries-old neighbours. 'It's lovely, isn't it?' she said, thinking the word a feeble expression of her true reaction. Like many another Cotswold settlement, the overt self-consciousness detracted from a wholesale enjoyment. It was as if an eye was forever open to the American tourists in their coaches, cameras clicking and whirring. Thea could not prevent herself from wondering what the fate might be of a resident who let weeds grow in their garden, or paint peel on their woodwork.

The pace slowed to a crawl as they savoured the scene. 'I was once a painter, you know,' said Mrs Gardner. 'I sold a lot of pictures of these houses, a long time ago. To the visitors. Some celebrity woman bought eight of them, and paid me two hundred and fifty pounds each. Can you believe that? But I gave it all up. It got boring quite quickly.'

Thea had not observed any paintings in either the main house or the cottage. That didn't prove anything of course, but in her experience painters could seldom resist displaying their own work on their own walls. She was caught short by the realisation that she was doubting everything Mrs Gardner told her. It was an odd, disturbing sensation, as if the world had tilted on a different axis and nothing was as it seemed. But the old woman was again striding out vigorously, the spaniel matching her pace contentedly.

'How wonderful,' Thea said. 'This must be

heaven for a painter.'

'You get tired of so much beauty,' came the deeply lucid reply. 'You start to crave for a bit of ugliness. Isn't that funny!'

'I think I can understand it,' said Thea carefully.

The success of her idea was exceeding her greatest hopes, with interesting conversation a bonus. They could be any two women enjoying a stroll on a spring day, with the well-behaved dog to complete the picture. They turned up beside the green area containing the playground, and right again along a pavement. Thea hoped there would be a way back through the churchyard, and thence a return to the High Street.

'There's Thomas,' Granny said suddenly. 'I don't like him.'

'Thomas' turned out to be an elderly man of military bearing, his spine so straight it looked as if it had been surgically enhanced with metal rods. Unfortunately the effect was spoilt by his waistline, which protruded from the top of his trousers like a huge over ripe peach, impossible to conceal. He was standing in the gateway of a handsome house. His face, as he registered the little group approaching him, was of blank astonishment. 'Gladys!' he squawked. 'What are you doing here?'

'Where's Julian?' the old woman asked him, her voice full of accusation. 'What have you done with him?'

A red flush covered the withered cheeks, and the square shoulders sagged ever so slightly. He looked to Thea for help.

'I'm Thea Osborne,' she offered. 'I'm house-sitting for the Montgomerys, and looking after Mrs Gardner. We thought we'd go out for a walk, it being such a lovely day.'

His distress seemed to deepen. 'But you *can't,*' he protested. 'I mean, she *never–*'

'I expect she just got out of the habit,' Thea said firmly, ignoring the flicker of disquiet that the man's reaction had produced in her. 'We're having a really nice time, actually. I'm hoping we can find a way back through the churchyard. It is all rather hilly around here, isn't it?' She laughed in a tone she hoped was disarming. The man's disapproval made her feel foolish and reckless.

He pulled his lips back from his teeth in an expression that spoke of scepticism and superior knowledge and the constraints around arguing with a strange lady. 'Well, I wish you luck,' he said and strode away.

'He's a stuffed shirt,' said Granny loudly. 'Pity about his beer gut.'

'Does he live here?' Thea asked, in an attempt to avert any further rudeness, and ready to be impressed by the discovery that he owned the handsome house.

'Not *here,* in this house, but here in Blockley, yes he does. He lives close to where I live. Across the street.'

There was a way into the churchyard, as she had hoped. Before reaching it, she paused again, to give Granny a rest and have another good stare at the village. The vista and character changed with every few steps, she was discovering, with the levels a complete chaos. To the south-east of the church there was a riot of roofs, houses crammed close together, many with creepers that would be flowering fabulously in another couple of months.

Hepzie strained at the lead, which was still in the old woman's hand, and they all moved rapidly for a few steps. The church rose before them, the square tower providing bland encouragement of a sort. Granny's breathing had become louder, and her face seemed flushed.

'Are we going to a wedding?' Granny asked. 'Or a funeral?'

'Neither. We'll go through the churchyard and out of the gate on the far side. Then we'll be nearly home again.'

Thea stopped and turned for another long look, back the way they'd come. She could see the ground falling away to where she supposed the former silk mills must be, on the small river that had provided power for the spinning machines and looms. The colours were all in the same spectrum from yellow to brown to red. A painter's paradise, by any standards. She started to say something to that effect, but Granny was not listening. Letting go of the dog, she sank to the ground, her legs crossing like broken scissors, her weight falling onto one outspread hand. 'Ouch!' she squealed, her voice high and childlike.

Thea's first reaction was utter horror at this sudden collapse. But it was immediately followed by an urge to laugh as she saw the old woman's face. Its expression revealed no pain, just surprise and a flicker of satisfaction at the drama of the occasion. Thea paused to assess the situation. 'Don't panic,' she muttered to herself. 'She's not really hurt. Come on,' she said more loudly, deliberately bracing. 'Up again.' She took hold of Mrs Gardner's arm and pulled, to no effect whatever.

Hepzie hovered close, tail wagging slowly, jaw dropped.

'Get up now,' said Thea, slightly cross. 'What's the matter with you?'

The old woman merely giggled, and then winced, clutching her right wrist in the other hand. 'Ow,' she said again. 'It hurts.'

'Problems?' came a voice. Thea looked up to see a very beautiful young man wearing a purple silk shirt and shoes that appeared to be covered in diamonds. His black hair was long and impossibly glossy. His skin was a kind of light black, his features sharp. A chunky gold chain hung around his neck.

'She won't get up,' Thea said. 'She landed on her hand, and now her wrist seems to be bothering her.'

'Hey, Granny! What's your bother, hmm? Let's get you standin', shall we?' The accent was a fascinating mixture of influences, most of which Thea could not identify. The voice itself was rich and warm.

'Hurt myself,' said Granny.

'Do you know her?' Thea asked. For a wild moment she wondered whether he might actually be Mrs Gardner's grandson.

'Hey, no. Course I don't. Just tryin' to assist, that's the whole thing.' The words emerged in an iambic rhythm that made everything sound like blank verse. Who *was* this man, she wondered. He moved behind the collapsed woman and tried to insert his hands into her armpits. She squealed and wriggled and clamped her arms tightly against her sides until he gave up.

'Not goin' to work,' he concluded.

'Well, it's very nice of you to try,' said Thea, sounding hopelessly prim and pinched to her own ears. 'We haven't got very far to go, but even so I can't see her walking back. And there's the dog,' she added foolishly. The dog was the least of her worries.

'Needs a doctor, seems to me.'

Thea huffed a scornful laugh. 'On a Saturday afternoon? Some hope. I don't imagine

there's a doctor in Blockley anyway, is
there?'

'Not so's I know about. I just staying here
a while, with another somebody.' Was it
deliberate, Thea asked herself, this mang-
ling of the language? Some kind of perverse
attitude, marking himself out as a stranger
in the heart of English countryside?

'So?' she demanded. 'What do we do? I
only got here today. I don't know anybody,
either.'

'You's got a car?'

'Yes. Just over there.' She pointed down to
the High Street. 'But I can't drive through
the churchyard, can I?' She forced herself to
think properly. 'But I could bring it to the
gates, I suppose.'

'Then you trots over and fetches it. I wait
with poor old Granny, keeping her amused
and happy, till you drive yourself up here,
and takes her off to the Casualty place.'

'Oh God! That'll be Cheltenham. Or
Gloucester. It's *miles*. Oh, damn and blast
it.'

She felt breathless with the nuisance of it
and the prospect of serious damage to the
fragile old wrist. Not to mention the
embarrassment of such a terrible beginning.
At this rate, her name would be blacklisted
across the whole region and she'd never get
another house-sitting commission. Already
she'd begun to regard herself as a jinx, the

way so much had gone wrong in previous assignments.

'It's getting better now,' said Granny, suddenly bright and considerably more focused. 'I need to stand up, don't I? It isn't ladylike sitting here in the street.'

Thea gave her a searching look. 'Go on then,' she said, not altogether kindly. The young man held out his narrow long-fingered hand, which had peculiar-looking callouses around the tips of the fingers.

'Let me help,' he said, sounding almost normal.

As if a lost spring had suddenly re-appeared, Granny drew her legs together, took hold of the proffered hand with her good one, and was miraculously resurrected. Thea moved closer, and inspected the injured wrist. 'Let me see this,' she said, with authority. Granny cooperated meekly as Thea manipulated the joints, prodding and questioning. 'It's not broken, that's for sure,' she announced. 'Very slightly sprained, at worst, I'd say.'

'You a nurse, then?' said the man.

'No, but I can tell when a wrist is broken,' she snapped. Then she remembered herself. 'Thanks again. I think we'll be OK now, if we take it slowly.'

He smiled, a wide display of wonderfully even teeth, accompanied by a complicated expression. He seemed to be waiting for something with a degree of puzzlement.

'We mustn't keep you,' said Thea, feeling ruffled by his look.

'OK, then,' he said. Disappointment was manifest in his drooping shoulders. Thea frowned. 'You were really very kind,' she repeated. 'It was obviously silly of me to bring Mrs Gardner so far. I don't think she ever really goes out.' As an afterthought she added, 'My name's Thea Osborne. I'll be here until the middle of next week. Maybe I'll see you again.'

He shrugged. 'Don't set your heart on it, lady. Not a lot of folks see Ick twice in a single week.'

Ick? Thea laughed awkwardly. 'Oh, well. Thanks again.'

Granny was a pale shadow of the exuberant self who had charged down the hill with the dog's lead in her grasp. Now she leant heavily on Thea, and mumbled something about bread and sausages. Thea made no attempt to engage in conversation, being too busy reproaching herself for the rash adventure and worrying about the consequences. Hepzie ran free ahead of them, keeping to the pavement, obviously following their scent back the way they'd come for the final few yards.

Safely indoors again, Thea heaved a deep sigh of relief. She doubted whether she'd have the courage to repeat the experiment –

certainly not before Jessica arrived, in any case.

Brooking no arguments, she made a pot of tea in Granny's little kitchen, noticing that the place seemed tidy and clean enough to pass any casual inspection. There were tins of soup and ravioli and pilchards in one cupboard, packs of rice and pasta in another. 'Who does your shopping?' she asked, unwarily.

Mrs Gardner looked at her blankly. 'Shopping?' she said.

'Where does your food come from?' An even dafter question, no doubt.

'The van,' came the reply as if Thea had asked what the big hot thing in the sky was called. 'The van brings it on a Tuesday.'

'Right,' said Thea with a forced smile. 'That's all right then.'

'He's called Sid. He's a very nice man, Sid is. He always has a joke and a wink for me.'

Choosing to believe every word, Thea presented the old woman with a mug of well-milked tea. It seemed the milk came more often than once a week. Two pint bottles of silver-top were in the fridge. Blockley must be one of the last outposts where the milkman delivered every morning – and the stuff still came in bottles.

There was essentially only one room on the ground floor, plus the kitchen and a small hallway which contained the stairs, the front door and the connecting door into the main house. The room was crowded with furniture: a table and three upright chairs, a two-seater sofa, an armchair, television, and a large antique bureau with a bookcase above it. 'That's nice,' said Thea, admiring the mahogany and briefly scanning the spines of the books. 'You have some interesting books, as well.'

Granny flapped a hand. 'Never been much of a reader,' she said. 'They were my father's mostly.'

Hepzie had automatically been included in the little tea party and was sitting up on the sofa, tongue lolling. 'The dog ought not to be on there,' frowned the old woman. 'Never let dogs on the furniture. My mother would have a fit.'

'Oh Lord, I'm sorry.' Thea lifted the animal onto the floor, knowing it would be a struggle to make her stay there. 'Down!' she ordered. 'Lie down!'

It worked for the time being, although large reproachful eyes were fixed on her face throughout the rest of the visit.

There was a neatly folded piece of canvas on the table, from which coloured wools peeped out. 'Oh, are you doing a tapestry?' Thea exclaimed. 'Can I see it?'

Without waiting for permission, she opened it out to reveal an exceptionally large piece of work. The picture was a mother and child, in the classic pose of the infant Jesus with the Madonna. It was more than half completed, the stitching neat and regular. But the colours were bizarre. The child had blue skin, and behind the figures a violent orange tree was taking shape. The Madonna's clothes were spattered with vivid patches of red which were a complete deviation from the colours stencilled onto the canvas. Her face and hands were yellow.

'Gosh!' Thea murmured. 'This must be keeping you busy.'

'Have to use up all my old wools before I die,' chirped the old woman cheerfully. 'And it upsets Yvette,' she added, as if that were a source of great satisfaction.

'I can see how it might,' Thea said. 'A bit different from your paintings, I imagine?'

'Paintings? What paintings, dear?'

Thea was learning quickly. She merely shook her head as if it didn't matter at all. 'Drink your tea,' she urged. 'Before it gets cold.'

'I'm worried about Julian,' said Granny, ignoring the tea.

Thea paused before taking her first sip. 'Yes,' she nodded. 'You said before. Can you telephone him?'

'What?'

'Give him a ring. See if he's all right.'

'But he lives here. Why would I do that? Anyhow, I hate the telephone. Always have.

49

Nasty intrusive thing it is.'

Thea was trying to remember what she'd already been told about the man. 'Here?' she repeated. 'What do you mean? Where exactly does he live?'

Granny waved a hand towards the next house. 'Other side of them. The next building.'

'Julian lives next door to your daughter? That house with the railings? The one that overlooks the garden at the back?'

'Yes, yes,' snapped the old woman. 'But where is he *now*? He *always* comes for lunch. He hasn't come. Has he?' she creased her brow, staring hard into Thea's eyes.

It was a quandary. For all she knew the man had not been in Granny's life for fifteen years. On the other hand, he did get a great many mentions; far more than Yvette or her husband. The old man they'd met had shown no surprise at Granny's reference to Julian, either. But she had detected no signs of life in the house in question since her arrival. It added up to a puzzle which she assumed would solve itself before much longer.

'Perhaps you made a note about it?' she suggested. 'On your notepad. Shall we try to find it?'

Granny Gardner narrowed her eyes. 'Who said you could look at my pad?'

'I don't want to look at it. I just thought it

might help if we could find it.'

'In the bureau, of course. That's where it is.'

'Shall I...?'

But the old woman was already on her feet. She pulled down the front flap, and reached inside. The 'notepad' turned out to be a leather-bound book, the size of a hardbacked novel. Mrs Gardner flicked the pages, showing almost all of them to be blank. Thea stared at it. 'I don't think...' she began. 'I mean, you haven't written much in it, have you?'

Granny hugged the book to her chest. 'Too good to write in,' she said. 'Except the most *special* things.'

Thea knew when she was beaten. 'What about your wrist? Is it better now?' There had been no signs of pain or reduced movement since they'd got indoors.

The old woman had evidently forgotten the whole incident. She looked down at her hands, still holding the book, without any sign of understanding the import of the question. Then she carefully replaced the book in the desk and closed the flap. Thea made her twist and bend the wrist before judging it to be fully restored.

'You're very strong,' she said admiringly. 'You might easily have broken it, falling like that.' But then she realised how light the old body was, putting little real weight on the bones of the wrist as she fell. Mrs Gardner seemed to be composed of skin and sinew and not much else.

Hepzie was on the sofa again, and Thea judged it was time to leave. 'I'm just next door,' she said, speaking too loudly. 'Shout for me if you need anything.'

Granny didn't look at her as she went to the front door and let herself out. Just before she closed it behind her, she heard the familiar question: 'Who *are* you, anyway?'

CHAPTER THREE

Armed with the information that the adjacent house belonged to the missing Julian, Thea decided she was fully justified in trying to locate him and tell him Mrs Gardner was worrying about his absence. It felt as if he could answer a great many crucial questions, at the same time. She shut the dog in the Montgomery house and strolled along the pavement to the next door.

There was no reply when she knocked. She stood at the solid oak door, with a feeling of déjà vu after the long wait that morning outside Granny's cottage. For good measure, she moved to the street window and tried to peer in. The curtains were closed, but a small gap down the middle gave her a glimpse of a shadowy room with normal-looking furniture and no sign of habitation. As she stepped back to the door, and reached to knock again, a very tall middle-aged man approached her. 'Good afternoon,' he said with a friendly smile. 'Can I help you?' He looked over a large bulbous nose at her, and spoke in a hoarse smoker's voice.

'Are you Julian?'

'No, no. I'm Giles Stevenson. I live opposite and a little way down the street.' He
pointed towards some smallish houses,
below the level of the pavement. Curious
little alleyways led down to one or two of
them, and Thea was momentarily distracted
by this detail. Giles Stevenson brought her
back to reality. 'Not answering again, eh?
He's a bit of a recluse, to be honest. Is it
something important?'

'Do you know Mrs Gardner? Mrs Montgomery's mother.' Thea pointed at the cottage.

'Of course! Poor old Gladys. I knew her
when she was a real force to be reckoned
with. Brilliant mind, creative, sure of herself. It's shocking the way she's gone downhill. Mind you, she is ninety-two.'

'Ninety-two! She can't be.' Thea was
stunned.

'It's true, just the same.'

'But I've just marched her all round the
town.' Thea's insides quivered with the
enormity of what might have happened. No
wonder Granny's poor old legs had given up
on her. 'Though it wasn't easy to get her
home again,' she added, with a rueful laugh.

'Well, well. Brave old you. For all we know,
you might have started a whole new trend. I
surmise that you must be the lady Yvette's
asked to come and keep an eye on things?
Did she *tell* you her mother needed to be

54

taken out for walks?'

'No. It just seemed like a good idea,' Thea said weakly. 'And yes, I'm the house-sitter. Thea Osborne. What shall I do about Julian, do you think? Mrs Gardner does seem quite worried about him.'

'Not a lot you *can* do. He might have gone out, I suppose. You never know with Julian.'

'Is he–? I mean – how old is *he?*'

Giles Stevenson laughed. 'He's a chicken in his late seventies, and yes, all his wits are completely intact. Local historian and archaeologist, traveller, bit of a celebrity in an old-fashioned way. He and Gladys have known each other almost for ever. She worked with him on his excavations for quite a while. There was even a little bit of a scandal at one stage. If it hadn't been for that wife of his, well...'

'There's a wife?' Thea looked at the door again.

'Not any more. She died last year. Look – don't worry yourself about all this. You'll never get to the bottom of all the goings-on around here. The thing about Blockley, you see – we're one of the few genuine communities left in this area. Guiting Power's another one. You only need to glance at all the posters around the place, to see how many clubs and activities we've got going. True, we get a lot of weekenders, but even they seem to blend in pretty well. We all watch out for each other here. Tell you what – Julian's almost certain to be out somewhere with young Nick – that's his grandson. They've got some project on the go, from what I can gather.'

'So he's around, you think? Mrs Gardner seems to think he's missed some regular appointment. Of course, it's difficult to be sure…' She paused, not liking to cast aspersions on the old woman's mental state if this was a friend of hers.

'He does drop in on her a lot, I know. But as you've seen for yourself, it's impossible to make firm plans. She gets confused about time. But don't make the mistake of thinking she's completely addled,' he advised. 'She's clever enough when she needs to be.'

'Thanks,' said Thea, not sure what she ought to do with this information.

'Don't mention it.' Giles scratched his large nose absently. 'Though I haven't seen Nick's car here since last weekend. He'd usually park it just about here.' He nodded at the street just below them. 'It's possible that Julian has decided to buzz down to see the lad. He likes a bit of a jaunt if the weather's favourable.'

Thea began to think her quest for the missing Julian was altogether hopeless. 'Oh,' she said. 'Where does Nick live?'

'Dorset, somewhere. Julian takes his jalopy there and back, when the spirit moves him.'

'Jalopy?' Thea found herself filing the word as a promising one for Scrabble. Although she played much less than she used to, the habit of collecting anything with a good collection of high-scoring letters was still with her.

'It's actually a magnificent vintage Rolls, worth about as much as a house. He keeps it in a lock-up garage the other end of town.' Giles sounded envious. 'It makes anyone who sees it go weak at the knees,' he added.

'Well,' Thea summarised to Hepzie when they were indoors again. 'So far we've met a stout old man called Thomas, a tall middle-aged one called Giles and a very peculiar young one called Ick. Not too bad for a first day, I suppose.'

She debated whether or not to report to Granny that Julian had almost certainly gone to see his grandson, driving a car to die for. On reflection, she came to the conclusion that it was best to leave well alone for the time being. She could hear a radio or television through the connecting door, suggesting that Mrs Gardner was contentedly settled. So Thea went out to the garden at the back of the house, and sat on a wicker chair, drinking in the view. Although Julian's house had no windows looking into the Montgomerys' garden, Thea could sense that it was empty. No sounds or smells wafted over the dividing wall, and she suspected that virtually no normal person would be able to resist a quick word to the strange house-sitter and her dog if he'd been there.

There were buildings at all angles around her. The High Street houses were mainly Georgian, if she was any judge, and several rose to three storeys in height. The Montgomerys' home was smaller, but the rooms were generous and the value of the property obviously shockingly high.

The sun was setting behind a patch of woodland that rose to a plateau which she could just glimpse behind more houses. All she could hear was birdsong, and the low mutter of televisions or radios from the surrounding houses, with sporadic car engines in the streets around her. A slight scent of frying onions mingled with the spring blossom in the garden.

Her thoughts repeatedly turned to the old woman next door, and the heavy responsibility she was already proving to be. The arrangement with Yvette and Ron seemed bizarre – a very inefficient means of ensuring that Granny was all right. Surely there must be times when they went out and left the house empty? Did they lock the street door somehow? Did they sedate her, or call someone else to watch over her? Or was the whole thing much more relaxed than Thea was assuming? After all, Granny's wits were not as addled as all that, and she seemed to be remarkably healthy in body. In most obvious respects, she showed every sign of being able to take care of herself.

Strange, Thea thought, how different a place always became once you'd embarked on a spell of being in sole charge. In every case, her initial interview with the owners of the houses she was sitting had gone perfectly smoothly, the tasks enumerated, trust accorded with no apparent reservations. Only later did the complications emerge. This time, she had made every effort to anticipate difficulties. She had asked for a list of useful names and phone numbers to be displayed prominently. She had even requested an introduction to Granny before the Montgomerys departed, but this had never taken place. 'She'll be dozing now,' Yvette had said, when Thea had visited. 'Besides, she'll have forgotten you by the time you turn up at the end of the month.' When the details of the takeover had been arranged, it had become clear that Thea would not be able to arrive until after the couple had left for a morning flight to Calcutta. 'I'm really sorry,' she said, 'but I've got an appointment I can't break on that morning.'

The truth was that Phil, her bloke/boyfriend/lover – whatever you called them when both parties were in their forties and the relationship had been far from form-alised – had stayed the night, Friday into Saturday, and she had no intention of throwing him out before first light in order to wave the Montgomerys off. They had given her a spare door key and the code for the alarm and seemed to be quite happy with the plan.

Thea and Phil had met during her first house-sitting assignment in Duntisbourne Abbots, and had been thrown together again at Frampton Mansell. Between the two encounters, some alchemy had taken place, and the second meeting had felt like being reunited with a missing possession of considerable emotional value. Their bodies behaved as if strong magnets had been implanted in them, and the resulting pull was beyond resistance. That had been eight months ago now, and the first heady pleasures were ebbing and transforming into something quieter. 'Reason is prevail-ing,' Thea had noted sadly. 'This is a lot less easy than I thought it would be.'

But they had parted that morning with reluctance. He was due back at the Ciren-cester police station where he held the post of Detective Superintendent, she to earn some useful cash watching out for a senile old lady. She had twined herself around him, just inside her front door, before he pulled it open and strode to his car. 'I'll miss you,' she'd whimpered, suddenly not wanting to do the Blockley job at all.

'I'll phone,' he said. 'Keep your mobile where you can hear it.'

Now she glanced at her watch. Six o'clock. He'd be back in his flat by this time, cooking himself one of his all-in-one-pan concoctions. She dug for her mobile in the bottom of a large bag and switched it on, feeling guilty. She had disobeyed his instruction, unable to train herself into the habit of leaving it on and charging it up regularly to keep it alive.

A message flashed onto the screen. *Change of plan, Momma*, it read. *Can I come Sunday about 6.00pm? Phone for explanation.*

She tried to guess what the explanation might be for Jessica bringing forward her arrival time. It felt unusual, but not quite alarming. It was, after all, good news. The company of her daughter was always a treat, a return, somehow, to the way things ought to be. The maturing and separating of a girl from her mother was presumably a healthy and natural process, but it mainly felt violent and painful. It was a sadness layered on top of the grief for Carl, killed on the road only two years earlier. It was the loss of these two best-beloved people that had sent her out on the series of adventures that the house-sitting turned out to be. Anything, she had decided, rather than moulder away indoors getting old before her time.

And now, instead of phoning Phil, she called Jessica. There was no need even to pause to question which one took priority.

Jess sounded terrible. Her voice was low and thick as if she was half asleep. 'Something happened at work,' she said. 'I made a ghastly mistake, and there's to be an inquiry about it. Mike says it will all blow over, but I think he's just being kind. I don't want to be here on my own tomorrow night. I hate this place.'

'So come now,' Thea urged. 'It's only an hour and a half's drive at most.'

'I would, but I've arranged to visit Uncle Damien this evening. They asked me ages ago and I can't let them down now. I'm staying the night, and there's something fixed for tomorrow as well. I won't get back here till nearly four, probably. I'll try to leave again within the hour, so it should be just after six, if I'm lucky.'

Jessica's capacity for complex planning astonished her mother. Damien was Thea's older brother, living in Derbyshire and steadfastly fond of his niece. Jessica was on an attachment with the Manchester police, renting a small flat in Altrincham. The zig-zag driving she would have to achieve over the coming twenty-four hours was impressive.

'I won't ask you to tell me exactly what happened,' she said. 'Soon enough tomorrow. I'm glad you're going to Damien's – he's a good listener.'

'They'll all be so disappointed in me,' the girl wailed. 'I've let everybody down – you as well.'

'Don't be silly. I can't believe you've done anything as bad as all that. You've only been with them a few months. What do they expect?'

'You won't say that when you hear the whole story. And Uncle James! How am I ever going to face him again?'

James was Carl's brother, another doting uncle, who had warmly encouraged Jessica to follow him into the Police Force. Like Thea's Phil, James Osborne was a Detective Superintendent. It felt, at times, as if rather too many of her nearest and dearest were dedicated to law enforcement.

'He'll stick by you, darling, you know he will. It isn't as if you've killed anybody.'

'How do you know that?' Jessica's voice rose hysterically.

'Because I know you.'

'I've got to go, Mum. I'll see you tomorrow. I hope it's a nice place.' Thea could hear tears thickening her daughter's voice. Against all her instincts, she made no attempt to offer consolation. Instead, she adopted a falsely bright tone. 'It's amazing,'

63

she said. 'Absolutely beautiful. You'll love it.'

'That's nice,' said Jessica miserably. 'See you, then.'

Saturday evening was ruined for Thea after that. She flicked through television channels, and then began to watch a DVD of an old movie favourite, *The Belstone Fox*, which she had been thrilled to discover on the Montgomerys' neatly arranged shelf. She had watched it a dozen times as a teenager, unable to account for its appeal, but enduring the mockery of her siblings to watch it whenever she could seize control of the equipment.

But the thought of her daughter suffering from something that sounded like a ghastly mix of guilt, humiliation and foreboding clouded her ability to concentrate on anything. The knowledge that Jessica would now be under the temporary care of Damien did little to console her. Damien and Shirley had no children, after an early miscarriage had apparently put them off the whole idea. They were therefore moderately affluent and surprisingly interested in their nieces and nephews, of which there were a healthy nine in number, thanks to Jocelyn who had no less than five and Emily with her three.

'Interest', however, covered a wide spectrum of attitudes and practices. In the case of the fatherless Jessica, Damien had clearly taken it upon himself to exert what he saw as paternal control. The thing that amazed Thea about this was that the girl seemed to appreciate being told what she should do, how she should think, where she should aspire to reach in the future. Damien was infinitely more prescriptive than Carl had ever been – a fact that Jessica seemed to regard as immaterial.

At least she would not be alone to obsess over her misdemeanour, whatever it had been. To Thea's knowledge, Jessica did not have a boyfriend or a close female confidante. And when things got seriously rough, there was, in any case, no substitute for family.

Methodically, she performed the usual end-of-day routines. Not so much from any worries about electrical fires, but more from a growing social pressure to reduce use of power in general, she switched off all the gadgets at the wall. She washed and put away the cup and plate and cutlery she had used. Then she took the dog out into the garden for a widdle. The air was nippy, with a bright starry sky overhead. Walking down to the further end, she looked back at the houses, noticing with relief that a light was on in Julian's house next door. He must have come back from wherever he'd been, and with any luck would visit Granny the next day. The cottage was in darkness. Returning to the house, she locked the back door and left the key in the lock. Then she climbed on the hall chair to activate the buzzer attached to Granny's front door, reminded briefly of her sister Emily's neurotic habit of monitoring her children with a device that picked up their every breath and broadcast it around the house. Maybe that would be the Montgomerys' next move, too – planting bugs in Granny's rooms.

She was in bed by ten thirty, letting Hepzie lie on the covers as usual. The dog was perfectly clean and only moderately moulting. With luck the shed hair would be confined to the blanket they'd brought for the purpose.

She had expected to fall asleep quickly, after an early wakening that morning. Instead the events of the day swirled around her head, and the unfamiliar mattress militated against complete relaxation. She found herself thinking about Phil and the unspoken expectations from all sides that their relationship would soon be formalised in some way. They ought to move in together permanently or show themselves as a couple more regularly. They should do more of the things that couples did, like entertaining other couples, sharing joint hobbies, buying things. She and Phil did none of that. They talked and walked and had sex. They watched DVDs and ate food and had sex. As far as Thea could see, that was enough for the foreseeable future.

The next thing she knew, there was a raucous buzzing filling the house. It continued on a maddening single note, like no alarm clock or doorbell she had ever heard before. She took several seconds to work out where she was, what time it must be and why there was such a ghastly noise. The light outside was pearly white, suggesting the sun had not yet risen. What *was* that noise?

Then it came to her. Door! She remembered, abruptly, the system connected to Granny's front door. The old woman was escaping, and it was Thea's duty to intercept her. Muzzily, she rummaged for her dressing gown, still in her bag on the floor. Down the stairs and out into the street, where there was no sign at all of Mrs Gardner, the errant geriatric.

CHAPTER FOUR

It promised to be another dry day in Block-ley, with people already stirring. Thea had managed a glance at the clock beside the bed, noting the time as just after seven thirty. Two cars passed the house as she stood on the pavement in her nightclothes scanning the street for a glimpse of her charge. There was no sign of her, and with growing agitation she ran back upstairs and threw on the same clothes as she'd worn the day before.

Followed by a puzzled spaniel, she galloped down again and clambered onto the chair to reach the 'off' switch for the infuriating buzzer. Then she went back out into the street to discover Granny's door standing wide open. With fleeting hope, she went inside and called 'Mrs Gardner? Are you there?'

The thorough silence that met her confirmed her fears. The old woman was out in the town, possibly wearing only a nightie, given it was barely daybreak.

Wondering where to start in her search, Thea walked into the middle of the street for a better view in the direction of the church. The only person visible was a small girl, holding a large bunch of flowers, waiting at the door of a house halfway along the street.

Something about the figure clicked in Thea's mind. Mother's Day! Good God, it was Mother's Day and Thea had completely forgotten to send her own mother a card. She groaned to herself, fighting the surge of feelings that the realisation gave rise to. Irritation at the whole stupid business was uppermost, followed by annoyance with herself and a sense of being burdened by the need to rectify the omission. She would have to telephone and listen to her mother enumerating the gifts and flowers the others had sent. Over the past twenty years or so, the importance of the day had burgeoned insanely. As children they might have made a card at school or remembered to buy a tube of Smarties between them, but there was none of this emotional blackmail that seemed so inescapable now. She ground her teeth in sheer exasperation. How much better it would have been to have forgotten entirely, until the day was safely past.

And Yvette Montgomery – had she forgotten, too? Was she relying on her batty old parent to be unaware of the occasion? It was probably a safe enough gamble; and yet Thea wondered whether the old lady's absence had something to do with it. Had she looked out of her window, and, like Thea, been alerted by some obvious little ceremony in the street? Unlikely, surely.

Determinedly, she set out in search of her charge. Unless somebody had taken her into their house or car, she would presumably be in full view somewhere. After the collapse of the previous day, it was probable that she would not manage to get very far. Forcing herself to think, she came to the conclusion that the first place to start would be the mysterious Julian's house – he had evidently returned from his absence and could well be treating Mrs G to a plate of eggs and bacon at this very moment.

But Julian's door was as firmly closed as before, and the interior just as silent, when Thea knocked. She tried again to peer through the front window, but could only gain the same shadowy glimpses of the room beyond as she had the day before. It seemed obvious that nobody was there.

With the vague idea that Granny might have followed the same route as their walk of the previous day, she headed along the High Street towards the church. Then, realising it would have been impossible for the old woman to have got far in the few minutes since the buzzer had sounded, she turned back and trotted urgently towards the woods at the other end of the street. Past the handsome old houses on the right, and noting absently an ancient construction labelled the 'Russell Spring' she peered towards the trees for any sign of movement. Again, there was nothing. Time was passing and with it a growing sense of urgency and worry. She supposed she would have to cover the rest of the town, not resting until the old woman was found.

Everything seemed quiet and closed up as she turned the corner and started down the hill towards the shop-cum-Post Office and the Green beyond. A car came up towards her, driven by a person she recognised as 'Ick' from the day before. The car was low-slung, very shiny and made a loud throaty purr as it slowed beside the coffee shop. The sort of car that turned heads, Thea registered dimly. Just the kind of motor such a flashy show-off *would* drive. He waved at her with a grin and she nodded back.

Then all at once she saw her quarry, on the pavement close to the red telephone box, arm in arm with the middle-aged man called Giles. Giles who knew Julian, and believed him to be visiting his grandson, and who had claimed that Granny was ninety-two years old.

Granny was wearing the same respectable trousers as the previous day, with a different top. Her hair was brushed and there was an irreproachable cleanliness to her face and hands. Her mouth carried a determined air, and her eyes flickered as if attempting to focus on a myriad of fleeting thoughts.

Confronted by such a normal scene, albeit rather early in the day, Thea was aware of a dilemma. She could hardly grab the old woman and march her back home with an admonition to stay there. But she was being paid to keep watch over her, and to simply turn around and leave her to Giles's care seemed irresponsible. So she strolled towards them with a smile.

'Hello!' she said. 'Nice morning, isn't it.'

Mrs Gardner gave her an appraising look. 'Do I know you?' she asked.

Thea sighed quietly, glancing at Giles for assistance. 'We met yesterday,' she said to the old woman, when it was clear that the man was not going to be of any use. 'We went for a little walk, with my dog. The spaniel, Hepzibah.'

The old woman showed no sign that this found any connection in her memory. She gave her head a little twitch, as if tuning herself to a different setting, and said proudly, 'I'm having a day out with my friend. He's taking me for a drive and then lunch. He says I can be his surrogate mother.'

Thea laughed. 'That sounds a splendid idea.'

'And we've just been looking at the flowers on the Green,' Granny elaborated.

Giles Stevenson pushed out his cheeks in

a rueful expression. 'She came knocking on my door about twenty minutes ago, would you believe? Lucky I was already up. I like to get a bit accomplished at the keyboard early on, then I can enjoy the day with a clear conscience.'

Thea had scant interest in Giles's routine, just at that moment. *Keyboard* suggested something musical to her, and nothing more.

'It's rather cheeky of you,' she said to her charge. 'Especially on a Sunday.'

'*Mothering* Sunday,' the old woman responded sharply. 'It's special. Have you got a mother, dear?'

Thea closed her eyes for a second. 'Don't ask,' she begged.

Giles chuckled – a pleasant gravelly sound which made Thea feel warm and grateful towards him. 'So – you'll be spending most of the day together, will you?' she asked.

He winked. 'Let you off the hook, won't it? Now, don't worry. Gladys and I go back a long way. I'll make sure she's all right, if you want to go off somewhere for a bit. Give that little dog I've been hearing about some exercise. I'll bring her back sometime after lunch. Mid-afternoon, let's say.'

Mrs Gardner leant against him, plucking at his sleeve like a small girl. 'I never really had a son, you know,' she confided. 'It's all a big pretend. I only had the two girls.'

Thea had no answer to that, but she gave

them a silent blessing, feeling buoyant with relief.

Hepzie was whining inside the front door when Thea returned to the house. It still wasn't even half past eight, she noted. Why was everyone out so early? Admittedly it was a fine morning, the sun warm enough to ripen buds and waken the hibernating, but it was a Sunday, after all. She resolved to indulge in a leisurely breakfast, using food from the Montgomerys' fridge and marmalade from their store cupboard. She made coffee in their machine and found some expensive-looking pineapple juice inside the fridge door.

But the inner buoyancy quickly deflated. Jessica! She was worried about Jess and whatever blunder she'd made at work. During her final year at university, the girl had gone for the assessment process for entry into the police. Thea had listened with mounting horror at the demanding exercises and interview that her daughter had willingly endured. The fact of a degree, she had been told, was regarded as barely relevant. A grim list of 'competencies' was produced, including 'personal responsibility', 'resilience', 'respect for diversity' and 'problem solving'. How, Thea wondered, could her little girl possibly satisfy such requirements? Reading the prospectus over and over, she found herself questioning not just the practical demands but the jargon-ridden ethos behind them. 'Do you *really* want to do this?' she had asked, more than once.

Jessica had been adamant. 'Absolutely,' she had insisted. 'Trust me, Ma, OK?'

'But if you want to be on the side of right, you could be a lawyer,' Thea had argued. 'That would be a far better use of your brain.'

Jessica had merely shaken her head and held up a hand to silence any further protest.

And she had passed all the tests and interviews and assessments and medicals, only to find that the West Midlands training centres in Coventry and Birmingham were both full for the next year. After an earnest few days of phone calls, however, a place was found for her in Manchester, where she had begun her initial twelve weeks of classroom instruction the previous October. From there, she had moved to a police station in Salford for a further ten weeks of more active work under the watchful eye of Mike Hamilton, a tutor constable.

Thea had tried to keep up with it all, but was aware that she had been less attentive than some mothers would have been, due largely to her deepening relationship with Phil Hollis. Phil himself had persuaded her to let Jessica fly free, finding her wings in the strange and murky world of the police probationer. 'She knows how to find you if she needs you,' he said. And now she did and she had and Thea was worried.

When she did finally leave the house with Hepzie, it was with an idea of exploring the Ditchfords – the group of lost medieval villages near Todenham, four or five miles away. Lost – although the more accurate term was surely *abandoned* or *deserted* – villages had been a passing interest of hers some years previously, discovered by accident during some idle reading. Her imagination had been fired less by the mundane detail of changing farming practices than by the slow disintegration of settlements which had once echoed to shouts and children's laughter and the ringing of the blacksmith's hammer. Thea had always possessed a sharp awareness of the fact that there was no inch of British soil that had not been trodden by human feet repeatedly for thousands of years. In the Cotswolds, where farmers had ploughed and harvested and husbanded their sheep, the evidence of this was overwhelming. Not a stone was in the position that nature had placed it, but every one had been used and reused for a cottage or a wall or a sheep pen, until it almost hummed with the traces of hands that had moved it and shaped it.

She drove to Todenham and left the car in

a layby below the village hall. A few clouds had gathered in the west, but it continued to be a thoroughly pleasant spring day. Grasping the map firmly, she located the footpath that led directly to the site of Ditchford Friary.

Even though she knew there would be little to see, she was disappointed. Some indeterminate bumps and troughs gave rather too much imaginative freedom to conjecture the former existence of small houses, animal shelters and field layouts. She sat down under a hedge for a few minutes, trying to tune in to the lives of the long-gone villagers, with very little success. All she was aware of were birds preparing for the breeding season and a solitary rabbit loping carelessly across the middle of the bumpy field. Hepzibah failed to notice it, burrowing idly as she was amongst some stalks of dry grass left over from the previous year. Letting her gaze roam across the landscape, she found the photographs in Ron Montgomery's study coming to mind. They had captured similar patterns of furrow and stone in the Gloucestershire countryside. Perhaps, she mused, he too had wanted to rediscover the long-gone settlements.

She recalled other walks with the dog on earlier house-sitting assignments, and held her breath for a moment, fearing the sudden production of a body part or mysterious piece of cloth as a result of Hepzie's burrowings, but nothing of the kind happened. It was Sunday morning – Mother's Day – and spring had arrived on cue. It would be hours yet before Granny was returned by the attentive Giles, or company arrived in the shape of Jessica. She could stay out here until hunger impelled her back to Blockley. And even then, she could buy herself a meal at the Farriers Arms in Todenham, a few yards from where she'd left her car.

But the prospect of sitting by herself in a pub – which might very well not permit dogs – was unappealing. Instead, at the end of a walk which she was forced to admit had been a somewhat negative exercise, she got back into the car.

Before she could turn the ignition key, there was a rapping at the window beside her. Startled, she turned to find herself almost nose-to-nose with a woman wearing a headscarf, tied in the fashion favoured by the Queen some thirty years ago. Her skin was weatherbeaten, the cheeks red and chapped, the teeth discoloured. Making a frantic twirling gesture with her hand, the woman conveyed an instruction for Thea to open the car window. She started speaking as the gap widened. 'Which way are you going?' she demanded.

'Er – that way,' said Thea jerking her thumb over her shoulder. 'To Blockley.'

'You can give me a lift, then. Thank Christ for that.' And she scuttled round the front of the car to the passenger door.

'Is there an emergency?' asked Thea, watching the woman push Hepzie unceremoniously out of her way. The dog jumped onto the back seat with no sign of resentment.

'Sort of. I've got a flat tyre, and my son's expecting me. I'm already about an hour late. I tried changing it, but the bloody spare's buggered as well.' She spoke with a west country lilt that must have been the normal accent for Gloucestershire not too long ago. Thea assumed her to be a local farmer, or at least someone who habitually worked out of doors.

'Where are we going?' she asked.

'What? Oh, yes. He's in Paxford. It isn't far out of your way. You must think I'm rude, but we all give each other lifts around here. Just like in the good old days.'

Thea doubted very much whether this was true, although she did recall the informative Giles also claiming that Blockley still retained a community spirit. She had no idea where Paxford was, either. 'You'll have to direct me,' she said. 'I'm a stranger here.' She turned the car around with a few deft manoeuvres and set off down the lane, back the way she had come.

'No problem. This is all because of blasted

Mother's Day. Doesn't it make you sick? It's like a KGB brainwashing exercise, the way everyone pretends to like their appalling old mothers all of a sudden.'

Thea snorted her amusement. 'Just what I was thinking,' she said. 'I forgot to send my mother anything.'

'Do you have kids?'

'One daughter. She's coming over to join me later today. I've tried to train her out of observing any of the usual nonsense. She might bring me some chocs, I suppose.'

'So what are you doing in Blockley? Staying there?'

'I'm house-sitting, actually. I only arrived yesterday. I've got to keep an eye on an old lady who's a bit – forgetful.'

'Lost her marbles, you mean. It's not old Gladys Gardner by any chance, is it?'

Thea gave her passenger a quick look. 'You know her?'

'Everybody knows her. I know about you, as well. Knew you were coming, in any event. You've got your hands full there. How come you got away today?'

'She's been taken out to lunch by a surrogate son. I grabbed the opportunity to do a bit of exploring.'

'The Ditchfords,' said the woman, as if it was obvious.

'You read minds, I see. Do you know my name as well?'

The woman laughed. 'I don't think I have gleaned that detail, but mine's Gussie. Short for Augusta, of all things. My parents were a good sixty years behind the times.'

'Thea Osborne. Pleased to meet you.'

'You were searching for the lost villages,' Gussie stated.

'That's right. But I couldn't really find them.'

'Looking in the wrong place, duckie. You needn't have come driving all over here – there's one right under your nose.'

'Oh?'

'Upton. You go through the woods at the end of the High Street, and there it is, not half a mile away. Been excavated, it has, unlike the Ditchfords. But there's nothing to see now. Even when you know where to look, it takes more imagination than most people have to make any sense of it. But it's better this time of year, before the crops start growing. They put it down to oilseed rape most summers, and then you'd never know anything had ever been there.'

'They can do that, can they? Grow ordinary crops over it?'

Gussie shrugged. 'Who's to stop them? It's private land.'

'Well, I'd still like to have a look.'

'Good girl. Got the map, have you? The one that shows all the paths and fields? It's on there, clear enough.'

'It's back there, look.' Thea jerked her thumb towards the ledge behind the back seat, where a jumble of objects was scattered. 'Thanks for the hint.'

'You're welcome. It's Blockley's best-kept secret, some people think. Goes back a way earlier than medieval times, according to the archaeologists. And, you might say, isn't quite as deserted as you might think.'

Thea was reminded of the Barrow at Notgrove, close to the village where she had spent a week with Phil the previous autumn. That dated back to Megalithic times, but still retained its pull on the contemporary imagination.

'So many of these lost places,' she murmured.

'They're not the only thing that's lost around here,' said Thea's passenger regretfully. For some reason, Thea found herself thinking of the missing Julian, and Granny's plaintive quest for him.

Paxford turned out to be little more than a fleeting knot in the road two or three miles east of Blockley. The sense of being in a time warp was as strong as in any Cotswold village, heightened by the bizarre retention of a large tin plate sign for Spillers Shapes over a defunct grocery store as well as a protruding notice advertising Hovis. It was less quiet than most, however, with a flurry of activity outside the Churchill Arms. 'That looks popular,' said Thea, thinking it rather early for lunch, still.

'It gets reviews for the food,' said Gussie carelessly. 'Brings out all the townies – except they mostly can't find the place. We're not too big on road signs around here.' Thea made a mental note to give the Churchill Arms a try one day during the week.

Gussie had pointed out another lost village site, entitled Upper Ditchford, as well as expounding on the Knee Brook, which was the river that had powered the Blockley silk mills.

'The Cotswolds vary so much, don't they,' said Thea. 'I was in Cold Aston last year, and this is quite different, even though it's just a few miles away.'

Gussie mumbled agreement before alerting Thea to their arrival at her son's house. 'Quick!' she said. 'Stop here, before they see us.'

Thea did as instructed, wondering what the mystery was about. Her first interpretation was that Gussie was afraid that Thea might get invited in for a sherry if the family noticed her.

'Too complicated to explain,' the woman muttered. 'Listen – I'm sure to see you again. Thanks for the lift. If I'd spotted the flat tyre earlier I'd have walked, of course. It's only three or four miles. Don't get too agitated about Gladys, will you. She's got a lot more sense than she lets on. She isn't going to come to any harm. Just try to be patient with the way she asks the same thing over and over.'

'Thanks,' laughed Thea. 'That was getting to me a bit.'

Gussie gave her a last searching look. 'Word of advice,' she muttered. 'Don't under-estimate her. There's a difference between forgetting what time of day it is and being stupid. Gladys Gardner definitely isn't stu-pid, and it would be wise to remember that.'

'Right,' said Thea, trying not to feel like a schoolgirl. 'Have a good lunch. It was nice to meet you.'

CHAPTER FIVE

The drive back into Blockley, along an unfamiliar road, took her over a handsome-looking river, and past a property entitled Hangman's Hall Farm, which set her musing cheerfully as to what the history of it might be. There were clumps of brown drooping snowdrops just visible through the new grass, no longer acting as harbingers of spring, but instead harking back to a winter that had been grim at times. Most of the expected flowers were late, the daffodils only just blooming and the leaf buds on the hedgerows very far from opening. But the past few days had brought great changes, which Thea had chosen to regard as signs of optimism for this particular assignment. The Montgomerys were paying her well, and despite the understating of Granny's condition, it did seem likely that she would manage to befriend the old lady and the people around her.

She made herself a light lunch, thinking that she and Jessica might venture out that evening for a meal at The Crown. Sooner than expected, she saw Granny and Giles pass the front window on their way back to the cottage, walking slowly. Quickly she went to the front door and threw it open. Calling to their backs, she said, 'Hello! Had a good time?'

Both turned to look at her without speaking. Granny's face was transformed from the bright-eyed animation of the morning. Everything drooped, and her eyes looked watery and unfocused. Giles's lips were clamped tight in what appeared to be exasperation.

'We overdid it rather,' he said. 'Poor old Glad's very tired now. She's going to have a nap.'

'Oh. Do you want me to...? I mean, can I do anything?' Thea was suddenly terrified that her charge was going to expire on her, and she'd have to summon Yvette home to arrange her mother's funeral. Except she was incommunicado in India, so that wasn't an option, whatever happened.

'No, no,' boomed Giles's deep voice. 'She'll be fine. It was all my fault. One tends to forget – well, you know.' He seemed to be trying to say more with his eyes, and a quick tilt of his head towards the exhausted Granny.

She *is* ninety-two, Thea wanted to say. What do you expect?

She let Giles take the old woman into her part of the house, and close the door behind them. He'd probably done it before, and from the look Granny had given her, she had yet again completely forgotten who Thea was and why she was there.

She could see The Crown from where she stood, noting a lot of people emerging and getting into cars. Voices floated along the street to her, families buzzing with the afterglow of a good Mother's Day lunch. Disaffected sons-in-law mollified by a bottle of Beaujolais, grandchildren glad to be liberated from the demands of manners and unfamiliar food. Thea thought again of the Gussie woman and wondered what her family consisted of, and how they felt about each other. It was odd, she realised now, that the son hadn't been summoned to collect his mother when her car failed her. Niggling questions occurred to her, and she hoped she'd have a chance to hear answers to them, over the coming days.

She and Hepzie went back into the house and remained indoors, listening out for sounds from the cottage. Giles left after a little while and all was silence after that. Inevitably, renewed worries about Jessica floated up, and there seemed no way of dodging them. The afternoon progressed steadily, however, with a mixture of reading, preparing the second bed in the spare room and browsing the Internet on her laptop for information on the lost Ditchford villages.

The last proved almost entirely fruitless, which surprised her, until she tried some lateral thinking and used the words *abandoned* and *deserted* instead. There still wasn't very much about the Ditchfords, but it seemed the closer settlement of Upton, mentioned by the Gussie person, had received plenty of attention from academics. She couldn't find the energy to read any of the learned papers listed, or the comparisons with other similar villages. Instead she closed down the computer and started to think about phoning her mother to grovel over her neglect. It was not an enticing prospect, so she deferred it while she boiled the kettle and buttered a Cream Cracker and worried a little bit about Jessica.

The knock on the front door startled her. It was only just after five, so it couldn't be Jessica. And yet it was. 'Goodness, you're early! What happened?' she greeted her unsmiling daughter.

Jessica pushed Hepzie away as the spaniel scrabbled ecstatically at her knees, and said, 'What do you mean? It's the exact time I told you I'd be here.'

'You said six.'

'It *is* six.'

'But–' Thea frowned at her watch, and then at the handsome pendulum clock hanging in the hall.

Jessica snorted. 'You forgot to put them

forward, didn't you? Have you been an hour behind everybody else all day?'

Thea felt a wholly disproportionate agitation at this small failure. The day she had just lived through acquired a completely new aura, stained with embarrassment and self-reproach. 'I've never done that before,' she said.

'Well, it doesn't matter, does it? Can I come in?'

Thea waved her in, still reassessing the past ten hours or so. It came to her that she had felt some sense of being at odds with everyone around her. They were having lunch too early – even Granny had apparently got the wits to reset her clocks, leaving the house so early that morning. And now it was six o'clock and somehow she wasn't *ready* for it to be that time. She felt cheated of something. And she felt incompetent, unfit for the world, and that was the most scary part.

'Happy Mother's Day, by the way,' said Jessica. 'I got you one of those chocolate orange things.'

It was a moment of embarrassment. Thea's refusal to permit any excessive gush inhibited them both. 'Thanks,' she said.

Between them lay Jessica's trouble, which somehow felt too big to talk about without due preparation, a gradual approach, to a scene where there might be tears or raised voices or ill-considered announcements.

'I'll show you the room,' said Thea. 'And make some tea. I thought we could go out for a meal – if we can find a table. Mother's Day is such a nuisance in that respect.'

'They mainly go out for lunch, I think,' said Jess. 'Did you have anywhere in mind?'

'Just The Crown, a little way up the street.'

'I saw it. You mentioned it in your directions.'

'So I did. It looks popular, at least. There was quite a little crowd there earlier on.'

Jessica sighed, and hefted the large bag that hung from her shoulder. 'Let's see the room, then,' she said.

Thea led the way upstairs and along a corridor to a medium-sized bedroom. 'It's very nice,' she said feebly. 'Good view over the back,' she added.

The window gave a long view to a hill rising to the west, beyond a row of houses on a road parallel to the High Street. 'The whole town's in a bowl – hills rise up on all sides,' she elaborated.

'Very pretty,' said Jessica. 'I'm sure I'm going to love it.' Her tone suggested quite otherwise, and Thea wondered whether her daughter was with her mainly from a sense of duty. After the ordeals of other house-sitting assignments, the whole family probably considered that she needed to be looked after every time she took on a new job. Her sister Jocelyn had asked her directly, a few weeks ago, why she went on doing it.

'For the money,' Thea had replied, not entirely honestly. The truth was she relished the constant changes of scene, the new people and the little snatches of history she collected during her brief sojourns in the various Cotswold villages. No two were alike, and she was already actively seeking further commissions, placing advertisements in magazines and creating a website for herself. One interesting woman had contacted her, wanting somebody to oversee her animals in Temple Guiting for a fortnight in early June.

'It was a centre of silk production,' Thea informed the girl, still intent on instructing her about Blockley, and resolving that she must take the visit at face value. Trying to read ulterior motives into people's actions was seldom a sensible line to take. She went on, 'There are huge old silk mills down at the very bottom of the hill, where there's a little river. I went for a look the last time I came here, when I met the Montgomerys. They've all been converted into apartments now, but you can see just what they must have been like. We can walk down there one day.'

'Fascinating,' muttered Jessica. 'Silk mills.'

Thea felt a dreadful urge to slap her. The reversions to adolescent mulishness happened very seldom now, but there were still moments when the twenty-one-year-old could slip back to fifteen – or even five at times. Thea supposed this was universal between mothers and daughters – perhaps between parents and children in general. The echoes and ghosts of those earlier years never quite disappeared.

Jessica was a good four inches taller than her mother, with her father's broad shoulders and long limbs. The look of Carl that sometimes flashed out was both sweet and sharp. His manner of tilting his head when thinking, the way he turned his left hand in towards his body to indicate impatience – to find them preserved in Jess had been a surprise. While he lived, Thea had never noticed that his daughter shared so many of his ways. It was a joy, mostly, despite the jolt it never ceased to give her. Another piece of the past forever captured. This, more than anything, was what bound families together. It was the same with her siblings. Damien was forever the older brother, sarcastic, protective, superior; Jocelyn the whining baby sister, struggling to keep up, quick to defend herself.

But she was losing patience rapidly. Until Jessica explained the reason for her loss of confidence, or whatever it was that might be going on, they couldn't hope to have a relaxed time together. And it seemed wise to combine it with a change of scene. It would, after all, be a shame if the atmosphere of the house were to be ruined by the emotions of an upsetting story. Besides, she was hungry and there was very little food in the store cupboard or fridge.

'So it's nearly half past six,' she said, with a little frown. 'I'd better give Hepzie her supper. Then we'll go out for a meal. OK?'

'You're allowed out, are you? Do you have to do any jobs first?'

Thea had forgotten Granny completely. She couldn't remember hearing anything from the cottage since Giles had left.

'There's an old lady next door. It's the Granny cottage, and she's the granny. She's ninety-two, and forgets things. She doesn't recognise me, but she fell in love with Hepzie the moment she saw her.'

'And?'

'And what?'

'Do you have to feed her, or put her to bed, or take her to the lavatory?'

'None of the above. I just have to try to keep her from wandering away and getting lost. There's a buzzer that goes off if she opens her front door. It went off this morning at half past seven.'

'How weird.'

'It is a bit. She's been out today, with a surrogate son called Giles. She looked terribly tired when he brought her home and she's been silent ever since.'

'You should check that she's still alive then,' said Jessica in a voice that was too normal for the words she spoke.

'I don't want to wake her if she's asleep. On the other hand, if she sleeps all evening, she'll be awake all night.'

'Does she wander off in the night as well?'

'I don't know.' Thea's voice rose. There were too many things she didn't know, she was starting to realise. Then she forced herself to concentrate on the question. 'Well, yes, I think she does. She was out incredibly early this morning. The buzzer woke me up. I think she'd been moving around for a while before that. There were sounds that I only half heard, before I woke up properly. Do you know what I mean?'

'Sort of.' Jessica frowned, and flicked the short hair behind one ear.

Thea detected a fading interest, which was irritating. She wanted to finish her story, to update her daughter on the ways of the house, to fill the space that would otherwise be occupied by Jessica's own story, which Thea did not feel quite ready for. 'You must know how it is in a strange place,' she continued, slightly more loudly. 'Your mind just accepts that there'll be a lot of strange noises and smells and so forth, so you don't react to them. If I had to wake up properly every time I heard something unusual, I wouldn't get any proper sleep. So I tuned it all out. But thinking about it later, there were a few thuds and rattles going on, which could have been her getting up before dawn, I suppose.'

'And what about you, eh?' Jessica gripped the spaniel round her soft throat and gave her a playful shake. 'Not a very good guard dog, are you?'

'She's useless,' Thea agreed. 'I always hear things way before she does.' Hepzibah beamed at her tormentor and wagged the feathery tail.

Jessica stayed with the subject of Granny. 'Can you get in without disturbing her? Did they give you a key?'

'I can go through the connecting door. There's a key on a hook above it – they keep it locked, which I know is another weird thing. They said I might frighten her if I appear all of a sudden, so best not to use it.'

'Mum, this is quite a peculiar set-up. That poor old lady is being kept prisoner.'

Thea recalled the cage-like fence around Granny's little garden area and couldn't help but agree. 'I suppose they've got their reasons,' she shrugged. 'The old girl certainly is terribly forgetful. I think they just want to cover themselves, having somebody here, in case she wanders off and gets run over or something. Mrs Gardner's pretty robust physically. I don't think I need check her now.'

'Did you bring your laptop?' The sudden switch of subject was typical. Thea nodded. 'Good. Let's Google The Crown before we take the plunge. It might be horrendously expensive. I saw another pub on the way in. Great Western, it was called.'

Thea's admiration for her daughter's powers of observation had always been high. It was one reason why she knew she would make a good police officer. Thea herself had not even noticed there was another pub in Blockley.

'Go on, then,' she invited. 'While you're doing that, I'll go and have a listen, just to see if Granny's awake.'

It was with considerable relief that she heard the muttering of the television when she put her ear to the connecting door into the cottage. She even caught a brief cackle of laughter that she was sure came from the old woman herself. When she went into the living room, where Jessica was reading the computer screen, she reported her findings.

Jessica interrupted her. 'Hey! This is wonderful!' she laughed. 'Somebody's posted a review of the restaurant at The Crown. It's incredibly rude. I'm surprised they haven't been sued for libel, the things it says.'

'Bad food?'

'Terrible. Inedible, it says. Greasy. Desserts brought straight from Iceland. The shop, not the country.'

'Oh dear! Does that mean we have to go somewhere else?'

'Of course not. We have to check it out. If they've seen this, they'll have smartened their act up, anyway. Though it's not cheap.'

'Never mind. We'll have a blowout tonight, and spend the rest of the week surviving on Marmite sandwiches.'

'We will not. This is my holiday. I want proper feeding, twice a day, thank you very much.'

Outside it was still broad daylight, thanks to the time change. Jessica walked slowly, inspecting the delights of Blockley. She paused at the house next to theirs. 'Curtains closed?' she noted. 'Do you know who lives here?'

'A man called Julian. Granny's best friend, apparently. She's been worrying about him. He was missing for most of yesterday, but his lights were on last night, so I assume he's back.'

'But you haven't seen him today?'

Thea shook her head. 'I still haven't seen him at all. But I've been out most of the time, so I wouldn't have done anyway. Giles Stevenson says he's a bit of a recluse and sometimes doesn't answer the door, even if he's in.'

Jessica tutted disapprovingly at this.

'Granny talks about him a lot. He's got a

grandson, and is a retired archaeologist and some other things. He's got a vintage Rolls Royce that lives the other side of Blockley.' Thea beamed proudly at all the information she'd gleaned in such a short time.

Jessica was peering through the gap in the curtains. 'Still closed at this time of day – that's odd,' she noted. 'It's nowhere near dark yet. Why didn't he open them this morning?'

'Perhaps he likes it gloomy. He sounded a bit like that from what Giles said.'

'Hmm.' Jessica sounded interested and alert, suddenly.

'What?'

'A lamp's been knocked over.'

Thea almost laughed. It was a cliché, surely? A classic Agatha Christie moment. 'Is there?' she said. 'How clumsy.'

'I'm going to knock,' Jessica announced. 'We can introduce ourselves to him. It's a perfectly reasonable thing to do.'

So she did, and just as before, there was no response at all. A chilly silence seemed to seep from the house which even Thea had to admit was unsettling.

'Can we get round the back, do you think?' Jessica asked.

Thea sighed. 'Quite easily, as it happens – but *why*? What possible justification do you have for doing such a thing?'

'There are definite signs of something not

being right.'

'But darling, you're not on duty now, and besides, I'm starving hungry.'

'Well I'm going back into our house, and out into the garden. Something feels fishy here. You don't have to come.' But Thea knew she didn't have a choice. Briskly she led the way through to the back door, across the lawn and over the wall into the next garden. They had to push through the bamboo curtain, which rustled loudly. Jessica strode to the back door, knocked on it and called 'Hello? Sir? Are you there?' Then she turned the handle and pushed the door, which readily opened.

Thea waited outside, sifting a clutch of emotions ranging from admiration to trepidation, all imbued with pangs of hunger. Jessica came back white-faced, fishing in her pocket for her mobile phone, and having got hold of it, quickly thumbing the buttons.

'Hello? Yes, this is Probationer PC Jessica Osborne, Manchester Division. I've just discovered a fatality. Suspicious circs. Blockley, Gloucestershire. High Street. Elderly male. Name unknown. No persons on the premises. Right. That's right. Thank you.' She pressed another button and faced her mother. 'There's a man in there. He's dead.'

Thea felt a wild desire to laugh. 'It'll be Julian,' she said. 'Bags I not be the one to tell Granny.'

CHAPTER SIX

Jessica prevented her mother from going into the house and seeing the body. She pulled the back door shut and bundled Thea through the Montgomery house and into the front room to watch for the police response. It took twelve minutes for a familiarly marked car to pull up in the street.

'You deal with them,' said Thea. 'I can't cope with this.'

With an impatient little toss of her head, Jessica went outside. But she threw back the comment that she would be bringing the officers through the house in the next minute or two.

She met them as equals, rather to her own surprise. 'You're the rookie who called this in, are you?' asked one. He was a uniformed sergeant, thirtyish, with kind eyes. Jessica nodded.

'Not on duty, then?' said the other one: a constable with ginger hair and a nervy manner.

'I'm here on holiday. I'm stationed in Manchester. I only got here this afternoon.'

'And the first thing you do is find a stiff. Clever!' smiled the sergeant. 'So where is he? Who is he?' He had a clipboard in his hand. 'You know about the G5, I suppose?'

'Vaguely,' Jessica admitted. 'The house looked odd to me. My mother's looking after this one, temporarily. The deceased lives next door. There's access at the back.'

'OK, lead on,' invited the sergeant. 'I'm Tom, by the way and this is Eddie.'

'Jessica Osborne,' she responded.

'Yes, we've got that,' said Tom, smiling again.

Briefly introducing the policemen to Thea, who was hovering in the hallway, Jessica led them along the same route as before. Elbowing their way through the bamboo gave rise to some remarks about jungles, but the atmosphere was essentially serious. Eddie grew more tense as they stepped into Julian's house.

The body was lying spread-eagled on the kitchen floor, wearing ordinary day clothes. The wide-open eyes staring blindly at the ceiling were all the confirmation required that this was a dead person. Carefully, Tom leant down and lifted the body's right arm. 'Rigor,' he noted. 'Been dead all day, then.' He glanced at the two younger officers. 'Don't touch a thing,' he cautioned them. 'Jess – what have you touched in here already?'

'Door handle, that's all,' she said. 'I didn't go close to him. It was obvious he was dead.' She was hypnotised by the staring eyes, filmed with the bombardment of tiny airborne particles that would normally be blinked away every few seconds. 'What killed him?' she wondered. 'Might it have been natural causes, after all?'

'Not for us to say,' Tom told her. 'But I can smell foul play here. You don't lie like that if you're having a heart attack or a stroke, or if you've just stuffed yourself with Paracetamol.'

Eddie was only half inside the room. His skin looked green. 'Go outside if you're thinking of chundering,' Tom warned him.

'It isn't at all disgusting, is it?' Jessica said softly. 'Poor old man. It's just terribly *sad*.'

'Good girl,' Tom approved. 'Is this your first?'

She nodded. 'You never know how you'll react, do you?'

Tom huffed a brief laugh. 'Eddie does. This is his third, and he's still going to pieces. Do you know his name? The old man, I mean?'

'Julian something, that's all. Assuming he's the occupant of this house, of course. He doesn't look like a burglar caught in the act.'

'Does your mother know him? Can she identify him?'

Jessica shook her head. 'She only got here yesterday. She's never seen him.'

'Neighbours?'

Jessica sighed. 'You'll need to check with my mother, but there's an old lady in the cottage attached to the house we're in. She's senile, though, as far as I can gather. Not likely to be a reliable witness.'

The aspect of the procedure that Jessica found most surprising was the lack of urgency. It made sense, she supposed, with the man past rescue, but if it was a murder, surely they should be pursing the killer more quickly? Bob seemed to read her mind. 'We have to get every detail right at this stage,' he explained. 'Otherwise we contaminate evidence, or make mistakes that wreck the whole investigation all down the line. Think about it.'

She nodded. 'I know,' she said. 'It's just...' she tailed off.

'OK, well we can't do any more until we've had the doctor and the photographer do their bit. Then Forensics get their turn. Then we remove the body and it gets its PM. That'll be first thing tomorrow.' He cocked his head at her. 'You could watch, I would guess – if you wanted to. You have to do it sooner or later. This might be a good one to start with.'

'Wouldn't I need clearance from Manchester?'

He shrugged. 'They'd be glad to get the box ticked, like as not.'

The ticking of boxes and generous inclusion of Jessica into the next hour and a half of police activity swept all thought of anything else from her mind. The forensic team arrived and offered her a protective suit and a grandstand view of their operation as they crawled all over the house, tagging and bagging, whipping fingerprints from every surface and generally turning an ordinary place of residence into the scene of a crime. The computer in a small office was taken away for analysis and several boxes of files quickly scanned and summarised.

The identification of the body was performed, at Thea's suggestion, by a tall sleepy-looking man called Giles. He had been quickly located and discreetly escorted through Julian's front door. Jessica took little notice of him, being more interested in the filling in of the vital G5 form.

'Any sudden death, you fill in one of these,' Bob explained. 'It goes to the Coroner eventually.'

The form invited a detailed description of the scene of death, name and address of the person identifying the body, last known sighting of the person alive.

Giles couldn't answer that point. 'I had a quick glimpse of him this morning, as it happens,' he said, with a glance at Jessica. 'The house-sitter lady was looking for him yesterday evening and I guessed he might have gone down to Dorset. But that is a pure guess...' he scratched his large nose and looked anguished.

'Where did you see him this morning?' Bob asked.

'Walking along to the postbox, at the end of the street.' Giles pointed towards the woods.

'And what time would that be, sir?'

'Early. Before seven. I was finishing an article in my office, up there.' He pointed again, to an upstairs room in a house on the south side of the High Street. 'I can see a lot from up there.' His stricken look intensified. 'How long would you say he's been dead?'

'Can't say yet, sir.'

'But he's stiff, isn't he? That means several hours. So unless Gladys ... no, that can't be right...'

'Don't worry, sir. We have an idea of the difficulties with Mrs Gardner,' said Tom.

He didn't, though, thought Jessica, having seen Thea's reaction to these words. She didn't herself, yet. The desire to meet this bewildered and bewildering old lady was getting increasingly strong.

The police doctor had at least settled the question of how Julian died. With the help of the invaluable Tom, the body had been rolled over, to reveal a wound just below the left shoulder blade. 'Right into the heart, I'd say,' nodded the doctor. 'Sharp little weapon, too.

See how it's sliced through the cloth of his shirt? Clean as a whistle.'

'Why so little blood?' asked Jessica breathlessly. She could feel the wicked metal blade entering her own back, in a ghastly piece of empathy. 'And how did he get onto his back?'

'Good questions,' nodded the doctor. 'My guess would be that the knife was left in place for a few minutes, until the heart stopped beating. It would act as a kind of bung, then. As for how he got turned over, we'll probably never know.'

'Would the killer have blood on him?' she went on, keen to maintain a professional manner.

'Unlikely. The weapon would, though.'

Everything moved on. The body was taken away, the people of Blockley became aware, rather slowly, that some crisis was taking place in their midst. And Thea had to deal with a suddenly animated Granny.

The buzzer betrayed the old woman's exit onto the pavement, and before Thea could intercept her, she was at Julian's front door, pushing between two white-costumed forensics officers to gain entry. 'Where is he?' she asked, in a normal-sounding voice.

At that point Thea caught up, and put her hands on Granny's shoulders. 'He isn't here,' she said.

'Why?' The tone was that of a curious six-year-old. 'Where is he?'

The officers looked worriedly at Thea, clearly conveying that this was not their area of responsibility and could she please deal with the situation quickly.

'They had to take him away,' Thea said, painfully torn between a desire to tell the truth and fear of an unpredictable reaction. 'Come back to the cottage and I'll try to explain.'

'Who are these men? They look like astronauts. Why are you pulling me like that?'

Thea felt a surge of resentment against the old woman and everyone else in sight. She was being asked to do the impossible, and it damn well wasn't fair.

Then help appeared in the shape of Giles Stevenson. He had been hovering at the edges of the activity for the past hour, not speaking, taking a few steps up and down the street, but obviously unable to tear himself away. Now the old woman had materialised, Jessica wondered if this was what he had been waiting for all along.

'Gladys, Gladys,' he crooned, coming towards her with his hands outstretched. 'It's all right my old dear. Come back home and we'll try to explain it to you.' He threw Thea a look that said she was expected to come as well.

Bystanders had slowly assembled along the

High Street, watching and muttering between themselves. 'What in the world is happening?' called a smartly dressed woman
standing on the opposite pavement.

Nobody gave her an answer. There was
only one vehicle left outside Julian's house,
belonging to the forensic team, demonstrat-
ing that the main action was past and there
would be little left to see from outside.
Inside the house, however, a lot was still
happening. Fingerprints taken, photographs
capturing the precise location of mundane
objects, drawers opened, paperwork examined. But this was invisible to the gathering
onlookers. They had to rely on rumour and
speculation to figure out the basic story, and
if that didn't work, someone would eventually ask Giles to enlighten them, when he
had finished soothing the bewildered
Gladys.

Jessica was left behind by the departing
Tom and Eddie, the undertakers and the
police doctor. She had an invitation to
attend the post-mortem at eight-thirty next
morning, and a warm ember of satisfaction
lodged in her breast at the way she had
performed in a time of crisis.

Now her mother beckoned to her, saying,
'Help us see to Granny, will you? We'll have
to get her back into her house and settled
down. I don't think it's going to be easy.'

In the event, Thea and Jessica stayed only

a few minutes, shooed away by Giles's insistence that he would manage better on his own. But not before they had both noticed a giant display of flowers in a tall ceramic vase on the living room table. 'My word!' gasped Thea. 'They weren't here yesterday.'

'Frances sent them,' said Mrs Gardner proudly. 'They're for Mother's Day. Isn't she a good girl!'

Thea gazed at the display. 'But when?' she wondered. 'When did they come?'

Giles cleared his throat. 'I was in on the secret,' he confessed. 'They were sent to me yesterday and I brought them over this afternoon. Nobody's going to deliver on a Sunday, you see. Not even such a special Sunday as this.'

'Well, they're gorgeous,' said Thea, and followed Jessica along the pavement to their own front door. 'Food,' she whimpered, standing in the hallway. 'I must have food.'

It was half past nine. They hurried to The Crown in the faint hope that something would still be on offer. 'It *is* a hotel,' said Thea optimistically. 'Surely the kitchen stays open round the clock?'

The bar was not busy. The staff seemed exhausted from the lunchtime family rush, and seemed half-inclined to refuse to serve any more meals that day. Thea talked them into something from the snack menu, pushing Jessica into a seat in a corner of the small bar and getting two glasses of white wine.

'I don't like white wine,' said Jessica. 'I wanted lager.'

'Drink it,' Thea ordered. 'It's medicinal.'

'Funny sort of medicine.' But she drank half of it in a few large gulps. 'God! What a day! What a *week!* There's obviously a curse on me.'

'You were wonderful out there,' Thea said with total sincerity. 'So professional! I was really impressed.'

Jessica nodded acceptance of the tribute, but gave a rueful grin. 'You were rather sidelined, I'm afraid. It must have been frustrating, just waiting for everything to get done. Why didn't you have something to eat while you were hanging about?'

'I didn't like to, in case I was needed. I could hardly just sit there eating scrambled eggs with the place full of police. I did have a couple of biscuits, though.'

There were three people in the small corridor-like bar next to the main one, easily able to overhear what Thea and Jessica were saying. A young man put his head around the doorpost and caught Thea's eye. 'You know about the murder then?' he asked. 'What's happened?'

Jessica put up a hand to ensure her mother's silence. 'We can't tell you anything,

I'm afraid,' she said. 'It's all being taken care of. If you live in Blockley, there'll probably be house-to-house questioning tomorrow. Anything you want to know will have to wait until then.'

The youth pulled a face expressing reluctant acceptance of her words. 'I live in Moreton, actually,' he said.

'Well, it'll be in the papers, I expect,' Jessica said with finality.

Mindful of his mates listening in, he had to make one last try. 'You a policewoman then?'

'That's right,' said Jessica, meeting his eye until he dropped his gaze and returned to his drink.

'We can't talk here,' Thea realised, looking round the small room, with only seven tables, packed closely together. Three of them had people at them, all within a few feet. It was as if they were assembled in a normal living room. It would feel almost rude to fail to include them in any conversation. The fact of a sudden violent death in their midst was plainly occupying all thoughts. The word *Julian* with its soft consonants floated from ear to ear, along with muttered interrogations about what could have happened and when he had last been seen and how hard it was to believe such an event could happen.

'No,' said Jessica. 'And it doesn't really

matter now, anyway.'

'Oh, yes it does,' Thea insisted. 'That's your real life, back there. This is all just a distraction. Whatever mistakes you might have made in Manchester are going to have to be faced. And I want to know the whole story.' She was muttering, her face turned down towards the table, but still she knew how audible she was to the other drinkers.

The food arrived and they ate it rapidly, with little interest in the quality. When she had finished, Jessica played with her wine glass, sliding it backwards and forwards over a damp patch on the table. Finally she began to speak, her tone flat, her eyes on the drink. 'I know I should tell you about it. Get it off my chest, or something. But it seems very remote, all of a sudden. Nobody died, at least. I just made a total idiot of myself, that's all.'

'Well, let's go for a walk, up to the church and back, and you can tell me the basics as we go.'

They were gathering themselves to leave when two people came down a flight of stairs running from the corner of the bar close to where they were sitting. Thea turned and saw the odd-looking man from the day before. The one who had called himself 'Ick'. With him was a girl. She was tall and thin and very pale-skinned. Her hair was black and long, her limbs loose. Her face was striking, with fleshy lips and wide-spaced eyes.

'Oh, hello,' Thea said without thinking. 'We meet again.'

He met her eyes, with the same faintly puzzled look she remembered from the previous day. 'You remember,' Thea prompted him. 'When the old lady fell over, and you offered to help.'

'Right, yes, right it is,' he smiled. 'And did the Granny lady get better? Some old partridge she 'peared to me. Tough feathers.'

Thea laughed. 'She's fine. I think it was mostly an act.'

'So what's going forward out in de street, then?' he asked. 'All that going on? Somebody hurt or what?'

Thea glanced at Jessica for assistance, only to find her daughter gazing worshipfully at the man, slack-jawed.

'A man died, actually,' Thea said, surprised the story hadn't reached every Blockley ear by this time, and too bemused by Jessica's weird behaviour to think before she spoke.

'No!' His handsome eyebrows rose, and some of his jewellery jingled. He looked at his companion. 'Hear that, Clee? People doing their dying in our little hidey hole!'

The girl just blinked and shrugged.

'No worries. We need to be gone.' He extended a forefinger at the barman, and cocked it as if firing an invisible revolver.

'See you later, my friend. Have the Drambuie standing by for when we fly home again, right?'

The barman almost saluted, and then watched with an expression just about as gormless as Jessica's as his patrons departed.

Jessica managed to speak a few seconds later. 'How do you know Icarus Binns?'

'He's Ick to me,' Thea teased. 'That's what he told me he was called.' She frowned. 'You'll hate me for this, but I've never heard of Icarus Binns.'

'He's a ... performer. A sort of rap singer with a guitar, but not quite. And that's Cleodie Mason with him. She's a model.'

'They make a fine couple,' Thea said carelessly.

Jessica wriggled in her excitement. 'They're both *terribly* famous,' she insisted. 'This is amazing.'

All Thea could think of was how enormously improved her daughter's mood had become, simply because she had found herself in the same room as two so-called celebrities. She remembered Granny Gardner asking her, 'Are you one of these celebrity people?'

'This area's full of them,' she told Jessica. 'You'll probably see a whole lot more before the week's out.'

Thea led the way out onto the street, still thinking about the encounter with Ick. 'Odd business, being famous,' she observed. 'What does it mean, when you really think about it?'

'He's very talented,' Jessica said. 'It's a real art.'

Thea remembered the bizarre linguistic habits of the man and raised her eyebrows. 'He certainly speaks very strangely. Where's he from?'

Jessica shrugged. 'Essex, I think.'

Thea giggled loudly. 'Essex! I should have guessed.' She felt a touch of hysteria lurking somewhere, and fought to subdue it.

'Come on,' she ordered. 'Through the churchyard, down to the left and maybe we'll explore around the back streets behind the High Street. That should give you time to spill the beans.'

'OK.' Jessica walked a little way along the empty street, not bothering to use the pavement. Then she took a deep breath. 'Here goes, then. Big sink estate, lots of minority issues, unemployment, single parents – you know.' Walking side by side, they did not look at each other. Thea made a slight murmur of encouragement, and Jessica went on, 'We get called to a domestic that's still going on when we get there. Eight in the evening. Screaming, glass breaking, kids crying. All the clichés rolled into one. Plus it's a black family.'

'Is that relevant?'

'Yes and no. It was meant to be useful for my training. Show awareness in action, sort of thing. Long lists of stuff we're not allowed to say.'

'Really? Like what?'

'Never mind that now. The *point* is, there's this big psycho, slamming his wife – I mean *partner* – against the wall, with three kids all pulling at him and kicking him. It had been going on a good hour when we turned up. The *noise!* You wouldn't believe it. Anyway, we walk in, shouting over the racket, and he ignores us completely.'

'How many of you?'

'Three. My tutor constable – that's Mike, and his team-mate Jake and me. Well, procedure says a whole load of stuff about appropriate force and risk minimalisation, and maintaining calm authority. None of which actually translates into reality in that sort of situation. So they just got hold of an arm each and dragged the bloke off the woman. They had to almost trample the kids to do it, mind you. Then the woman – who didn't seem to be hurt much – launches herself at him like a cat and digs her nails in his face, while he can't defend himself. The scratches were incredible and she's yelling and screaming worse than ever. That's when clever clogs Probationer Osborne loses it big time.' She paused, eyes closed for a moment. Thea felt rather than saw that she was shaking.

'What on earth did you do?'

'Got between them. Pushed her off, and tried to subdue her. One of the kids jumped on my back, and I didn't even think. I just shook him off and smacked his face when he came back at me again. I smacked him quite hard, to be honest.' She laughed bitterly. 'If I'd slapped the woman it might have been OK. But violence towards a kid is way out of order. There must be about ten reasons why it's taboo.'

'How old was he?'

'About seven.'

'But you can't have really hurt him.'

'He acted as if I had. Jake yelled at me to get back to the car, the woman grabbed the kid as if he was dying, and the psycho grabbed his chance and started accusing us of assault against a defenceless child. They are so savvy – they know all their rights, and all the things we're not permitted to do. At least it all went quieter after that.'

'But what happened? I mean, was anybody arrested?'

Jessica shook her head. 'The woman wouldn't press charges, and the neighbours all melted away as soon as we got there. I'm up for a disciplinary and Jake says he doesn't want to work with me any more. It's all a ghastly mess.'

Thea tried to smile. 'I can't believe you'd be in any real trouble for such a minor thing. You were only trying to help, after all.'

'You don't understand,' said Jessica sadly. 'It's set back relations between the force and the community. The story's all round Salford by now, and the kid's a hero.'

'And you? What effect has it had on you?'

Jessica's eyes filled. 'I'm not sure I can do it, Mum. It's too hard. Everyone's against us, right through society. The harder we try to give everyone due respect, the more they take advantage. I don't want to spend my whole life being hated.'

Thea struggled to find something to say that would be convincingly reassuring. While she was still thinking, Jessica's gaze was drawn to the street they were in, somewhere to the south of the church. The lighting was subdued, and there were no people anywhere to be seen.

'You'd never know anything had happened, would you?'

'What?'

'This place. People safe in their beautiful houses, telly on, cat on their lap, jobs to go to, money in the bank. It's a dozen worlds away from that estate where I smacked the kid. Even when there's been a murder a few doors away they're not seriously bothered. Where I work, there'd be a riot by now.'

'Maybe they're so scared, they can't think what to do except lock the doors and sit in front of the telly.'

'And tomorrow they'll hold a meeting and double the activities of the Neighbourhood Watch. They'll all start accusing each other of stabbing the old man and some won't speak to each other again for years. Is that more like it?'

'Probably,' said Thea. 'Giles told me this is a close community. And these noticeboards everywhere certainly show how much they've got going on.' They were passing one of the boards as she spoke – although strictly they were not boards at all, but handy wooden doors leading to a garage or a shed, opening onto the street and freely offered for publicity material. Thea had seen three already, and assumed there were more in other parts of the town.

'I shouldn't knock it,' said Jessica wearily. 'This is how we all want the world to be, after all. Quiet and pretty and safe and friendly. It's a wonder the police could even find it – they probably haven't been called out to Blockley for years.'

'Which makes the fact of a murder all the more terrible,' Thea observed.

'Yes,' said Jessica. 'And now all I want is to go to bed. I've got to be at the mortuary for eight-thirty tomorrow.'

This was the first Thea had heard of the appointment, and she fought down the impulse to protest against it. The light was fading fast as they emerged once again onto the High Street. Trying to ascertain exactly where they were, she heard Hepzie yapping inside the Montgomery house.

'Oh, God,' she said. 'I wish she wouldn't do that. She'll disturb the neighbours.'

'Some neighbours,' said Jessica wryly. 'A dead man and a senile old crone.'

Thea did not even have the energy to laugh.

But the day was still not quite over. Thea and Jessica both carried mobile phones in their bags, and both had them switched off throughout the evening. Jessica, however, automatically checked hers for messages before going to bed. 'Oh!' she gasped, as she listened to a recording. 'That was quick!'

'What?'

'Uncle James. He's already heard what's happened. He wants to know if I'm OK.'

James Osborne was Thea's brother-in-law. Since the death of Carl, he had taken it upon himself to keep a protective eye on both women, favouring Jessica in particular. With no children of his own, his niece had gained a special place in his affections from the day she was born. It had been a family joke the way Jessica was blessed with two doting uncles, one from each side. Damien and James scarcely ever met, but sometimes it felt as if they were competing to give their shared niece the greater share of consideration and concern. Thea knew she should be grateful for the attention they lavished, and the help James gave Jess in her pursuit of a career in the police. 'Does he know about you being in trouble at work?' she asked.

Jessica nodded, slightly sheepish. 'I saw him last week. He came up for an evening and took me out for a meal. You know what he's like. As soon as he heard about it, he rushed up to get the whole story and see if he could smooth things out.'

Thea's feelings of jealousy took her by surprise. Her daughter had waited days and days before telling her what had happened, and yet her uncle had known about it from the start.

'Did you tell Damien all about it, as well?' she asked.

'Of course. How could I not?'

'Hmmm,' was all Thea allowed herself to say. It was not in her character to complain openly about being the last in the family to know about her daughter's problems, but from Jessica's slightly sheepish look, she knew there was no need to spell it out. The girl already understood how she felt. 'And you told them both you were going to be here with me, I suppose?'

Jessica nodded again, slightly defensively. 'Why not? It isn't a secret, is it?'

Thea shook her head. 'Of course not. And

now James has heard about this murder.'

'Obviously he has. He's the Superintendent.' A thought struck the girl. 'Actually, Mum – do you think that's why they were so nice to me, the cops who let me watch everything just now? Do you think they made the connection with the name, and worked out who I was?'

Thea wasn't sure which would be the correct answer to this. 'They could have done,' she prevaricated. 'Would it matter?'

'I don't want special treatment,' Jessica worried. 'That's one good thing about being attached to Manchester. Uncle James means nothing up there. Oh, damn it! That must be why they're letting me go to the post-mortem tomorrow, as well.'

'Surely not? Did they say anything to make you think that?'

'Not really. They just offered me the chance to observe it. I can't refuse, can I? It's always difficult to get a slot for probationers.'

'And you're all right about it, are you?'

'I won't know till I try,' the girl admitted. 'But I think it'll be OK.'

Out of a feeling of wanting something of her own to balance a sense of being sidelined, Thea fished out her own mobile and switched it on.

'Looks as if I've got a message as well,' she said. 'It'll be Phil.'

She was right. With an odd sensation of symmetry, she listened to her own Detective Superintendent's words on the recording. They were bland, affectionate and quite un-worried. 'At least he hasn't heard the news,' she said, with a mixture of relief and dis-appointment.

'Give him time,' said Jessica.

CHAPTER SEVEN

The post-mortem was only mildly unpleasant, and most of the nasty aspects were eclipsed by the interest Jessica felt at the revelations it produced. The pathologist was a silver-haired man in his mid-fifties, with very clean skin and a gentle manner. He shook hands with her and introduced himself as Bill Morgan. 'This your first?' he asked her.

At her nod, he prodded the body and gave his own responding nod. 'Nice and fresh,' he commented. 'Shouldn't be too stomach-churning.'

A uniformed constable was also present, notebook open, chin held high in an effort to display confidence in his ability to withstand the coming onslaught.

And then it began, with very little ceremony, but with a prevailing atmosphere of respect and due care which Jessica found reassuring. Bill Morgan dictated into a microphone that hung from the ceiling as he made his examination. Jessica hung back a little, steadying herself, until it came to looking at the fatal wound. This was far from straightforward. Anxious to retain the entry wound intact, access to the heart had to be from the front. The body was flopped from front to back, to front again.

Finally, the pathologist began peeling away the flesh to trace the trajectory of the weapon, dictating constantly. 'Lateral stab wound between the fourth and fifth thoracic ribs. Right ventricle of the heart penetrated to a depth of approximately half a centimetre.'

The heart, when it was eventually revealed, was smaller than Jessica had expected and paler in colour. 'How exactly does it kill you, when you're stabbed through the heart?' she asked.

'You bleed to death. Blood goes into the thorax at immense pressure if the left side of the heart is punctured. Less so if it's the right side.'

'Which is this?'

'See for yourself.' The pathologist deftly exposed more of the damaged heart, drawing back to give Jessica space. She tried to make sense of what she was seeing. 'The right?' she hazarded.

'Well done,' he smiled at her.

'So how quick would it have been? How long from the stabbing to losing consciousness and dying?'

'A maximum of thirty seconds. Even though the wound's on the right, it still doesn't take long. This heart has had some battering in its time – see the scarring where it's had to repair itself?'

Suddenly she couldn't maintain the clinical detachment any longer. Shaking her head, she took a few steps back. 'Sorry,' she gasped. 'Give me a minute. I'll be all right. It's just...'

The pathologist gave a small shrug of disappointment as if a promising pupil had let him down. 'Take your time,' he said. 'It doesn't matter.'

For the next few minutes, Jessica averted her gaze from the metal table, and contented herself with listening to the commentary. 'The entry wound's clean borders indicate a very sharp single-edged knife. Width of blade likely to be no more than a centimetre, and the depth of the wound a little under five centimetres.'

'Small knife,' Jessica ventured.

'Not necessarily. People seldom drive them in to the hilt. In this case, the resistance from the intercostal tissue – between the ribs, that is – would have probably slowed the momentum. It was a lucky blow, I'd say – managing to find the space between the ribs first time. They're pretty close together.'

'Or someone who knew exactly what they were doing.'

Bill Morgan stared at the body. 'What was he wearing?'

'A shirt,' Jessica said. 'The knife went right

through it.'

'Hmm,' said the pathologist. 'Then I'd say it was a very lucky blow.'

'There was no visible blood anywhere on the floor,' she said. 'Is that usual, not to bleed at all?'

The pathologist looked at her with mock severity. 'I showed you the heart, didn't I? And the cavity full of clotted blood?' She gulped and nodded. 'That's where it all went. The skin is quite elastic, so if he was effectively dead when the knife was pulled out the wound would shrink in size a little and it's quite feasible for blood not to escape. It's impossible to say for sure, but I'd guess the knife stayed in situ for perhaps ten minutes after the stabbing. There are indications of that from the smaller blood vessels in the tissue just inside the wound.'

'And can you tell when he was turned onto his back?' she remembered to ask, having gulped down the latest portion of reality with some difficulty. 'When we found him, he was face up.'

The pathologist studied the skin of the back more closely. 'More or less immediately after the knife was removed, I'd say. See the pooling effect? Gravity makes the blood collect at the lowest point. Jolly useful thing, gravity.'

'But he couldn't have turned himself over, because the knife would still be in him...'

Jessica shuddered, and fought a brief battle with herself. 'It seems a funny thing to do.'

Bill Morgan shrugged. 'All kinds of explanations. He might have been lying on his side, and the effort of removing the knife rolled him back. Not deliberate at all. A dead body is heavy and difficult to manipulate. And most people, having just stabbed someone to death, would be in a highly agitated state. Yanking on the knife in such a state ... well, you can perhaps imagine what it might have been like.'

Jessica forced herself to try, imagining one hand on the dead shoulder, the other pulling the weapon free, stepping quickly back when it came, worried that a gout or even fountain of blood might follow, letting the body flop where it liked, perhaps not even noticing in the haste to escape and try to forget the terrible details of what you'd done. Only when she became aware of Bill's eyes on her face, did she understand how fully she'd accepted the challenge. 'Alarmingly easy, isn't it?' he said gently.

'Scary,' she admitted.

The removal of the stomach and careful collection of the contents again found Jessica's lurking nausea overlaid by her intense interest in the findings. 'No recent food consumed, but signs that he had a drink. Looks like tea.' Jessica tried to recall whether there had been unwashed cups in Julian's

kitchen. Had his killer drunk a companion-
able cuppa with him before knifing him to
death? She remembered items on a draining
board, washed and left to dry in their own
time. She thought there had only been one
mug, one small plate and a saucepan.

When it came to the hands, things became
even more interesting. 'Fluff under the
fingernails – which are a little longer than
normal.' Bill extracted samples with a
curved metal probe.

'Would he have clutched at the carpet as
he died?' Jessica wondered aloud, visualising
the reflexive action.

'He was found in the kitchen, which isn't
carpeted,' said the constable, consulting his
notes. 'I thought you were there?'

Jessica flushed. 'I was. Sorry. I forgot. So –
he might have been stabbed in the living
room and crawled through to the kitchen?'

'Just possible, if he was quick,' agreed Bill
Morgan. 'But it would have taken the last
seconds of his life.'

'Right,' said Jessica, gulping again. 'I see.'

They excused her after that, despite the
post-mortem having some way still to go.
She drove back to Blockley without noticing
a single thing along the way. Her head was
full of the images of violent death, and the
puzzle created by this particular one. The
task was obvious: discover the identity of the
person who drove the knife into the old

man's back. Her training up to that point had included nothing about detection of murderers. Uniformed police constables had only a background involvement in murder investigations, in any event. The routine door-to-door questioning, the trawling through endless computer files, perhaps the eventual arrest of the villain – but little or none of the meticulous assembly of tiny forensic clues, building a case, closing in. And where would this one start? The post-mortem findings painted a confusing picture of a man in his seventies, up very early on a Sunday morning, drinking tea. Then stabbed in the back, probably whilst lying on a carpet, and either crawling or being dragged into the next room and left to die, the knife being removed from the scene. A lamp in the carpeted living room had been knocked over and left where it fell.

She knew nothing about him. The contents of his house had suggested an orderly man, bookish, solitary, reasonably well off financially. She had noted his surname at the mortuary – *Jolly*. Mr Julian Jolly. Identified by a Mr Giles Stevenson, neighbour. Well known to Mrs Gladys Gardner, elderly friend and neighbour, unreliable witness.

She felt very little emotion during the thirty-minute drive. It was all too cerebral for that. The mystery of what had happened possessed her, under the influence of the cool dispassionate post-mortem. The testing of a wide range of hypotheses consumed her attention. The back door of Julian's house had been unlocked, and there was access into his garden from a small street through a door in the wall. The front door had been locked and bolted on the inside. The killer had taken the knife away with him, and was unlikely to have a single drop of Julian's blood on his person. But there were always traces. Her sketchy knowledge of forensics told her that. Everyone left a thread or a fleck of skin or a hair. There could be no escape, in the long run.

Thea had woken with the same sense of mild disgruntlement that she had felt the previous evening. The facts of Julian's death were skittering away from her, leaving her to plod along behind everyone else, fighting to gain enough information to construct a sensible story for herself. Jessica had told her a few basics before they went to bed, but she had clearly not wanted to rerun everything she had seen and heard during the aftermath of discovering the body. The knife in the back was the central detail. And the absence of any blood. And then the revelation that her daughter was invited to attend the post-mortem had obliterated everything else. Thea hated the idea of the girl witnessing such a gruelling procedure, being forced to confront the full reality of human mortality. It seemed corrupting somehow, tainting Jessica's youthful innocence.

But when Jess came back, at half past ten, Thea's distress took a different form. Her daughter was not upset or disgusted, as expected, but fired with curiosity and determination to tackle the puzzle of Julian's death. She answered Thea's concerned questions – 'Was it horrible? Did they take proper care of you? Did you learn anything?' – impatiently. 'I want to try and work out exactly how it happened,' she said. 'Why did he get up so early? Didn't you hear anything? It was all going on just a few yards away from you.'

Thea waved a hand before her face, as if swatting cobwebs aside, experiencing an impatience of her own. 'I've told you already – it was my first morning here. I didn't know which sounds were normal, and which might be something sinister. All I remember is that buzzer going off loud enough to rouse the whole street.'

'What time was that?'

'Half past seven or thereabouts.'

'Old time or new?'

'Pardon?'

'The clocks went forward that night. Was it half past seven or actually half past eight?'

Thea sighed. 'Half past eight, I suppose. There were people out and about. I saw a little girl carrying some flowers for Mother's

Day. I wondered why they were all so early. All day, people were doing things at the wrong time.'

'Honestly, you're getting as senile as the old bat next door.'

'I hope not,' said Thea gloomily. 'She's fifty years older than me.'

Jessica laughed at that, but kept up her questions. 'So before the buzzer – you didn't hear anything?'

'That's what I was trying to tell you yesterday, soon after you arrived. There *were* some noises early on. Thumps and bumps, which I still think were probably Granny getting up. Her bedroom's through the wall from ours, I think. Which reminds me,' she said abruptly. 'The police phoned and they want to come and interview her. They thought I should be there, with her daughter away. I tried to explain how impossible it would be, but they wouldn't be told.'

'It's got to be done,' Jessica nodded. 'And I'm keen to meet the old thing properly at last. I've hardly seen her yet.'

'You'll get your chance,' Thea assured her. 'That looks like the police car now.'

Out in the street, a few feet below the level of the pavement, the top of a car was visible. As they watched, both front doors opened and the heads and shoulders of two police officers appeared. One was female.

'Come on then,' said Thea. 'Let's just hope

she remembers me.'

They managed to persuade the officers to stand back slightly while Thea knocked on Granny's front door. It was opened with comparative alacrity, and something akin to recognition dawned in the old woman's eyes. 'Hello, dear,' she said. Something about the *dear* rang false to Thea, despite it having been used before. Somehow Gladys Gardner didn't strike her as a person who would have used the word very naturally at any point in her life.

'There are some people here to talk to you,' she said, trying to make it sound quite a normal event. 'Could we come in, do you think?'

'I expect so. Giles told me I should. He wrote it all down, you know. That was kind of him, don't you think?' She proffered a sheet of paper with several lines of large black writing on it – the calligraphic version of shouting.

'Very useful,' said Thea, wishing she'd had a similar idea two days ago.

The four of them crowded into the living room, making it seem very small. The Mother's Day flowers seemed as fresh and exuberant as ever, and Thea found herself speculating as to whether they really had come from Frances, or whether Giles Stevenson had taken it upon himself to get them on her behalf, in the hope of pleasing Granny.

The old woman consulted her crib sheet. 'It says "Don't be worried by questions. Answer them to the best of your ability." That's clear, isn't it.' She looked chirpily from one face to another. 'Go on, then. Ask me.'

'Does it say anything there about Julian?' Thea wanted to know.

'Oh yes!' Granny was almost eager. 'That was the whole purpose, do you see?' She held the paper under Thea's nose. The top line read, 'Julian is dead.'

'A bit stark,' Thea murmured faintly.

Granny shook the paper irritably. 'Facts are the thing,' she said. 'If he's dead then I need to remember, don't I?'

The police woman nudged her way forward, eyebrows raised patronisingly. 'When did you last see him?' she asked. 'Can you remember that?'

Granny narrowed her eyes, but another glance at Giles's instruction kept her on track. 'Possibly last week,' she said. 'He came here often, you see. We were friends. He and I worked together in the past. He understands me and how my poor brain doesn't work so well. He can help me.' Only Thea appeared to have noted the slip into present tense, and understood the significance. Granny's gaze wavered, and the hand holding Giles's notes dropped to her side.

'Where is he? I'm worried about him. Did something happen to him? And where's Yvette? My own daughter's left me all alone, and now my house is full of strange people.'

As if to compound the situation, someone knocked briskly on the door, startling everyone in the house. Jessica, being nearest to the door, went to answer it. Granny, with some sense of domestic courtesy, elbowed her way after her.

A loud male voice could be clearly heard. 'Oh, Gladys, there you are! What's been happening here? Are you all right? Did something happen to Julian?'

'Thomas,' said Granny, as if to herself. 'Thomas is at my door.'

Jessica took charge. 'I'm afraid this isn't a very good moment,' she said. 'The police are here.'

'Police? But Gladys can't – I mean, she won't be able to–' he floundered. 'And who are *you?*' he finished.

'It's a bit difficult to explain,' Jessica said. 'If you don't mind waiting a few minutes, I'm sure we'd like to have a word with you. Are you a neighbour?'

Thomas waved an arm across the street. 'I live down there,' he said. The *down* suggested one of the cottages approached via a small lane leading off the main street. 'But please tell me. I need to know the truth. Julian and I – that is, we've always been such friends, and now they're saying he's dead.' He quivered uncontrollably for a few seconds. 'Dead! Can that be possible? I *must* speak to Gladys. Why did nobody come to tell me? Me – his best and oldest friend.' His voice cracked, and his head drooped forward with the weight of his emotions.

Jessica put a hand on his wrist, and said gently, 'I assume you haven't been interviewed yet?'

'Interviewed?' He mumbled the word as if it made no sense to him. 'What do you mean?'

'The police will be calling at every house in the area, as part of their investigations into the sudden death of Mr Jolly.'

'So he *is* dead.'

'I think you knew that already, didn't you?'

'Perhaps I did.' He raised his eyes to meet hers. 'And if they're interviewing us all, then that must mean he was murdered.' Jessica made no attempt to contradict him.

Granny had been standing alongside Jessica throughout this exchange. 'Murder?' she echoed breathlessly. 'You mean manslaughter, don't you?' She smiled earnestly at Jessica, and then turned a stern face on Thomas. 'Not murder, you see. Not at all.'

Thomas gave her a long mournful look, shook his head, and turned to go. 'I'll wait for my interview, then,' he said. 'I'm sorry to intrude.'

Jessica watched the shambling figure as it retreated across the street, and then went back into the house, ushering Mrs Gardner ahead of her.

Granny was impossibly animated after that. Despite repeated references to her notes, in particular the top line of them, she appeared quite unaffected emotionally. 'Dead,' she mouthed, as if tasting the word. 'Julian is dead. Well, well. It comes to us all, of course. We mustn't feel too sorry for him. Where would be the sense in that?' Her peculiar reaction to the word *murder* had evidently already slipped away beyond recall.

The police officers were completely out of their depth. One of them urged Jessica out into the hall, and whispered, 'Is she for real? Can she possibly be acting?'

Jessica rolled her eyes. 'Your guess is as good as mine. It's a brilliant performance, if it's all for our benefit. But does it really matter? She's no use as a witness, is she? Even if she's treating the whole thing as a game, that makes her unfit. Either she really can't remember, or she's deranged in some other way.'

'Yeah.' The woman scratched her hairline fiercely. 'Never met anything like this before.'

Jessica, flattered to be consulted, hurried to agree. 'She's such a sweet old thing, isn't she? Like a child.'

'Right,' said the officer dubiously. 'Though I don't know about you, but I've seen some of the things children can do when the whim takes them. It isn't very sweet, usually.'

Jessica remembered the savage little boy she'd smacked, and shuddered. 'That's true,' she muttered.

'So what do we do about this old Granny? She's the closest to the victim – the only friend we know of up to now. Quite likely the last to see him alive, come to that.'

'You'll need to talk to my mum. She came here on Saturday and spent most of the day with the old girl. She's got a better idea of how her brain works – or doesn't work – than I have.'

'OK. Well let's have one more go.' The woman squared her shoulders and marched back into the room.

Granny was sitting on her sofa, with Thea beside her. The other police officer – a sergeant – was bending towards her. 'Can you tell us everything you remember about Mr Jolly?' he was urging her.

Granny met his gaze, wide-eyed. 'Every-thing?' she repeated. 'That might take a while.' She began a disjointed litany of facts, most of them concerning Julian's career as an archaeologist dating back to the nineteen fifties or thereabouts. 'And he's writing about Joanna Southcott's Box,' she threw in, apparently for good measure. 'With Thomas.

Did I see Thomas recently? I can hear his voice in my head. Awful man. Fat Thomas.' She giggled. 'He and Julian are always fighting. Like boys, they are. What was I saying?'

Everybody sighed. Thea patted the blotchy old hand, remembering the injured wrist from Saturday afternoon. There was no sign at all of any lasting damage. The grip on her own hand was strong, almost clawlike.

'Well, I think we'll call it a day,' said the police sergeant, flipping his notebook closed. 'I've tried to get most of that down.'

Thea smiled sympathetically at him. The jumble of information could be vitally important or utterly irrelevant and how was anybody to know the difference? The snippet about Thomas, which did in fact chime with the encounter on Saturday afternoon, was the only remark that seemed remotely to pertain to current events.

'Mrs Osborne?' said the police woman, tilting her head slightly. 'Could we–? Do you think we could go next door and have a little talk?'

'Give me a minute,' said Thea, gently withdrawing her hand from the old woman's grip.

Awkwardly, the party left the house, with Granny nodding and smiling at their retreating backs. Thea turned to her on the doorstep. 'I'll come and see you again later on,' she said, knowing such promises meant nothing. If she failed to honour it, Granny would never notice. Or would she? The frequent gleams of intelligence in the small dark eyes were impossible to ignore.

CHAPTER EIGHT

The 'little talk' never properly happened. 'We were basically only sent to assess the old lady,' said the sergeant. 'I just wondered whether there's any more you can tell us that might help with that?'

Thea sagged helplessly and shook her head. 'Not really,' she said. 'What you see is what you get, more or less. She's very changeable.'

'OK,' he nodded. 'We'll have to report back, and they'll send a CID team to go on to the next stage.'

'When?'

'Right away, I would guess. Our job now is to get on with the door-to-door. Last sightings, unusual noises, suspicious characters – all the usual.' He sighed. 'That old girl's really off with the fairies, isn't she?'

Thea grimaced unhappily. 'It's a bit more complicated than that, I'm afraid.'

'Yeah,' he huffed carelessly. 'It usually is.'

Thea and Jessica slumped together on the sofa, trying to catch up with events. 'So we can take it that it definitely wasn't suicide,' said Thea, after a few minutes. 'Can we?'

'Absolutely definitely, it was not. Even if

he attached the knife to something and rammed himself onto it backwards, he could hardly have pulled it out and hidden it before dying. The pathologist said he'd only have about thirty seconds, at the very most. As it is, he seems to have crawled from one room to another, which was remarkable.'

'Pity,' Thea sighed. 'Suicide would be such a relief. So much better than a murder.'

'Christ, Mum – listen to yourself. The man's *dead*.'

Thea defended herself. 'Yes, I know. And suicide is violent and selfish and shocking and all that. But murder's an enormous crime against the rightful order of things. It shakes everything up. It never really goes away – the trace persists for decades – sometime *centuries*.'

'You don't have to tell me that,' the girl complained. And then the doorbell rang. 'It'll be the police again,' said Jessica with certainty.

Even though the man on the doorstep was not in uniform, she remained convinced that he was from the CID. 'Are you Miss Osborne?' he asked.

'That's right,' she confirmed, throwing back her shoulders. 'How can I help you?'

The man's manner quickly alerted her to her mistake. He dropped his gaze, chewed his lower lip and shifted his weight from one foot to the other. 'Well ... um ... I don't expect you can, really. My name's Nick Jolly. I've just driven up from Dorset.'

'Oh! You must be a relative of Mr – I mean, the name's the same. Jolly.' Jessica found herself almost as tongue tied and upset as the visitor.

He nodded. 'My grandad. The police phoned me. I came–' he forced a watery smile, 'I suppose I came to make sure it was true.'

'Come in,' she ordered him. 'You look awfully shocked. And you've driven all the way from Dorset?'

'I must have done, but I can't remember much about it. I just kept getting this picture of Gramps as I last saw him. He was really fit, you know. And they wouldn't tell me what happened,' he burst out. 'I've been visualising the most terrible things.'

Thea appeared and helped Jessica to usher him into the sitting room and onto the sofa.

Nick shook himself. 'I still can't believe it. I only saw him last Saturday. I came up for the day, and we went out to – for a little walk. He was on good form, considering.'

'Considering what?' asked Thea.

Nick wiped a large hand down the side of his face. 'Oh – well, he was never particularly *cheerful*. You know Gramps. I think the word is *curmudgeonly*. In a nice way, of course. Nobody really minded him. What

144

on earth *happened?'* he finished loudly.'

'We never met him,' Thea said gently. 'I only got here on Saturday and Jessica arrived yesterday. Almost the first thing she did was to find his body.'

'Mum!' Jessica warned in a low voice. She gave Nick an apologetic look. 'Sorry, but I don't think we can tell you very much, until after you've seen the police. It's up to them, you see.'

'But it must have been violent?' he hazarded. 'There wouldn't be all this beating about the bush otherwise. The man who phoned said they were pursuing enquiries, or something...' Again he swiped a hand slowly down his cheek. 'It sounded as if they were hinting that he was ... well, *murdered.'* He turned mournful eyes onto Jessica. 'Can't you tell me that much, at least?'

Nick Jolly was in his mid-thirties, with very thick dark hair growing long at the back and sides. To Jessica's eyes he was a man genuinely in shock, trying to keep pace with events, and maintain his frail composure. She shook her head regretfully. 'To be honest with you, I'm not sure you should have come here,' she said. 'I understand why you did, but it's important that you speak to the officers involved with the case before I tell you anything.'

He frowned at her in confusion. 'You sound very formal,' he said, with a hint of a

145

boyish whine.

'Jessica's in the police as well,' Thea explained. 'That's why she has to be careful to stick to the rules.'

'Oh! How–? I mean, that's a surprise.' His face grew even paler and his fingers started a little dance where they rested on his leg. 'What about Gladys? I suppose that's why you're here,' he realised slowly. 'If Ron and Yvette are away. She must be in a real state, poor old girl.'

'She doesn't seem to understand, actually,' Thea said. She bit back the questions she wanted to ask, after another repressive glance from Jessica.

Nick got up from the sofa. 'I'd better go. It was out of order to come so soon. You must be pretty shaken up yourselves. Anyway, I got what I came for, I suppose.' His shoulders slumped as he turned towards the door. 'There's no doubt about it, I see that now. Gramps is dead, and it's a case for the police.' He sighed. 'In a way, he'd probably have enjoyed the drama. He wasn't the sort to look forward to a slow lingering death from some disease finishing him off by inches.'

Mother and daughter merely smiled, and stood out of his way.

'Well... This is...' He stumbled into the hall. 'I shouldn't really have come, I know. But I was bothered about Gladys. I needed to know if she was all right.' He glanced towards the cottage, as if hoping to see through the wall into Granny's quarters.

Jessica had followed and was standing protectively close to Nick. 'It's nice of you to be concerned about her,' she said.

'Oh, well. I've known her all my life. She's always been a bit like another Granny to me. And Frances – I always *adored* Aunt Frances.' He sighed again.

Halfway into the street he looked back, and said, 'I've booked into The Crown for a couple of nights. Perhaps I'll see you again.'

'I'm sure you will,' Jessica agreed. 'And ... we're really sorry, you know. It's a rotten thing to happen.'

'Yeah,' he choked, before stumbling down to his car.

'Poor chap,' said Thea, as they closed the door. 'He seems very genuine. Sorry if I almost put my foot in it. I didn't understand the rules.'

'I know you didn't. By rights he ought never to have come here. They'll have told him to go straight to the Incident Room for interview. At least, that's what I assume. I was so scared of messing up by saying too much to him. I expect he thought I was rude.'

'He was in too much of a state to notice,' Thea assured her. 'Fancy driving so far in that condition.'

'People do it all the time,' said Jessica absently. 'Do you think he really was genuine? I got the feeling he was hoping to see Granny for some reason.'

'What – more than a normal concern for her?'

'Possibly. It felt odd the way he mentioned her again right on the doorstep.'

'I don't think that meant anything,' said Thea. 'You're reading too much into it.'

Jessica shrugged. 'I expect you're right. But I would love to sit in on his interview with the police. I get the feeling he could be extremely interesting.'

'Oh?' Thea's tone was abrupt. 'Can you say why?'

Jessica blinked. 'No special reason, except he's bound to tell them a whole lot more about Julian than they know so far. They'll get all kinds of stuff out of him.'

'But he's only just heard that his beloved grandfather has died.' Thea stared at her daughter. 'You make it sound so cold and callous.'

'Don't start that again, Mum. They'll be careful with him, of course. But they do need to know the facts of Julian's background. Surely you can see that?'

But Thea had become entrenched. 'No, I can't. That poor man can barely form a complete sentence, the way he is now. And when he comes here for some reassurance, you clam up and quote police procedure at him.'

Jessica gritted her teeth. 'It wasn't at all like that. I think you're talking absolute rubbish. I'm going upstairs now, before I say something I'll regret.'

Watching the girl disappear, Thea was left with a residue of uncomfortable feelings. While Jessica had been at the postmortem, she had done little more than rerun events of the past two days and worry that her daughter was having a ghastly time. Now they seemed to have stumbled into a pointless argument that left them both sulky and silent. She went outside, thinking a change of scene would help.

A quick walk to the end of the garden with the dog brought her unpleasantly close to the scene of Julian's demise. The bamboo screen had been mangled by the comings and goings of several officials, even though most of them had used the front door. The damage to the plants seemed symbolic of the sadness hanging over the house. Gradually Thea's attention became entirely absorbed in the appearance of the two gardens, and its implications for what had happened to Julian Jolly the previous day.

She began to force her mind to construct possible explanations for how the man had met his fate. As far as she was aware, the front door had been bolted from the inside, so even if the killer had been admitted by Julian willingly, surely the escape after his death could only have been through the back, with the door left unlocked. Slowly, she examined the possibilities. On the further side of Julian's garden there appeared to be a small wooden door in a high wall, where, she had noticed earlier, there was at least a theoretical egress onto the street beyond. But when she examined it closely, it was obvious it had not been opened for years. Ivy twined robustly around the hinges and across the small space between door and wall. The act of opening it would have torn away several tendrils and been impossible to conceal. This left her concluding that nothing short of an athletic climb over the back wall could have taken place. The wall was close to eight feet high, with another house immediately beyond it, which made this theory highly improbable. She would have to ask Jessica to find out from the police whether they had evidence to show how the killer got away. Without that, she could not avoid the notion that he had fled through the unlocked back door of the Montgomery house, and out of the front onto the street while Thea was asleep up-stairs. Except – she had locked the front door and bolted it. Nobody could have fastened it again from the outside.

Jessica had returned to the kitchen and was reading her lecture notes. Hostilities forgotten, Thea joined her, intent on talking through her latest findings. She began with an account of her garden explorations.

'Do the police know how he got away?' she asked. 'Because as far as I can see, it's a real mystery.'

Jessica teetered between irritable dismissal of the question, and something more cooperative. Her mother, like most mothers, had an uncanny knack of asking the wrong thing at the wrong moment. But there was already too much unpleasantness floating around, and the balance came down on the side of good sense.

'No,' she said. 'I hadn't even thought to wonder about that until now.'

Thea laid out her alternative hypotheses on what could have happened. 'It's a dreadful thought,' she said, 'but the most likely one is that he ran through this house, in at the back and out at the front.'

'You'd have heard,' said Jessica earnestly. 'That can't possibly have happened. Besides, surely you locked both the doors?'

Thea had been braced for this. 'Front yes, back no,' she said concisely. 'And don't lecture me. Ron himself said he doesn't usully bother with the back. He said nobody could get in that way,' she added miserably. 'But it still doesn't work, unless I was so distracted by the buzzer going off that I never even noticed the front door was unlocked.'

'Can't you remember?'

Thea's face tightened in an effort at recollection. 'I *think* I had to turn the key, and unbolt it, to get out. But you do that stuff so automatically, I can't be totally sure.'

Jessica scratched her nose thoughtfully. 'There aren't many alternatives,' she concluded. 'From Julian's back door, the only ways to go are into this house, or over the wall at the far end of his garden, or into the next house along the High Street.'

Thea nodded. 'That's right. I just hope it's the last option – although from what I can see, there isn't any escape from the next house along. It's got solid walls on all sides.'

'Solid? And high, I suppose.'

'Looks like it. I suppose the police have explored it by now. They'll tell us what they've found eventually, will they?'

Jessica grimaced. 'They will if they decide the killer came through here. Now take me to see this door you've found.'

Jessica had no need to say anything, having inspected the door just as Thea had done. Her eyebrows did the talking, as she stared up at the wall.

'You see what I mean,' said Thea and her daughter merely nodded.

In the house again, reluctant to talk through the alarming likelihood of what had happened, the two remembered the wider world at the end of their respective mobile phones. 'We'd better try and catch up with James and Phil,' said Thea. 'Or they'll be banging on the door by tea time.'

'At the latest,' Jessica sighed. 'But we'd miss them if they didn't exist.'

They went into separate corners of the house with their mobiles and tried to rectify their omissions. Jessica had more luck than her mother. Detective Superintendent James Osborne had been waiting anxiously for the call, so much so that the woman on the switchboard put her through in a second. 'Jess? What's happening? You *are* in Blockley, aren't you? Your name's here on the screen as having found a body. Homicide victim. For God's sake, sweetheart – what's going on?'

Calmly, she told the story. 'Although I expect it's all on your screen anyway,' she concluded.

'Most of it,' he agreed. 'So you're all right are you?'

'I'm fine. Don't fuss,' she said, trying to sound convincingly firm and evidently failing.

'Jess – I'm here to help you. You ought to come to me when there's any trouble, not try to deal with everything on your own.'

'Stop it,' she sniffed. 'You'll make me cry.'

'Listen. What happened in Manchester – you have to believe me when I say it's not important. It's practically forgotten already. You'll get a bit of a reprimand, admittedly, but there won't be any follow-up.'

'Thanks. But that isn't really – it isn't really that side of it that's bothering me. It's *me*. I lost it. I lost control.'

'And scared yourself. I know. It's *normal*, love. We all do it. We're not robots. And people can be so bloody infuriating at times.'

Despite herself, she felt better, and giggled. 'That's true.'

'So take a few days out, let your mother spoil you. There's sure to be some fascinating bit of history she'll latch onto. Go for long walks. Try some of the local eateries. There's a great place at Paxford I've heard about.'

'That's all fine,' she interrupted him. 'Except that the man next door's been murdered, and there's a senile old Granny here, as part of Mum's package for the house-sitting. Granny-sitting is more like it. And we've just had a visit from the victim's grandson, which set us at each other's throats for some reason.'

She heard James tapping a keyboard. 'Nicholas Jolly. Fontmell Magna, Dorset. That grandson?'

'The very one. He's probably quite nice when he isn't in a state.'

'Bit old for you, pet.'

She gritted her teeth at that. Even her devoted uncle suffered from the general

154

obsession with sexual cliché that seemed to run right through the police force. If she ever thought about it at all, she supposed he might be somewhat starved of sex, because his wife, Rosie, was a semi-invalid with a chronic back problem. James Osborne was not happy – that was the basic essence of it. Childless, required to be eternally patient and caring towards Rosie, the survivor of two brothers who had always been devoted to each other, he seemed battered by fate and unable to find any haven from his troubles.

'Mum forgot all about Mother's Day,' she said, snatching at random for a change of subject. 'Don't you think that's funny?'

'Silly business,' said James inattentively. 'Just a racket created by florists and greetings card people.'

'Like Valentine's Day,' she agreed.

'Right. Not to mention Christmas.'

'Don't mention Christmas,' she pleaded. 'Now I'll let you get on with your work. Thanks for being so nice. Don't worry about me any more, OK?'

'I'll worry until they've caught that killer. And be sure to lock all the doors.'

'You think it's a burglar who'll come back for more loot?' She thought she'd managed to inject enough bravado into her tone to convince him, successfully hiding the lurking nervousness that wouldn't go away.

'I'd like to think it was a very frightened burglar who's now two hundred miles away.'

'But you can't believe that.'

'No,' he said gently.

'So who was it?'

'Somebody who had a grudge against old Mr Jolly, perhaps. Or wanted him quiet about something – for ever. Or got into the wrong house by mistake. You know this isn't the first time your Mum's been caught up in something nasty.'

'So?'

'So think about it. People away – strange woman, not knowing anything about the place or the locals. Golden opportunity to nip in and do the dirty deed.'

'You sound like a – I don't know. A cheap paperback thriller from the Fifties.'

James snorted. 'And what would you know about the great Rex Stout? Or John Dickson Carr? Or–'

'OK, OK. I'm going. See you soon.' And she disconnected him. With a deep breath she tried to push away the apprehension that had been growing ever since the post-mortem had forced the reality of the situation upon her. Somebody was out there with a murderous weapon, and she and her mother were staying in the very next house. And however much Thea might joke about the dog defending them, they were essentially defenceless. Daytime was all right – their eyes and ears would alert them to any danger. But the night would be very different, and Jessica was already inwardly shuddering at the prospect.

'Mine's having a bit of a panic. How about yours?' said Thea, coming into the room a few moments later.

'The same. He means well, I suppose.'

'I know.' Thea sighed.

'You're missing him,' Jessica accused. 'If I wasn't here, you'd have asked him to come and stay, I bet.'

Thea was emphatic. 'No I wouldn't. I wanted this time with you. I haven't seen nearly enough of you since last summer. Phil can wait. He's not going to go anywhere.'

'You sound awfully sure.'

Thea smiled complacently. 'I am.'

'So when's the happy day?' Jessica tried to speak lightly, but it came out wrong. She turned away to hide the sudden hardness on her face.

'No happy day, Jess. I've told you that before. I don't want to be married again. I like being on my own. And Phil's got too much baggage, as the saying goes. Not to mention his job.'

'Right,' muttered Jessica. 'So what are we doing for lunch? It looks like rain out there.'

Thea ducked her head to peer at the sky through the front window. 'Rain? Surely not!'

'And wind. Look at those bushes.'

'Bummer. Well, let's go to the shop and buy some lunch and then I should probably pop next door. After all the excitement, I really need to make sure she's alive. What if the shock's finished her off?'

'That would be all we need. Did the people leave the number of a local undertaker?'

Thea slapped her daughter's arm. 'Of course not. I was joking. She's going to be fine. I won't allow anything else to happen. And since the police haven't been back, we might even assume they've caught Julian's killer hiding in a ditch over at Aston Magna or somewhere.'

Jessica shook her head 'Sorry, but no such luck, according to Uncle James. There isn't really a place called Aston Magna, is there?'

'There really is. I'll take you to see it tomorrow, if you like. It's near Upper Ditchford – that's one of the lost villages. Won't that be interesting?'

'Fascinating,' groaned Jessica.

CHAPTER NINE

They went together to the village store, as it began to rain gently, and bought assorted convenience food that would need little cooking. Fray Bentos pies, frozen Ready Meals and a large victoria sponge made by a local woman. 'Lovely!' enthused Jessica. 'All my favourite things.'

Thea had almost got to the point where she no longer quizzed her daughter on her diet, and whether she was eating properly, with plenty of fruit and not too much alcohol. Jessica looked as if she managed at least as well as Thea did, her skin clear and her figure neither too fat nor too thin. The most zealous mother would be hard pushed to find any cause for concern, at least on the physical side.

'Hello,' came a voice behind them. The tall lugubrious figure of Giles Stevenson stood there in a bulky jacket, the hood over his head, making him seem oddly ageless and indefinable.

Thea found herself wanting to hug him, as an unlikely rescuer, a familiar sharer in the crisis that had overwhelmed them. 'Hello,' she said, standing her ground. 'Are you all right?'

He stooped to bring his face closer to hers. 'Are *you?*' he rejoined.

'Just about. Aren't we?' she enlisted Jessica's support. 'It's all very nasty, though.'

'How's Gladys today?'

'She was all right this morning. The police came to try to interview her, but I'm afraid it didn't go very well.'

Giles smiled painfully. 'No,' he said. 'I don't suppose it did.' He gave the impression he could say more, but was reining himself in.

'There doesn't appear to be very much reaction in the village,' Thea commented. 'I mean – everything looks as if it's carrying on as normal. In the shop just now – nobody asked us about it. Surely they know who we are by now, and what happened last night?'

'Bad form to talk about it,' he said with a cynical kink on his lips. 'What would you expect them to say?'

Thea nodded. 'I see what you mean.'

Jessica seemed restless, beside her, but Thea was not inclined to abandon the conversation quite yet. She was asking herself at what precise moment she had concluded that Giles Stevenson was on their side, a good and useful person, and realising it had been close to this very spot, the previous morning, when she had been frantically searching for Granny, only to find her on the man's sheltering arm.

'Your list was a good idea,' she said next. 'Did you write it last night?'

He nodded. 'It usually works quite well.'

Jessica hefted the bag of shopping, before asking him, 'Is she really as senile as she seems? I mean – the police were wondering if it's for real, this morning. There just isn't any *logic* to it,' she complained.

'*Au contraire*, my dear,' said Giles softly. 'The logic might not be apparent to you or me, but I assure you it exists. Gladys is the same person she's always been. Her instincts are unchanged, her mannerisms and even, I think, her values. She might forget her name, sometimes, but she still knows who she is.'

The obscurity of this silenced the women for a moment. 'It is very mysterious, though,' said Thea at last. 'It makes everything so unpredictable.'

'Oh yes,' Giles smiled sadly. 'It does that all right. Which is why I admire Yvette for being brave enough to go off and leave her, the way she did. We all warned her it might have drastic consequences. Gladys doesn't like changes in the routine – not unless they come from her, of course.'

'But you can't possibly have expected something like this – can you?' Thea stared at him, suddenly aware of the depths of her ignorance about the people, the place, the connections between them. 'You don't mean that, do you?'

He closed his eyes for a moment, turning his face to the mild drizzle that was falling. 'Unpredictable, remember,' he said. 'I had no idea what to expect.'

Something cold settled on Thea's heart, a suggestion of horrible proportions, which she actually tried to brush away with the flat of her hand.

'It's raining, Mum,' said Jessica. 'I'm getting wet.'

But Thea still wasn't quite ready to separate from the man who she believed knew more answers than she had questions. 'How long has she been like this?' she asked. 'With her memory the way it is?'

He almost seemed relieved, and his reply came readily. 'Just about five years now. It isn't Alzheimer's, you know. It was the result of an accident.'

'Accident? How?'

'The idiot GP prescribed the wrong drug for her. All she wanted was an anti-inflammatory for a sore shoulder. He gave her some new stuff, didn't check the dosage, and it knocked her for six. You should have seen her! She was like a different woman within days of taking it.' The indignation was stark.

'My God!' Jessica was suddenly animated. 'Didn't they strike him off for negligence?'

Giles shrugged. 'Not so far. You know how slowly these things grind on. He's blaming

162

the manufacturers and the pharmacist, equally. The makers say they listed the possible side effects quite clearly, with all the contra-indications. Gladys drank several shots of scotch while she was taking them, which didn't help.'

'So he says it was her own fault?' Jessica suggested.

'Not in so many words, no. And of course nobody can prove for sure that she wasn't already getting senile, and had managed to mask it. It's left a lot of ill feeling.'

'And a woman who doesn't know what time of day it is,' said Jessica.

Giles huffed a gentle laugh. 'Oh, she knows that, all right. That's just one of her games.'

Thea wondered about this remark. Granny had definitely been confused about the time of day last Saturday, when Thea had first arrived.

Giles was in full spate. 'Gladys lives in a perpetual present, you see,' he expounded. 'She knows precisely what time it is *now*. Just don't expect to get anywhere if you want to know about yesterday.'

'Although,' Thea said, even more doubtfully, 'she talks about her own past. She told me she came here when she was sixty, that she worked with Julian, and was keen on painting.'

Giles raised his eyebrows tolerantly. 'I'm sure she did,' he said. 'And tomorrow she'll tell you she was born here and spent a lifetime as a potter.'

'It isn't true?'

He shook his head. 'How much of anything that one person tells another is true?'

Jessica had had enough. 'I'm going back,' she said. 'The shopping's getting wet as well as me.' She took a few steps, clearly expecting her mother to follow.

But Thea was gripped by the question, eager to enter into the philosophy of it. 'Facts,' she protested. 'Surely you can trust the facts a person tells you?'

Giles put up one hand. 'No more,' he told her. 'Your daughter's right. This is not the time or the place. Besides, I have to return to the grindstone. This won't butter the parsnips, will it?'

'What do you do?'

'Oh, I'm just a hack. Weekly columns here and there, you know. Had a piece in the *Telegraph* last week, for a change. Not usually quite so upmarket as that.'

Thea remembered his reference to a keyboard, and understood her mistake in thinking it had to do with music.

'Celebrity interviews?' Thea asked with a mischievous smile. 'Have you done Icarus Binns?'

'That nincompoop? I might slide a little way down market now and again, but I never get so low that I'd find him a suitable subject, believe me. For a start, I can't understand anything he says. And for another thing, these celebrity types are no-go when they're over here. It's an unspoken agreement that we pretend they're just like the rest of us.'

Thea smiled. If this man earned enough from his so-called hack writing to afford to live in Blockley, he was probably something of a celebrity himself. 'Very civilised,' she said. It was a parting shot, and with nothing more said, they went their separate ways.

Having caught up with Jessica, Thea began to apologise for being annoying. But Jessica cut her short. 'There's something very odd about that man, don't you think? All that old-fashioned charm feels like an act. Nobody behaves like that any more.'

Thea gave this some thought. 'They do, you know. In places like this, the men still wear ties even if they're not going anywhere, and they open doors for women. I like him. He seems *trustworthy*.'

Jessica laughed scornfully. 'This place is in a time warp. In Manchester they just leer at you and call you names.'

'If I had to choose, I suppose I'd go for the time warp, then.'

Thea had been thinking a lot about the increasing gulf between country areas such as the Cotswolds, and the urban frenzy that was now her daughter's habitat. There seemed to be nothing in between, no bridge from one to the other, and very little mutual comprehension. Her house-sitting episodes, in small affluent villages, where a good proportion of the properties were owned by town-dwellers who escaped for some fresh air and silence, had only highlighted the great divide. She had found herself in farmyards and tiny local pubs worlds away from the centre of Manchester or Birmingham. People in the villages of Gloucestershire still understood the rhythms of the seasons and the malodorous realities of meat production, even if they were not directly involved. But, she had discovered, they basically behaved the same as their urban cousins. They became addicted to harmful chemicals, they felt rage and fear and jealousy. They closed and locked their doors and huddled over their computers. The languidly patronising Giles seemed a perfect case in point.

'You like these places, then?' Jessica asked.

'I love the *look* of them,' said Thea carefully. 'And the history, and the way they seem so permanent and incorruptible. These houses have been here for two centuries or more, and they're going to last at least that long again.'

'But they're going to be more and more like film sets – just hollow sham, with nothing really going on behind the façades. Tourism is sure to ruin everything that's genuine about them.'

'That's already happened to a few. But tourism is by nature blinkered, one-track sort of stuff. There are dozens and dozens of little places tucked down country lanes, where the tourists would never dream of venturing. No, it won't be tourists – it'll be the rich second-home people. But there's some good things about them. They preserve the appearance of the houses, for a start.'

'And you think the main virtue of them is the appearance,' observed Jessica. 'Isn't that a bit sad?' They were passing one of the doors on which had been pinned several notices concerning village activities. 'Look at this,' Thea invited. 'They have them in a lot of places. Somebody offers their street door as a community noticeboard like this. And see what they've got going on. Bridge, film club, yoga, first aid course, even a discussion group. They do actually meet each other, from the look of it.'

'And they indulge in some good old-fashioned murder, too,' said Jessica. 'Just like where I live.'

'I was hoping we wouldn't talk about that,' sighed Thea.

'Tough luck. Look what's parked outside our house.'

It was a police car containing Tom and Ginger Eddie. 'Them again,' said Thea. 'Don't we even warrant the CID?'

'Don't!' Jessica shuddered. 'What I'm dreading is your Phil and my Uncle James arriving together and giving us more lectures about safety. Don't they realise how much more scared it makes us?'

'I think that's the intention,' said Thea. 'They don't like women to be fearless. It unsettles them.'

'You could be right. It must make them feel redundant.'

'It's another example of what we were saying about men and the way they treat women. If you ask me, they're all pretty much the same, deep down. They think we need protecting and rescuing every five minutes.'

'Oh well,' Jessica sighed. 'Maybe there are times, just now and then, when we do.'

Thea thought back to her alarming house-sitting commission in Frampton Mansell, where she definitely had needed rescue. 'Yeah,' she said. 'But those are just the times when they're off doing something else.'

They were close enough to the house to hear Hepzie barking inside, a high reproachful sound, accusing the world of abandoning her to the annoyance of police officers at the door.

'Still no sign of Granny,' said Thea. 'Do you think they've tried to speak to her?'

'Let's ask them,' said Jessica, going to the driver's side of the car and bending down to catch the man's eye. 'Hi, Tom,' she said. 'Fancy seeing you again.'

With a single movement, the two men left the car and Jessica stood back to accommodate them. 'Could we come in and talk to you for a minute?' asked the sergeant, without much of a smile.

'Of course,' said Jessica with the faintest hint of irony. 'We're completely at your disposal.'

Thea unlocked the door, and deactivated the burglar alarm that Jessica had made her set before they went out. 'Stupid thing,' she muttered.

The policemen seemed slightly bored by their assignment. Just an old man bumped off, nobody too upset about it, village life carrying on more or less as usual. 'I gather they didn't get far with the old lady this morning,' said Tom. 'And I should ask how the post-mortem went – if that isn't insensitive of me.'

Jessica looked at the ginger-haired Eddie who had scarcely said a word in her hearing thus far. He gave her a flickering grin, ready for the sympathy.

'It was fine, thanks,' she said. 'Really interesting. And I wanted to ask you something – did I get the offer of attending the pm because of my uncle?'

Tom blew out his cheeks in a parody of innocence. 'I don't know what you mean,' he said, and then winked. 'Don't knock it, love – that's my advice. If you're any good, it can't hurt, and if you're rubbish, it isn't going to save you.'

Jessica giggled her relief. 'Thanks,' she said. 'Now, are you coming in?'

'So where did we get to with the old lady?' Tom asked again, once inside the door. 'We could really do with some answers from her.'

Thea and Jessica both gave him repressive looks. 'Even if she answered your questions, you couldn't rely on what she said,' Thea emphasised. 'She makes a lot of it up. Or dreams it, maybe. She's ninety-two, for heavens sake.'

'Age isn't regarded as an impediment in itself,' Tom said, as if reading an invisible book of rules. 'And her memory can't be too bad if she's still living independently.'

'Well, see for yourself,' Thea said. 'It's not for me to decide, is it? For all I know you've got a whole set of procedures for interviewing senile witnesses.'

'No, they haven't,' said Jessica, with a suppressed chuckle. 'Even I know that much.'

Thea lost patience. 'Well, it's not up to me, is it? You go and question her. Maybe she's having a lucid day today. Maybe she saw the whole thing and it's come back to her, clear as crystal.'

Tom remained unmoved by the sarcasm. He held his ground, planted solidly on two large feet. 'So how do we get hold of her? We knocked on the street door, and nothing happened.'

'She usually answers the door,' Thea said. 'Even though it can take a long time. I suppose we could try the connecting door, but she doesn't like it, according to her daughter. It's only really for emergencies.'

'How do you define an emergency?' asked Eddie, as if waiting for his moment in the limelight.

'I have no idea,' snapped Thea. She led them to the door halfway along the hall, and took the key from the hook.

'This is a weird arrangement, don't you think?' said the sergeant. 'Keeping your poor old Granny locked away all lonely and neglected?'

'I suppose they've got their reasons. They seemed like very nice people. They said something about firm boundaries. She's quite fit physically, after all.'

'Hasn't she got her own key to this door?'

'It seems not. That would defeat the purpose, wouldn't it? Although–' she remembered 'she did have one originally, and apparently lost it. Maybe it turned up again.'

'Maybe she never lost it at all,' Tom suggested.

Thea gave him a startled look. 'That's a bit cynical, isn't it?' she said.

He shrugged. 'Maybe. So let's assume she

really has lost it. How does she contact them if she needs to? What if she falls out of bed in the night, or forgets where she is, or runs out of milk? What's she supposed to do?'

Thea flapped a hand at the Sergeant, trying to make him stop while she explained, aware that she had asked precisely the same questions of Yvette, some weeks earlier.

'She'd have to shout. They'd hear her in the night. It's all one house originally, after all.'

'And don't forget the buzzer,' said Jessica.

'What buzzer?' asked Tom.

Thea showed him. 'It's very loud. Rather a good idea, in some ways.'

'Hmm,' said the policeman. 'So she isn't allowed to go out of her own front door.'

'I took her out for a walk on Saturday afternoon,' Thea said, as if in self-justification. 'It wasn't altogether successful.' She laughed ruefully. 'She fell over, which was very scary at the time. That's when that Ick person showed up. He offered to help, which was nice of him.'

'Icarus Binns,' Jessica translated importantly. 'We saw him in The Crown. And Cleodie Mason was with him.'

The sergeant was perhaps thirty-four, the constable six or seven years younger. There was no doubt whatsoever that they would know the two celebrities.

Both men struggled to appear nonchalant.

172

'Yeah, I heard something about that. We like to keep an eye on these high-profile figures. They can be vulnerable.'

'You mean somebody might kidnap them?' laughed Thea. 'And hold them to ransom?'

'It isn't unknown,' said Tom stiffly.

Beside them came a sudden banging on the locked door. 'What's all that noise?' came a shrill voice. 'Who's doing all that talking?'

Thea called back, 'It's all right Granny. I'm going to open the door, and you can see for yourself.'

'Who do you think you're calling Granny?' came an angry reply. Thea remembered that she had been careful to stick to the more formal 'Mrs Gardner' until then.

'Sorry,' she said, pointing to the key hanging just too high for her to reach. Tom lifted it down, and put it in the lock. It turned easily, but when he tried to open the door, it wouldn't move. 'Hang on,' he said. 'It wasn't locked after all.'

'Yes it was,' said Thea. 'I checked it on Saturday and I haven't touched it since then.'

'Well, you saw what I just did. I turned the key, and now it's locked.' He reversed the process, and the door opened. 'I turned it back, and it's open. I don't think you can argue with that.' He looked to Jessica and Eddie for support, which they both gave with unreserved nods of their heads.

When the door was pulled fully open, Granny Gardner was revealed, standing very upright, dressed in clean cord trousers and a bright pink jumper. She looked alert, fit and about seventy-three.

'Police!' she said, eyes wide. 'Has there been a robbery? Did Yvette lose the Minton plates? I told her not to leave them on full view.'

'No, no,' Thea said. 'Nothing's been stolen.'

'You've been driving too fast then,' she stated as clear fact. 'That must be it.' She gave Thea a penetrating scrutiny. 'You're the person with the long-tailed spaniel,' she said.

Thea almost clapped. 'That's right!' she said. 'We went for a walk together.'

'No, I went for a walk with Giles. Silly man,' she added. 'Told me Julian was away with that grandson of his. I knew that wasn't right.' Her face clouded. 'I remember his notes,' she quavered. 'They say Julian is dead. Can that be right?' She looked from face to face, stepping back to give admittance to the policemen.

Sergeant Tom gently ushered Mrs Gardner into her front room, and leant himself casually against the back of a chair. 'Yes, that's right,' he said. 'And we came to talk to you about him.'

She frowned at him, a wilful child with pouting lips.

'Julian was your good friend, is that right?'

She nodded. 'He helped me with my lists. He was like you – bossy,' she quipped, with a little smile.

'And was he going to help you when your daughter went on holiday?'

'Is Frances on holiday? I haven't seen her for ever so long. But she sent me flowers, see.'

'No, it's *Yvette* who's on holiday,' Thea insisted. 'And I'm here to keep an eye on you. The policeman wants to know whether Julian would have done the same.'

The blankness that met this question seemed to Thea tragically genuine. The old woman didn't even shake her head, but simply lost herself in thick clouds of bewilderment.

'Did he have a key to your house?' Tom repeated.

The old woman's eyes narrowed. 'Key? What key? Did who have a key?'

'Mr Julian Jolly.' Tom pushed a hand into a side pocket of his jacket. 'Because I think he did. I think this is it.' With a magician's flourish, he produced a shiny door key, which Thea recognised immediately. She took a breath to speak, but he quelled her with a look.

Mrs Gardner failed even to focus on the object. 'Never mind,' said Tom. 'We won't bother you any more. Thank you for letting us talk to you. And, if I may say so, you're looking extremely smart today.'

'I always put this jumper on for Julian,' she said, looking down at herself. 'This one's his favourite.'

Leading the way, the sergeant conducted his little party back through the connecting door into the main part of the house. Closing the door behind Jessica, he removed the key that Thea had used, and inserted the one from his pocket. But his expectations were dashed. The key refused to turn.

'What are you doing?' asked Thea.

Tom tapped the key against his teeth for a moment, and then looked towards the back of the house. 'There's a lock on the kitchen door, I assume?'

'Of course,' Thea nodded.

Without waiting to explain, he marched through and repeated his experiment with the key. This time it fitted perfectly, turning in the lock and doing everything a good key should.

Tom flashed a triumphant smile at his audience. 'This was in Mr Jolly's pocket,' he said.

CHAPTER TEN

Before leaving, the police officers' attention was caught by the cage outside the back door of the cottage. For Tom, it seemed to be more evidence of strange behaviour on the part of the Montgomerys towards their aged mother. Thea made no attempt to defend them, still struggling to connect the fact of the key with the theories she and Jessica had developed earlier in the day concerning the escape route of the killer.

The two women talked about doors and keys for quite a long time after the policemen had gone, but with no constructive conclusion. Their theories tended to the circular, with so many distracting convolutions that there was plainly no sense in sharing them with the police – who in any case could work it out just as easily for themselves. Or so Thea insisted, when Jessica worried that they should at least check that Julian's garden had been thoroughly explored.

'That would be telling them how to do their job,' Thea objected. 'Not a good idea, in my experience.'

After they'd made and eaten a hearty

lunch, Hepzie was showing signs of cabin fever, so Thea suggested a walk through the woods to the higher ground, where they could look across to what had once been the village of Upton. 'It's stopped raining,' she pointed out. 'And there's a whole lot of day still to go. Hepzie can have a good run up there, as well.'

Jessica agreed with scant enthusiasm, and they set out towards the end of the High Street with a final glance at Granny's door. 'We'd better not be long,' said Thea.

It was obvious that the girl was preoccupied, as they passed several attractive houses and gardens without her seeming to notice them at all. Thea deliberately pointed out interesting features, as if to a young child in a sulk. She began with the Russell Spring, from which clear water constantly trickled. 'I bet it's lovely to drink,' she said.

Jessica didn't reply, and was barely even turning to look at the landmarks. Thea persevered, on the assumption that the silence was due to the girl not wanting to go out at all. The weather was far from perfect, reminding them that it was still only March, with all the mood swings that implied.

'Oh, look at this,' she went on, coming to a sudden stop beside a wide entrance to a steeply climbing driveway. *Joanna Southcott lived here. 1804-1814.* Where have we heard that name just lately?'

Jessica blinked. 'Never heard of her,' she said.

'Yes, you have. I'm sure you were there. Something about a box. Yes – I know! When Granny was talking about Julian this morning. She said he wrote a book about it, or something. With Thomas. Didn't she?'

'A box?' Jessica frowned. 'Joanna Southcott's Box. Yes, I remember. There was a file in Julian's house when it was searched. That was the title on the front. What do you know about it?'

'Hardly anything,' Thea admitted. 'So when we get back, you can look it all up on the Internet. It sounds intriguing. I have heard of her, somewhere, but I have no idea who she was.' She scratched her cheek, groping for a mental link. 'I thought she was some sort of witch, or a wise woman. Something like that.'

'Nice house,' observed Jessica, standing back for a better look. The big rectangular property was some distance above them, backed by trees, with terrace gardens between it and the road. 'Some climb to get up to it.'

Inside the gateway, to the right, was an arrangement of low stone walls which had no obvious purpose. 'What's that for?' asked Jessica.

'It's like a little area for people to sit in,' said Thea. 'Maybe she held her consultations there – for people too feeble to struggle up to the house.'

'Right. In 1814,' said Jessica. 'And her ghost keeps it tended even now.'

'Either that or Julian Jolly's been doing it,' said Thea lightly. 'It looks important, though – don't you think. Something we could find out about.'

Jessica sighed. 'Mum – that key. You do realise how bizarre it makes everything, don't you? Bizarre and scary. The dead man had a key to your back door in his pocket when he died.'

So *that* was the cause of her preoccupation, Thea realised. Not a continuing annoyance about one of her mother's gaffes, nor a worry about what awaited her back in Manchester. The girl was frightened.

She aimed for a gentle reassuring tone. 'You don't know that. The killer could have popped it in after he was dead.'

'Oh, yes – and why in the world would anybody do that? That's a daft suggestion.'

'I don't know!' Thea almost shouted in her frustration. 'Now leave it for a bit and let's get on with the walk.'

Meekly, Jessica followed, as Thea led the way confidently to the right and up a wide pathway to the end of the woods and out into a wide open field. The dog ran cheerfully ahead of them, and the breeze tossed their hair more in play than chilly malice.

They strode out, passing a pretty farmhouse with a massive barn facing onto the pathway and a picturesquely ruined outhouse the other side of a low stone wall. 'Isn't that gorgeous!' trilled Thea. 'If it's true that Granny was a painter, she must surely have painted this.'

'Did she really say she was a painter? When?'

'On Saturday, when I took her out for a walk. She said a celebrity woman paid hundreds of pounds for some of her work.'

'Not Cleodie Mason, I guess. She doesn't look as if she'd know what to do with a painting. So where's this Upton place?' Jessica switched subjects as if one was no more interesting than another.

Thea dug the map out of the bag on her shoulder, and carefully located the right section. 'Two more fields and down to the right.'

Jessica looked over her mother's shoulder. 'That's not a right of way,' she pointed out. 'We can't go down there.'

'We'll say we're lost if anybody sees us. It probably happens all the time.'

'How would you like it, if it was your land?'

'We're not doing any harm. Just let's see if we can recognise anything, OK?'

They walked for ten more minutes, passing a small Dutch barn on the track leading to Upton. A few yards further on,

Jessica baulked. 'We'd be able to see by now if there were ruins or anything,' she objected. 'And all there is is a field, the same as any other field. I'm tired. Let's go back. It's going to rain again, as well, look.'

Forced to admit that there was truth in every word, Thea allowed herself to be turned around and marched back the way they'd come. 'Imagine it, though,' she attempted. 'Living up here in neolithic times. Like being on top of the world.'

The way back felt longer than before, despite it being downhill. Thea talked about abandoned villages, and the various theories concerning them. Inevitably they reverted to the topic of Julian Jolly, archaeologist. 'Maybe he made a stunning new finding, and was murdered because of that,' she suggested, in a gothic sort of tone. 'They didn't just abandon their homes because there was no more work – but some terrifying disease struck them down.'

'Or they were abducted by aliens,' said Jessica, reviving somewhat.

'Or they were removed forcibly by some agency of the government who wanted to conduct some kind of secret activity here.'

'Did they have agents of the government in medieval times?'

'Definitely,' said Thea, with much more conviction than she really felt. All she could recall was Aphra Behn, spying in the seventeenth century, which was completely irrelevant.

'More likely they couldn't stand the weather,' said Jessica, facing into a sudden squall, shoulders hunched. 'Look at that cloud. It's going to pour.'

'We'll be home in ten minutes if we bustle,' said Thea.

A minute later, the cloud had passed by, to the south, and flickers of sunlight were forcing their way through the thinner covering overhead. 'We can slow down now,' panted Thea. 'I want to savour the view for a minute.'

Jessica stopped her headlong march, and sighed. Wind tossed her light brown hair. Her moods appeared to be every bit as changeable as the weather, and for the first time in over an hour, she smiled. 'It is rather impressive,' she conceded. 'All this open countryside – miles and miles of it. You never think about it, do you? It's just a kind of background blur that you see very vaguely from the motorway or the train.'

Thea said nothing, trying to adjust to the change of temper.

Jessica turned in a slow circle, scanning the woods between themselves and Blockley, the wide rising fields to the north and west, the vanishing path over the brow of a hill to the south. 'I can see precisely two buildings,' she announced. 'No roads. A few telegraph poles. It's a whole different world from where I live now.'

Thea and Carl had regularly taken their daughter on country walks from her earliest years. Carl had been a naturalist, eagerly showing her birds and flowers and fishing newts out of ditches. 'Yes,' said Thea. 'You knew that already.'

'I forgot,' said Jessica simply. 'You forget.'

'Oh,' said Thea. 'Maybe you do.'

'The *point* is,' said Jessica patiently, 'that there's stuff *happening* out here.'

Thea still hadn't quite caught the drift. 'What – nature red in tooth and claw, you mean? Things eating each other in the hedges?'

'Not really. I was thinking of people, tucked away in those houses, completely private. They could be doing absolutely anything, and nobody would know about it.'

Thea felt a cold shiver run through her. This was the voice of a police officer, imbued with the necessity of surveillance around the clock. Every moment documented, recorded, monitored. People forbidden from covering their heads, for fear the CCTV couldn't register their faces. People scanned with electronic devices to see what was in their pockets. People stored on databases by their iris patterns and their DNA. People filmed as they drove in the illusory sanctity of their private cars, not even able to pick their noses

184

in peace.

'And good luck to them,' she said with feeling. 'Little do they know that Big Brother is working as we speak to discover a way to watch over them.'

'There's the satellites,' said Jessica, thoughtfully. 'They can read the headlines on a newspaper from up in space. DEFRA pays them to report people digging holes where they shouldn't, or growing the wrong crops.'

'God help us,' said Thea, feeling suddenly painfully middle-aged. 'Where will it all end?'

'If they've nothing to hide, then they've nothing to worry about,' said Jessica.

'That's all very well, but show me the person with nothing to hide.'

'Nothing *illegal*, I mean.'

'And who's to say where the line comes? Today's little bit of eccentricity might be tomorrow's criminal act.'

'Not my problem,' said Jessica. 'I'm just meant to be enforcing the law as it stands today.'

'But that makes you no better than an automaton. You'd willingly go on one of these terrible dawn raids, would you? Hundreds of armed police battering down doors of totally innocent people?'

'Of course I would.' Jessica turned to give her mother a fierce look. 'That's my job. And they're not totally innocent.'

'Often they are,' Thea insisted. 'What about neighbours of the suspects? They get "evacuated" at gunpoint, smacked on the head if they're slow or argumentative. Jess, it's happening every week, here in this country. Stories that ten years ago would only be told about the KGB or Saddam Hussein.'

'I didn't think you'd gone so political,' said Jessica stiffly. 'When did this happen?'

'I haven't gone political. I just don't like the way things are going. And it upsets me to think you've joined the enemy.' Even as she said it, she knew she'd gone too far. 'Sorry, sorry,' she said urgently. 'I didn't mean that exactly. Although...' she paused wretchedly. 'I do wish you'd give it some objective thought.'

'We do, Mum. We have whole mornings in the classroom thinking about it. We know what people like you think of us, as it happens.'

'People like me,' Thea echoed slowly. 'That's most of the legal profession and the House of Lords these days.' She forced a laugh. 'Not the sort of company I ever expected to keep. But, darling, don't you see what that means? How far wrong the legislators and law enforcers have gone?'

'I think we'd better stop this conversation,' said Jessica. 'If you must have your say, then use Phil as your punchbag, not me. I'm still learning the job. Talk to me again when I've been on one of your dawn raids.'

'OK, sorry,' Thea managed, through a throat that was suddenly thick with distress. Where had all that bile come from? Through no more than a normal casual interest in the headlines, a few Radio Four discussions, increased awareness of the ubiquity of cameras – no more, surely, than the bulk of the population? She hadn't known the strength of her own feelings until this moment. 'Sorry,' she said again. 'That was awful of me.'

Not a word was uttered as they walked back down to the High Street. Thea assumed Jessica felt much as she did herself: aware of a gulf between them that had to do with some very basic divisions. But she had got it completely wrong. As they crossed the bridge on the eastern edge of Blockley, the girl said, 'I have a dreadful suspicion about the murder, you know.'

'What? I mean – is that what you've been thinking about for the last ten minutes?'

'Mainly, yeah. I started off thinking about that ding-dong we just had, but then I got onto crime solving, and the fact of a murder a few feet from where we're staying. That's the reality of my work, you see. Anyway, I ran through it all again, the bits I know about the people here. And I had a very nasty idea, that won't go away.'

'Which is?'

'It'll sound completely stupid. Remember

I haven't done any sort of detective work yet. So I'm not exactly thinking as a CID officer here.'

'Right. Go on.'

'First point–' She held up a forefinger, '–the Montgomerys are away, so the routine is sure to be different.'

Thea nodded wordlessly.

'Second point–' another finger '–that means the body could have been undiscovered for up to ten days.'

'Does that follow? I suppose Ron and Yvette could have popped in to see Julian every day when they were at home, but nobody's said they did. And don't you think I might have noticed a smell after a week or so, across the garden fence?'

'Doubtful. Anyway, then I started thinking about that door, and the key in Julian's pocket. It means he had free access to the house. That he probably popped in to see Granny through the Montgomerys' section. And *that* means he must have also been able to open the connecting door whenever he liked.'

'Obviously he could,' said Thea. 'The key was right there, hanging on a hook above the door.'

'Oh yes.' Jessica was deflated for a moment. 'In which case, we seem to be making it all much more complicated than it really is.'

'It seems pretty complicated to me,' said

Thea. 'But I keep going back to Saturday morning. Granny was obviously expecting Julian then. She was worrying about him. And why did they hire me, if Julian usually did what they were asking me to do?'

'Precisely,' said Jessica, casting no illumination onto Thea's confusion.

'Precisely what? It's still all a hopeless fog to me.' Thea felt herself wanting to withdraw from the whole conversation. She did not want to discuss murder, or hear Jessica's horrible idea. She wanted to get away from anything nasty and enjoy the spring with nothing to trouble her. She had had enough of trouble over the past two years, and was starting to resent it.

'I think Granny did it,' said Jessica, loudly, her voice deep and blunt. 'I think she's faking a lot of that senility. And I'm not sure I believe she's really ninety-two. Who told you that?'

'Giles Whatnot. On Saturday evening. Why would he tell me a lie like that?'

'He probably believes it's true.'

'But darling, it *is* a stupid idea. How could she have the strength, for one thing?'

'We don't know how strong she is. Maybe he more or less fell on the knife while she was holding it.'

'A suicide pact – something like that? He wanted her to do it?'

'That's possible. But it wouldn't fit with

the lamp being knocked over. That suggests some sort of struggle in the living room, before he died in the kitchen.'

'Wait,' begged Thea. They were standing at the front door of the Montgomerys' house, and Thea fished in her pocket for the key. 'I still don't follow any of your reasoning. I'd be more likely to think it was that Giles – or even Thomas. When we met him on Saturday, the first thing Granny said to him was "What have you done with Julian?"'

'Really? Remind me which is Thomas?'

'The old gent with the beer gut, who came to Granny's door this morning. She told me she didn't like him.'

Jessica went into the house and dealt with the burglar alarm. Thea glanced around for the dog, only to see her a foot away, nosing intently up and down the pavement to either side of the front door. 'Somebody's been standing here,' Thea noted. 'Somebody she recognises.' And then, as if to confirm her words, a man emerged from a car parked further down the street, slamming the door deliberately loudly, to attract attention. The spaniel bounded ecstatically up to him, leaping at his legs, scrabbling at his thighs with sharp toenails.

'Good God, it's Phil,' said Thea, surprised at the way her heart had started to pound, and the blood to rush to her cheeks.

They ushered Detective Superintendent Phil Hollis into the living room. 'How did you find me?' Thea asked, with a giggle.

'Easy,' he said. 'You're next door to the scene of a murder.'

'And that address is on the police computer,' said Jessica. 'Otherwise you'd have a job to find us. There's no yellow tape across the front door, and no sign of any police activity.'

'There is if you know where to look,' he corrected her. 'But never mind how I found you – are you both all right?' He gazed into Thea's eyes. 'You must be feeling a bit persecuted.'

'Not really,' she disagreed robustly. 'I don't feel particularly affected by it, to be honest, except for the difficulties over Granny – that's the old lady next door who I'm supposed to be keeping an eye on. I never met the man when he was alive, and I'm still finding my way around the village. It feels as if I only just got here, in a way. And the really weird thing is that nobody in Blockley seems very bothered by the fact of a murder in their midst. There's a sort of collective denial going on, and I seem to be included. If it wasn't for Jess, I think I could more or less ignore the whole thing.'

Phil looked at Jessica. 'So you're rocking the boat, are you?' He knew her well enough by this time to recognise her sturdy refusal to admit fear. Even after some alarming experiences in Frampton Mansell – where he had woefully let her down – she had managed to reason herself back to fearlessness. It was a trait he knew he was always going to find unsettling.

She rolled her eyes at him, and sighed. 'Not at all. But it was me who found the body. I can't pretend it never happened. It's funny you turning up like this – I expected it to be Uncle James.'

'Don't worry. He'll be along,' said Phil. 'Sooner or later.'

'Are you part of the investigation?' Thea asked him.

He shook his head. 'Definitely not. There's a big operation ongoing in Birmingham, and my team's been sent in to help. I ought to be there now, by rights. But–' he twinkled boyishly at Thea, making her wonder whether she could find some excuse to go upstairs with him. Could she send Jessica out for some more shopping, perhaps?

'It's good to see you,' she breathed. 'And such a surprise.'

'I'm pleased to hear it. I wasn't sure what my reception would be. Women can be funny about surprises.'

Thea did not do flirtation. She did not say *Oh, and which women are you referring to?* She did not play the usual games, or tell the usual lies. 'I don't mind them,' she said.

'Actually, the whole point about a surprise, surely, is that nobody knows how they'll react until it happens.'

'Oh, Mum!' groaned Jessica, meeting Phil's amused eye. 'You're so–'

'What? What am I?' Thea genuinely wanted to know.

'Literal,' said Jessica. 'That's the word. You take everything at face value.'

'Sorry,' said Thea. 'Although, to be honest, I'm not really sorry about that at all,' she added. 'You'll just have to take me as I am.'

'Oh, I know *that*,' said Jessica. 'I was born knowing that.'

'Girls!' Phil reproached them. 'Enough. Go and make a pot of tea, one of you. It's nearly four o'clock.'

But the tea was barely made before Phil happened to glance out of the window and observe a man in his late thirties hovering near his car. 'Oh-oh,' said Hollis. 'That looks like somebody for me.' He went to the door and called out to the man.

'Sorry, sir, but you're needed,' came the reply.

'Why didn't they just use my phone? Where's your motor?' Phil asked him.

'They phoned us at the Incident Room up the hill, assuming you'd be there. I'd heard a whisper that your ... friend ... was in Block-ley, so I took a gamble and trotted down here. I thought ... I mean, it gave you a bit more time, that way. I knew your car when I found it.' He deliberately avoided looking at Thea, his face slightly pink.

Phil sighed, and turned to meet Thea's gaze as she stood in the hallway behind him. 'Sorry,' he said. 'Duty calls. It was good to see you, if only for a few minutes.'

'It was wonderful,' she said unguardedly. 'An unexpected treat.'

'I know I'm wasting my breath, but stay out of trouble, OK? How long are you here?' he asked Jessica.

'Till Thursday, all being well,' she told him. 'It's a bit uncertain, but that's the general idea.'

'So keep an eye on your old Mum, right? I don't want to hear about any heroics from either of you. The chances are the old fellow next door interrupted a burglar, and the bloke's back in Solihull or somewhere long since. Nothing to sharpen your detective faculties on. Rotten thing to happen, but no great mystery.'

He approached Thea, arms wide, and she folded herself into them for a thorough hug. Phil's body was nothing like Carl's had been. The two men smelt different, wore different clothes, put their hands in different places. But there was still, in a lurking corner of her heart, a sense of betrayal. She had truly and profoundly intended, when she married Carl, never to get as close as this to another man.

Jessica averted her gaze, bending down to the dog, watching a young woman with a baby across the street.

'See you, then,' said Phil at last. 'Not sure when.'

'We'll let you know if we solve the murder,' said Jessica lightly, and Thea held her breath. But no more was said, and the police car sped away. When they'd gone, Thea turned to Jessica. 'You didn't feel like giving him your theory about who killed Julian, then?'

'I didn't get a chance, did I?'

'Were you planning to?'

'I don't know,' the girl admitted. 'Very probably not.'

'Better have that tea, then,' said Thea hoping she sounded more stoical than she felt. 'Maybe we could give the patio a try.'

'The seats'll be wet,' Jessica objected. 'Haven't you had enough fresh air for one day?'

'I'll wipe them. I like the quiet, and the garden's so pretty, it needs somebody to admire it.'

'You're mad,' said her daughter, but she followed her out with a plate of biscuits.

They sat at the small wrought iron table for five minutes, before Jessica shivered and announced she was going back indoors. But before she could move, the silence was cracked into ear-splitting shards.

'What's that?' Jessica squealed.

'Oh, Lord. It's Granny's buzzer. She must have gone out.' Thea got up and hurried through the house. The buzzer was making its maddening sound just over her head as she threw open the front door. Hepzie was at her heels and she turned to order the spaniel to stay indoors. The dog seemed hardly to notice the noise, until Thea caught the strange look in her eyes. Apprehension and something like pain filled them. 'Stay!' she ordered. 'Go and talk to Jessica.'

But Jessica was already following her into the hall. 'What a ghastly din,' she complained, at the top of her voice.

'Can't you turn it off for me?' Thea shouted, pointing at the switch. 'I'll go after her.'

Thea could see no sign of Mrs Gardner, until she looked to her right and caught sight of a bow-legged figure heading towards the woods at the end of the street. The old lady was moving at quite some speed, she noted, and seemed very purposeful.

Putting on a spurt of her own, she drew level with her quarry within sight of the trees ahead. 'Off for a walk?' she puffed. 'You look as if you're dressed for it.' Mrs Gardner was wearing stout shoes that looked as if they'd been made around 1946, and a felt hat with a very droopy gauzy flower attached to it.

'That's right,' chirped Granny. 'I thought I'd go bird's nesting. I know all the different eggs,' she added proudly.

Thea entertained a flash of early memory, where her brother had come home with three different eggs from three different nests and their father had chastised him with astonishing violence. That had been, she supposed, during the Seventies, when wild birds were disappearing rapidly, thanks to the chemicals and hedge-removal involved in farming at the time.

'You're not allowed to collect eggs any more,' she said, trying to work out when Granny's egg-collecting heyday must have been. 'The birds need protecting from that sort of thing. Besides,' she realised, 'I think it's still a bit early in the year for it.'

The old woman pulled in her chin, and gave Thea a beaky stare of reprimand. 'I don't *take* the eggs,' she sniffed. 'I never did. That was the sort of thing boys did – blowing out the yolk. Very messy business. I just like to *look*, and watch the mother bird with her babies.'

'Can I come with you, then?' Thea asked, resigned to retracing the route she and Jessica had taken less than an hour before.

'I suppose so, if you're quiet.'

There followed sixty minutes of peculiar magic. A nostalgia that went back to a few brief years of Thea's childhood where she had been a country child. Not only did it remind her of her own experience, but it conjured her husband Carl and his stories of growing up on a farm in the sixties, where even then he had been unusual. Most of his peers had already caught the television bug and seldom went outside. He, however, had been born with a fascination for the outdoors.

With a shock Thea found herself revelling in her strange companion, who did indeed know where to find birds' nests amongst the patch of woodland so close to human settlement. And although Thea had been partly right in thinking late March was rather early for such activity, there were signs that the birds were gathering themselves for the breeding frenzy that was almost upon them. They sat on a fallen tree, quietly watching a robin flitting to and fro with dry grass in its beak. They listened to a bullfinch clattering in some overhead branches, and Granny pointed out three or four other species which Thea would never have noticed.

What must Jessica be thinking, she wondered? Had she followed unobserved for a few minutes, enough to understand what was going on? Or had she decided to make the most of an interlude on her own?

It took days for Thea to fathom everything she learnt from that enchanted hour in the woods with a very old woman whose brain only partly functioned. The emotion that surfaced first, and was initially hard to name, turned out to be *respect*. Respect for a person who knew she was defective and vulnerable and liable to lose herself in the tangle of contemporary realities – and who still got herself mobilised every morning and followed whatever the urge of the moment might be. It gave Thea a soaring sense of discovery to feel this, as well as something close to complacency. She was impatient to explain it to Jessica and others, until it dawned on her that this might be what Yvette Montgomery had been hoping to convey, without actually uttering any words that might be taken wrongly or dismissed as foolish.

It would explain the comparative freedom that Granny was still allowed, for one thing. And it would also account for the relationships she appeared to have around the village. Giles, her occasional surrogate son, for example, and the elderly Thomas, who Granny claimed to dislike. They had both treated her with dignity. Even the bizarre Ick, with his glittery shoes and strangled English, had taken her seriously. No age discrimination in Blockley, it seemed.

And if that was how it was, then Jessica's outrageous suspicions concerning the murder of Julian Jolly might not be so unthinkable, either.

CHAPTER ELEVEN

Monday seemed to stretch unnaturally, thanks to the change to British Summer Time. Jessica had settled in the living room with a dusty-looking police textbook, and the spaniel on her legs.

'You've only been here twenty-four hours and it feels like *weeks*,' said Thea restlessly.

'What's the matter with you? You can't be bored already. How will you manage after I've gone?'

'Good question,' gloomed Thea. 'I expect I'll go on a lot more nature rambles with Granny.'

'You'll enjoy that,' said Jessica encouragingly. 'You came back really happy just now.'

'It was lovely,' Thea agreed. 'Totally unexpected. Like time travel back thirty years.'

'Sounds more like a hundred years to me.' She closed the book with her thumb marking the place. 'She's a complicated character, isn't she?'

Thea considered her reply. 'I guess everybody is, once they've got to her age. Think of all the things she's seen and learnt in her life. Even if she forgets ninety per cent of it, there's still plenty left. And it isn't a normal sort of forgetfulness in her case. She hasn't got Alzheimer's. It's more like one area of local damage to her brain. If Giles is right about the cause, it isn't likely to get any worse over time. It might even get better.'

'Which would explain why she isn't kept completely under lock and key,' Jessica nodded. 'When I first met her, I thought she should be in some sort of home.'

Thea winced. 'Where she could never again go and watch birds building their nests,' she said forcibly. 'Kept sedated and patronised around the clock.'

'OK,' Jessica held up a hand. 'I get the idea.' She glanced at her book. 'I was hoping I could have a few minutes to revise a bit. Is that very selfish of me?' She squinted at her mother doubtfully.

'Haven't you finished with all that class-room stuff? I thought it was all practical now.'

'It is, but I still have to know it.' She flourished the book. 'It isn't enough just to pass the assessment and then forget it all. I have to keep refreshing my memory.'

'I see,' muttered Thea. 'Very commendable. I bet none of the others spend their time off "refreshing their memories".'

'I don't care what the others do.' Jessica sighed. 'To be honest, I'm worried they might send me back to the classroom after what happened last week. They might think

I'm not ready to be let loose on the streets.'

'Does that ever happen? It sounds pretty unlikely to me.'

'I don't know. And I'm scared to ask.'

'James didn't say anything, then?'

'Not about the course, no. He did his best to reassure me. All the usual stuff about everybody making mistakes.'

'Which is true, of course.'

'Except–' Jessica gave up, and let the textbook drop to the floor. 'Except I can't imagine ever having the nerve to go to a real incident again. It's too *messy*. Nothing happens according to the book. People are impossibly unpredictable. And there's so much we're not allowed to do.' She turned a tormented face to her mother. 'I have been thinking a bit about what you said earlier on, you know. Some of it might be right. I don't want to spend my working life torn by ethical dilemmas and seen as the enemy by my own mother.'

Thea writhed and tried to interrupt, but Jessica forged on. 'I think I might just give the whole thing up and find something else to do. Maybe law. I could be a solicitor.'

'Where practically everything happens by the book,' said Thea drily. 'How dull would that be?' Her sudden flare of hope that Jess might actually leave the police was quickly doused by concern for the girl's loss of confidence and sense of purpose.

'The way I feel now, I might prefer dull-
ness to all this – *anguish*.'

Thea bit back the easy words of consolation that she instinctively felt like offering.
She had not especially wanted Jess to go
into the police. Not many mothers would,
she suspected. But she had only gradually
come to see it as a threat to their relationship. And that was perverse, given that she
was the girlfriend of one senior police
detective and the sister-in-law of another.
With Jessica it was different. The constant
danger was an obvious anxiety, but it was
more the unsavoury influences that could so
easily blunt a young woman's spirit that
Thea feared. Her daughter had been a fairly
average teenager. She had not joined
political protests or raged about the state of
the planet. She had shown little passion
about anything, as far as her mother could
see. There had been two boyfriends, but
both had been labelled 'annoying' after a
few weeks. Shortly before Carl was killed,
Jessica had written from university saying
she had enrolled for a short course in Latin,
which would run just for a year and count
for a handful of points towards her degree.
'It's like nothing else I'm doing,' she'd
written. 'A complete change from Sociology
and Economics. I could never have guessed
what fun it could be.'

But when Carl died, she missed too many

Latin classes and never took it up again. Thea hadn't given it another thought, in her own black hole of grief.

'Can you remember why you opted for the police in the first place?' she asked.

Jessica shrugged. 'To please Uncle James, probably.'

'Don't give me that. James never put any pressure on you. He was always very good about it. None of us knew how delighted he was until after you got accepted. It came from you, and don't pretend otherwise.'

'Well, I don't remember why I wanted to do it, now. Something about a challenge, and being a bit different from the rest of the crowd.' She looked up. 'I got full marks in the Law module you know. I *could* be a lawyer instead.'

'It's entirely up to you,' said Thea, knowing how irritating she was being.

'Thanks for the support,' Jessica muttered with a scowl.

'Don't mention it,' snapped Thea.

The tension was not so much broken as diverted by the manic jingling of Thea's mobile. She rummaged in her bag for it, feeling as if she'd been wrong-footed in some way.

'Hello,' she said briskly.

'Thea? It's me. Just to say how good it was to see you today. I'd been missing you.'

Her response to the soft romance in his

voice was far from what Phil might have been expecting. *He's too old for all this,* she thought. *And so am I. It should be my daughter having mushy phonecalls, not me.*

'I'd only been here two days,' she said. 'We often go longer than that between seeing each other.'

'True,' he agreed. 'But I was anxious about you doing another house-sit. You know how accident prone you can be.'

'Phil, I'm not actually in a very good mood at the moment. That's the trouble with telephones – they never sense the atmosphere, do they? It's not your fault, but you're managing to say all the wrong things.'

'Oh!'

Yes, yes, I know – honesty hurts. I ought to be able to switch on the sweet nothings at a moment's notice. She gritted her teeth. Suddenly she seemed to be surrounded by landmines, and with every step her temper grew shorter.

'Sorry, Phil. It isn't you at all. And yes, it was very nice to see you so unexpectedly. But I'm actually not at all accident prone. I thought we agreed months ago that by its nature, house-sitting involves walking into the unknown. When people go away, they create opportunities for other people to misbehave.'

'Right. And that puts you at risk.'

'And I've got a big strong police probationer daughter to watch out for me. And a ferociously intelligent cocker spaniel for good measure.'

The jokiness must have reassured him. 'Oh, I don't know what I'm to do with you,' he said lightly.

'Don't do anything,' she said, not quite knowing what she meant by that. All she knew was that she felt an urge to push him away, at least enough to let in a bit more air and light. She knew that he was starting to think they should set up home together, and that she came over cold whenever she tried to imagine it. And that the conversation about it was drawing inexorably closer with every passing day.

'I really want to take you to lunch one day this week,' he persisted. 'At that Churchill Arms place in Paxford, preferably. Jessica would like it,' he added unfairly.

'That would be lovely,' she said. 'Jess leaves on Thursday, though, so you haven't got many days to choose from.'

'I'll give it top priority,' he said firmly. 'Work permitting,' he added, as he so often did.

'OK then. We'll await your pleasure.'

She terminated the call and looked at her daughter. 'Phil's taking us to the Paxford place as soon as he can get away,' she said. 'Is that all right?'

'Why are you so horrible to him?' Jess was

staring accusingly at her. 'He's a perfectly nice man, and you treat him like dirt.'

Thea shook her head wearily. 'Don't you start,' she begged. 'I was only being honest with him. What's the point of a relationship where you can't be honest?'

Jessica rolled her eyes, and leant off the sofa to retrieve her police textbook from the floor.

The scratchy atmosphere was sustained for another hour, during which Thea mainly stayed in the kitchen, giving Hepzie her supper and sitting at the table with a *Chat* magazine she had found in the living room. It seemed an odd journal for the Montgomerys to have in their house, given that most of the stories in it concerned people famous for going to parties and having a lot of love affairs. It was only halfway through that she understood. A half-page photograph featured the two young celebrities from The Crown the previous evening. The caption was unambiguous:

Supermodel CLEODIE MASON captured last week at Annabel's with her new beau ICARUS BINNS.

Underneath, a small piece of text elaborated further.

When questioned about their relationship, Cleodie coyly admitted that she and Icarus were seeing each other "on a regular basis". Icarus's former girlfriend, heiress Georgina Graham, is reported by close friends to be "seething" at the speed in which Icarus has replaced her in his affections. Since this picture was taken, there have been rumours that the couple plan to live together virtually full time. The whisper is that he is in the process of buying a handsome Georgian mansion in the Cotswolds. Where it is exactly is a closely guarded secret.

Thea examined the photograph with minimal curiosity. What must it be like, she wondered, to have one's every move followed by mindless journalists who produced simpering pieces of prose like this? Had they known what they were getting into when they set out to become famous? Did either of them have a scrap of genuine talent to justify the money and attention that they now wallowed in?

Thinking to smooth things over with Jessica, she took the magazine into the living room. 'Look what I found,' she said.

Jessica had evidently arrived at the same resolution to effect a rapprochement. With a smile, she took the magazine. 'Oh!' she chirped. 'How exciting. Do you think they're still here, then? In Blockley, I mean? Is this where their Cotswold hideaway is?'

'I have no idea,' said Thea. 'But Ick seemed to know his way around when I saw him on Saturday. And they were obviously staying last night at The Crown.'

'I hope we see them again. I might get to *talk* to him.' Jessica's eyes sparkled and she looked about fourteen. 'Imagine that. Icarus Binns!'

'It makes me feel horribly *old*,' Thea confessed. 'I've honestly never heard of him. Too much Radio Four and BBC2, I suppose.'

'You never were into that sort of thing,' Jessica said kindly. 'You always took more interest in the past. Dusty old history, I used to call it.'

'Did you? I never noticed.'

'Only to myself,' laughed Jessica. 'I was glad, really. My friend Caz's mum was a rally driver and never at home. I preferred you to that a thousand times over.'

'That's good to hear. I think I might have relished a rally driver for a mother, actually.'

'And Fran's mum was a headcase. She spent most of the time in hospital. Imagine that!'

'I remember her. Poor thing. I used to worry that I'd have to have Fran to live with us.'

'Oh, well,' Jessica shrugged. 'You didn't push the history down my throat, after all.

And it was nice when you'd stop the car and point out some crumbling old building where a famous speech was made or a riot happened in 1809. You seemed to have quite a thing about riots. I used to lie awake at night and try to imagine what they were like.'

'Good God! The things one never knows about one's children.'

They both laughed, harmony restored.

At seven, during a discussion about their evening meal, they had a visitor. Thea opened the door warily, to find a man she only half recognised, standing on the doorstep. He ducked his head, in a strange echo of an old-fashioned bow, and said, 'Good evening. We met briefly this morning, although it was your – daughter, is she? – was the one I spoke to. My name is Thomas Sewell. I was a good friend of Julian's.'

'Oh yes,' she said. 'Of course. Would you like to come in?'

'Only if it isn't a bother. I shouldn't be troubling you like this, I know. But the young lady did say I might– It's just– I was so very fond of Julian, and you two saw him– I mean, yesterday– I understand– I was wondering...'

Thea was slow to grasp the import of what he was saying, but Jessica, appearing behind her, caught on instantly. 'You mean we saw the body,' she said. 'Actually, it was only me.'

'Oh!' The old man's face looked loose and grey, his eyes large and heavy in their sockets. Everything about him, from his pendulous belly to the wattles under his chin sagged and dragged downwards. 'Yes. His body.' The eyes became wet, the low lip tremulous.

'Come in,' Thea ordered briskly. 'Have a cup of tea, or some sherry or something.'

'Thank you.' He entered the house on shaky legs, and sat down in the first chair he came to. Thea recalled the way he had comported himself on Saturday, his back straight, his gaze direct, and marvelled at such a collapse.

'You must be very upset,' she said awkwardly. For the first time, she experienced a pang of sorrow for the death of Julian Jolly, a man she had never known or even seen. He had had friends, and family and been loved at least by this old man.

'The police have been asking questions, of course,' he said, staring at the floor. 'Anybody they could find who knew Jules, I suppose. I've known him for fifty years.'

Thea exchanged glances with her daughter. It surprised her to think that these two men might have spent all their lives in Blockley. Like most Cotswold villages and small towns, there was a sense of impermanence amongst the residents. The buildings outlasted their occupants by a dramatic margin. They were briefly inhabited by people like Icarus Binns, not used as lifelong homes.

'Oh?' she said. 'Were you always here in Blockley?'

He shook his head, confirming her first assumption. 'Coincidence, mainly, that we both fetched up here. He spent decades working on the lost villages, and I'm a chartered surveyor. Retired,' he added with a rueful smile. 'Our paths crossed, as you might imagine.'

Jessica was clanking bottles in a drinks cabinet at the further end of the room. 'I'm sure we're allowed to use the sherry,' she said. 'Aren't we, Mum?'

Thea shrugged. 'Seems a bit rude,' she said. 'But if there is some...'

'Ron won't begrudge it,' said Thomas Sewell. 'He's a generous chap. Good hearted.'

Jessica poured a single glass of pale sherry and put it on a small table close to Thomas's elbow. 'We met Nick,' she said casually. 'Julian's grandson. He came here this morning. You know him, I suppose?'

'Barely. First met him when he was about twelve, if memory serves. Pudgy-faced lad, with jet black hair. His mother's got a touch of the tarbrush, I fancy. Indian – something like that.'

Thea saw Jessica tense at this unreconstructed reference to race.

'Doesn't he – *didn't* he, I mean – come here quite often to see his grandad? I rather got that impression.' Thea smiled, hoping she didn't sound like another police interviewer.

Thomas nodded slightly. 'Might have done. He's taken up the same line of work, which Jules was glad about.'

'Archaeology?'

'That's it.'

'And you were working with Julian on a book? Have I got that right, too?'

The blank look suggested otherwise. 'Book? Where did you get that idea?'

'I think Mrs Gardner said something to that effect.'

One or two pennies appeared to drop. 'We were doing a bit of research,' he said tightly. 'That must be it. You don't want to listen to everything Gladys tells you. I rather assumed you'd have worked that out by this time.'

'He had a big file on Joanna Southcott, according to my daughter, and we saw the plaque further along the street. We've been meaning to look her up on the Internet, seeing that she appears to be Blockley's claim to fame.'

The old man's rheumy eyes acquired a momentary gleam of interest. 'Great woman, badly neglected. But I can't pretend I've ever encouraged Julian's researches in that direction. A bit too close to whimsy for my liking. Attracts the wrong sort of person altogether.'

'Oh?'

But Thomas had lapsed back into his grief, reminding Thea of Granny and her inability to stick to the subject in hand. 'I won't know how to carry on without Jules,' he moaned.

'Give yourself time,' Thea tried to soothe him. 'It's all very raw at the moment. More sherry?'

She chose to interpret the ambivalent nod as acceptance, and signalled to Jessica to refill his glass. 'Did he have any other family? Besides Nick, I mean?'

'Abroad, mostly. And there's his mother.'

Thea thought she had misheard. 'Mother? Surely...? I mean...'

'She's in a home in Bristol. Ninety-nine, she is. She and I used to get along famously. Still do, when I can get there for a visit. We go in the Rolls, you see, and take her out for a spin.'

Thea had forgotten the Rolls. 'What's going to happen to it now? The car?'

'It comes to me,' he said simply. 'But it won't be the same without Julian to drive it.'

For a daft moment, Thea ran a scenario where Thomas had killed his friend for the sake of the car. But it was quashed by his unmistakable sadness.

'I expect I shouldn't have come,' he went

on heavily. 'You must be finding the whole business bewildering.' He looked at Jessica. 'But you were kind this morning, and seemed, if I may say so, to have some understanding. It is right that you're a police officer?' He squinted at her from beneath bushy eyebrows. 'They say the police get younger every year.' He attempted a smile that might have been roguish in happier times.

Jessica completed the thought for him. 'You came because you want me to tell you about his injuries? Precisely how he died? Whether he looked peaceful? That sort of thing?'

'That's right, my dear. I can't settle, you see, until I know a little bit about how...' His voice cracked and he dropped his head to hide his loss of control.

'He must have died very quickly,' Jessica said. 'It wouldn't have been completely painless, but very nearly.'

Thea looked at her daughter in admiration. How careful she had been to omit any actual details of how the murder had been committed. Was this her police training, or an instinctive caution? It seemed to Thea unlikely that there had been any tuition in the management of murder cases in the first months of the course. Jessica was merely being intelligent, which made Thea feel even more proud of her.

Thomas heaved a deep sigh, and dashed a hand beneath his nose. 'I hope that's true,'

215

he murmured. He raised his eyes slowly to Thea's. 'Have you ever thought how desperately important it is to die well?' he asked her. 'How it can undermine the whole of the life that went before, if death is ignominious? And how much more true that is when it's an old person?'

Something in the words made Thea think of Granny Gardner in her cottage. 'I haven't thought about it until now,' she said. 'But I can see how important it is.'

'It ought to go without saying,' the old man said, his voice stronger, as if Jessica's frankness had revived him. 'Nobody wants to be remembered as a leaking bag of bones, without wits or dignity. Because that *is* how you're remembered. All the past achievements and wisdom are wiped away as if they never happened.'

'I'm sure that isn't true,' said Thea. 'Think of Churchill, or Clark Gable, or – or–'

'Exceptions,' he waved an impatient hand. 'Think of your own grandparents – anybody you've known who reached eighty or more. What's the first picture of them that comes to mind?'

Thea met his watery gaze. 'I see what you mean,' she whispered. 'It never occurred to me before.'

'But what can you do about it?' Jessica demanded robustly. 'Give everyone a lethal injection before they start to crumble?'

Thomas Sewell smiled sadly at her. 'The answer to that is too big for one old man to provide,' he said. 'All I wanted to know was that Julian died as he lived – worthy of respect and dignity.'

'I saw nothing that would indicate otherwise,' said Jessica stiffly, and Thea thought again of Granny Gardner.

'Mrs Gardner was very fond of him,' she ventured. 'And I suppose she thinks of him in his prime, not as an old man.'

Thomas jerked his head forward impatiently. 'Julian *was* in his prime! He might have been in his seventies, but he was fit and well. We'll *all* remember him like that. There isn't anything else *to* remember.'

He put both hands on the arms of the chair, preparatory to standing up. His great belly seemed to surge ahead of him, rising into the air as his weight shifted. 'Thank you for the sherry,' he said, once he was upright. 'And the information.'

Jessica went to him, reaching a hand gently towards his arm. 'I hope it helped,' she said. 'And I'm sorry for your loss.'

He looked her full in the face. 'You can have no idea how great a loss it is,' he murmured. 'I have loved that man for fifty years.'

Once more Jessica was admirably careful. 'You and he – were you, um – *partners?*'

Thomas made a sound of irritation.

217

'Partners my foot! What a foolish word to use. We were never lovers, if that's what you mean. Julian loved his wife, and when she took to her bed and then finally died, he gave most of his attention to Gladys Gardner. No, we were never *partners*, as you mean it. We were mates, colleagues, brothers – there is no word that describes it properly. But I'm damned if I know how I'm going to manage without him.'

And before the threat of female sympathy could reach him, he was out of the room and fumbling with the front door.

CHAPTER TWELVE

Thea made a large omelette with salad and bread for their supper, and afterwards they slumped together on the sofa, debating whether to search for something congenial on one of the plethora of TV channels. 'We've earned some mindless entertainment after today,' said Thea. 'It seems to have gone on for ever.'

'It has been an amazingly long day,' Jessica agreed. 'I can't believe it was only this morning that I was at that post-mortem.'

'It's taken me most of that time to really believe there was a murder next door,' Thea mused. 'I think I just wanted to pretend it hadn't happened, to start with. To let other people sort it out and leave me out of it.'

'Well, you could do that. You're not really involved. We could try to carry on as normal, whatever that is.'

Thea shook her head. 'They won't let us,' she said.

'Who won't?'

'All these people who keep coming to the door and phoning us. We've got to stay and watch out for Granny – or I have – and while I'm in this house, I'm involved. No escape possible. Besides, I was talking about how I felt at first. Since then I've been hooked. Now I really want to know the whole story.'

Jessica grinned. 'That's a relief,' she said. 'I thought I'd have to do it all on my own.'

Thea narrowed her eyes. 'Do what?' she asked, with a wholly false innocence.

'What do you think?' replied the girl.

But their banter was a variant on whistling in the dark, and they both knew it. Together they went around the house, firmly closing every window, and employing every bolt and lock on doors back and front. Jessica switched the buzzer on, and checked that the connecting door to the cottage was definitely locked.

'Nobody can get in now,' said Thea. 'Not without smashing a window and waking the entire street.'

'I still feel a bit wobbly,' Jessica confessed, as she climbed into bed. 'I keep hearing funny noises out there.'

Thea listened to the night sounds of Blockley. 'I can hear a car quite far away,' she reported. 'And some sort of animal, even fainter. And water pipes gurgling in the roof. Nothing to worry about. Go to sleep. There's nothing to worry about.'

And within minutes, Jessica had done as instructed. Thea lay awake for a little while longer, relishing the warm weight of the spaniel against her feet, and steadfastly refusing to face the knowledge that there were only two more nights to go before she and the dog were on their own again.

Tuesday morning dawned cloudy and cool. Thea woke first, her mind instantly informing her that she was in a strange house, sharing a room with her daughter and her dog, responsible – sort of – for an old woman next door and trying to navigate the shoals of a relationship. The last to occur was the one she gave her attention to for the next five minutes, before Jessica was stirred by the spaniel. Hepzie knew Thea was awake and was suddenly all too energetic, shaking out her tangled ears and giving her hindquarters a seeing-to, which made far more noise than might be expected.

Phil Hollis was increasingly the default subject of Thea's thoughts in any quiet moment. She understood that the dilemmas and inconsistencies were the standard package for anyone in her situation, and the pitfalls no less inevitable for being able to foresee them.

He could turn her legs to marshmallow at one moment and crack her teeth with grinding frustration the next. There was a lot between them that worked, that was worth preserving. But she had found herself looking forward to the Phil-free times, too. Times when she could sit up until three in the morning with a book, or make herself a thick warm soup at three in the afternoon, without having to explain herself. Couplehood demanded routines and expectations that she found irksome. And for Phil it was the same, as she had forced him to admit a few weeks before. His erratic working patterns, profound preoccupations and sudden dives into depression were – much to his surprise – less bearable for having to give an account of them to another person.

'Don't make me give you a running commentary of how I'm feeling,' he'd begged her. 'Moods come and go, generally they're of no significance. If I have to describe them, and bring them to the front of my mind, that distorts everything. Do you see?'

'OK,' she'd agreed slowly. 'That makes a kind of sense – although I don't know what a couple counsellor would say.'

The word *couple* lay at the heart of their difficulties, she realised. After two years as a single person, she still took it for granted that the ideal situation in the eyes of the world was to be half of a couple. It was the default position, surely? Only when she stopped to examine what this meant did she discover that it might no longer be true. There were single people everywhere she looked, and they seemed perfectly happy with their condition. The couple word had gathered associations which were not altogether appealing. Phil, single for a few years longer, seemed no further forward in working out precisely what he wanted. In the end he had summed it all up. 'We're thinking too much about it,' he concluded. 'Why don't we just *live* and stop trying to give everything a label?'

And Thea had striven to do just that, only to discover that she resented the endless struggle to remain in the present, when a large part of her wanted to know where they would be in ten or twenty years' time. She could not entirely quell the fantasies where they were both in their seventies, retired and relaxed, taking grandchildren on adventurous holidays and agreeing completely about all the big topics of life. Every time she caught herself at it, she replaced the dream with alternatives, where she still lived alone with a dog or two and a flourishing garden and stacks of fascinating books to read.

But her musings this grey morning concerned Phil as police detective. She had met him during one murder investigation, and fallen for him during another. She knew him for a patient committed professional, albeit prone to sudden flaring frustrations and serious mistakes. His mind worked methodically, he was an organised leader with a streak of kindness that did not go unnoticed. But he was no Sherlock Holmes, she had quickly realised. Small details passed him by, connections and implications had to be worked at, and frequently led him in the wrong direction. Perhaps it was just as well that he appeared to have no involvement in the investigation into the killing of Julian Jolly. As far as she could tell, no senior officer had dropped all other work to solve this crime. It felt as if it was being fitted in around the edges of more important cases, assigned to sergeants and the occasional inspector, with plenty of input from the uniformed sector. Little pressure was being exerted from the public, or the family, or the newspapers to find the deranged knifeman who had stabbed the harmless old historian in his own kitchen.

And this felt wrong to Thea, as she let her thoughts slide from Phil to Julian. Somebody other than his devoted friend Thomas ought to care that the man had been killed. Jessica thought so too. Well, Thea decided – from now on, *I* am going to care. Before Jessica had properly opened her eyes, her mother was speaking.

'Hey, it's half past eight,' she said. 'Time to shift yourself. We've got a murder to solve.'

Jessica raised her head and grinned, with all the energy and tolerance of youth. 'Just what I was thinking,' she agreed.

Over breakfast they tried to compile a sensible action plan. Jessica quizzed her mother on every person she had met in Blockley since Saturday morning, and what her impressions of them had been.

'It's a short list,' said Thea. 'Granny. Giles. Thomas and Ick. That's it.'

'Are you sure?'

'Oh, and Gussie from Todenham, with a son in Paxford.'

'And did they all know Julian?'

'Gussie didn't mention him, but it's bound to be safe to assume she did.' Thea spread her hands helplessly. 'We can't possibly take it for granted that one of these people is the murderer.'

'No,' Jessica nodded, 'but we have to start somewhere. Granny and Thomas both claim to have been his friend more or less for ever. Giles as well, probably. And we forgot Nick. He has to be on the list.'

'And the police have surely interviewed all of them.'

Jessica shook her head. 'Not Gussie, for a start. Except maybe for a basic house-to-house, which might still be ongoing.'

'I don't see any point in counting Gussie. She's a red herring, I'm sure. It was entirely random that I happened to pick her up when I did.'

Jessica narrowed her eyes. 'Not necessarily,' she said. 'That was Sunday – right? Julian had been dead for only a few hours by then. She might have been in on it, knowing full well that you were the house-sitter. You could have been followed when you went to Todenham, and waylaid by her for some reason.'

Thea laughed. 'That's crazy,' she protested. 'You could work anybody in if that's your method.'

'Anybody who's met you, yes.' Jessica was serious, bouncing her pen on the table as she analysed her notes. 'Whoever did it will know you're here. Isn't it almost certain that the departure of the Montgomerys was the trigger for the attack on Julian?'

'And what if your idea about Granny is right?' Since Jessica's alarming assertion on their return from Upton the previous afternoon, no more reference had been made to the theory of senile old woman as murderer. Thea flung herself back in her chair. 'It's no good. It's like trying to do a jigsaw with more than half the pieces missing. We don't know enough to even guess what happened.'

'Not true at all. We have to start with some hypotheses, and test them out, based on what we *do* know. Some won't work, but others might.'

Thea frowned sceptically. 'Is that the approved method for solving a murder, then?'

'Very likely not, if you've got access to the police records and all the rest of it. If you're investigating privately, I don't see what's wrong with it.'

'Oh, I see.' Thea gave her daughter a penetrating look. 'You've decided to abandon
your training as a police officer, and become
a private investigator instead. Jessica Osborne, PI. No case too trivial, no crime too
terrible. That sort of thing?'

'Not at all. Don't be stupid.'

'Sorry,' Thea backed off, knowing she'd
gone too far, cursing herself for failing to
take a murder sufficiently seriously for her
daughter's liking. Somewhere there lurked
the abiding idea that she was on holiday,
despite being paid to take care of the house
and the old woman in the cottage.

'What we need to do is to make things happen,' Jessica asserted. 'Put people together
and see what they do. It's no good talking to
them one at a time. They can tell all kinds of
lies if you do that. You get a much better idea
of what they're capable of if you let them
spark off each other.'

'I can see that,' Thea said. 'But how do we
manage it? Throw a party? I'm not sure Ron
and Yvette would approve.'

'Dunno,' said Jessica. 'I'm still at the
hypothesis stage.'

'Doing it your way will end up with us just
playing a game for the next three days.
Hardly different from Cluedo – Granny
stabbed him with one of his own knives
because he knew her daughter was really her

grand-daughter. Grandson Nick did it with an archaeological pick, because Julian had evidence that Nick's research was rubbish. Icarus Binns did it because Julian had seen him having sex with Thomas Sewell and threatened to tell the tabloids. The landlord of the Crown did it because he thought Julian had written that terrible review of the food. Gussie did it because Julian refused to give her son a job reference.' She paused for breath. 'And those are just off the top of my head,' she added after a few moments. 'I could probably think of four or five more at least.'

Jessica's eyes were sparkling. 'They're all brilliant!' she applauded. 'What an imagination you've got!'

'And that's all it is. Even if one of them was true, we'd never prove it. Leave it to the police, love, and forget the whole thing.'

'But I thought you *wanted* to do it. You said – only an hour ago–'

'Yes, I know I did. But now it seems silly. It's bound to have been a burglar he interrupted in the early hours of Sunday.'

'Burglars hardly ever kill people,' said Jessica. 'That much I *have* learnt. Maybe I ought to ask Uncle James if there've been any developments. Do you think he would tell me?' Jessica played with her pen for another minute, and then answered her own question. 'No, he wouldn't,' she admitted.

'Would he?'

'I can't imagine why he would,' Thea confirmed. 'And asking him would bring him over here with a long lecture about minding our own businesses.'

'Mmm.'

They washed and dried the breakfast things, gave Hepzie a bowl of milk, and listened for sounds from the cottage. 'She is a quiet old thing,' Jessica remarked. 'No telly or radio that I can hear.'

She was standing with her ear against the connecting door. 'Maybe she isn't up yet. I wonder what she *does* all day.'

'I wonder that about a lot of people,' said Thea from the kitchen. 'I think they can make a magazine last all morning, for a start.'

By a rapid association of ideas, Jessica asked, 'Do you think Icarus has gone back to London? It'd be great to see him again. After all, he is on our list of murder suspects. We ought to try to catch another glimpse of him.'

Thea sighed. 'And then what? Ask him for his autograph and embarrass the poor chap?'

'He *expects* it. I bet he thought you were really weird when you didn't, on Saturday.'

Thea recalled the bemused expression on the rap artist's face, and could only agree. 'I think he did. He gave me a very funny look. I had no idea at all who he was.'

'You're a dinosaur,' her daughter told her, 'and you ought to be ashamed.' She was idly opening and closing a drawer in a rather fine antique side table, on which sat the telephone and a notepad. Her ear was still cocked for sounds of Granny Gardner. The drawer slid smoothly in and out, causing Thea some irritation, as she stood in the kitchen doorway.

'Do you have to?' she asked at last.

'What? Oh!' Jessica looked down at what she was doing. 'I was just playing with it.' Then she peered closer at the actual contents of the drawer. 'My God!' she said.

Thea went closer, and tried to see what was there. The hall was shadowy, and the drawer only half open. She put her hand out to pull it further.

'Don't touch it!' cried Jessica.

'What is it?'

Jessica took a tissue from a pocket and covered her fingers delicately with it. Then she lifted out the article by the very edges of its handle. 'Strangely enough, it looks like a knife,' said Jessica.

'But not covered in blood,' Thea observed. 'Why wouldn't there be a knife in a hallway drawer? Useful for cutting parcel string and sellotape.'

'It *has* got blood on it,' said Jessica in a low voice. 'See.' She pointed at the junction of handle and blade, turning the instrument towards the light. Thea could see a slight brown stain. The rest of the thing seemed very clean and shiny.

'How do you know?' she demanded, feeling no excitement or even much interest. 'It could be anything.'

'Mother,' said Jessica, using a term reserved for moments of profound impatience, 'does this look to you like a knife people would normally keep in a hall drawer?' She brandished it in Thea's face. 'Look at it!'

Thea did as instructed. It was an old-fashioned carving knife, sharpened so often that the blade had become narrow and curved, and very sharp. The sort of knife that cut through meat as if it were margarine in a tub. The tip was pointed.

'But wouldn't it bend?' she wondered. 'If you tried to stab with it? It isn't intended for that. See how narrow it is, after so much sharpening.'

Gingerly, Jessica fished a sheet of paper out of the drawer and wrapped it loosely around the knife. Then she tried to flex it. It would scarcely bend at all. 'It would work perfectly well,' she concluded. 'And there *is* blood on it.' She twisted it again. 'It's been recently cleaned, but they haven't done a very good job. They missed a bit, look.'

Thea gave a quick glance, feeling unexpectedly squeamish. 'So why would the knife used to kill Julian Jolly be here?' she asked, all her imaginative skill deserting her. 'That's crazy.'

'First we have to find out whether it *is* the murder weapon. I'll have to hand it in at the Incident Room. Did that chap say it was in the Village Hall? Where's that?'

'I don't know exactly. Past the shop and turn left, I think.'

'Come on, then.'

Before they left, Thea spent a few minutes worrying about Granny. 'I ought to be sure she's alive, at least,' she said.

'Why wouldn't she be?' said Jessica unfeelingly.

Thea just gave her a look.

'All right. Go and knock on her door, then,' Jessica conceded. 'Or whatever it is you usually do.'

'There isn't any *usually* about it. I have to make it up as I go along. At least the buzzer hasn't gone off, so we know she hasn't gone out.'

'Tell me again why you can't simply go through this door, and make sure she's OK? It seems daft not to use it.'

'I know. But those were Ron's instructions. He said it would scare her if I just appeared through it without warning her.'

'You could knock first, or sing, or something. After all, we used it yesterday.'

Thea looked at the door consideringly. 'It

seems even more odd now,' she said. 'Finding the back door key like that in Julian's pocket, and then this door being unlocked. And the knife right beside the door. We should be able to work out what happened from all these clues.' She blinked at the idea which suddenly came to her. 'What if somebody popped through from the cottage and put the knife in the drawer, as the first hiding place they came to? After they'd murdered Julian early on Sunday. We know that the door got unlocked at some point.'

'You realise the obvious answer, I suppose,' said Jessica.

'Do I?'

'I was right about Granny all along. She killed him, and came through the door with the knife while you were out or upstairs, and popped it in the drawer after she'd cleaned it. We have to remember this door was unlocked, when you assumed it wasn't.'

'If she did all that before seven on Sunday morning, she's a bloody good actor,' said Thea, wondering why she felt so cross. Then a memory flitted across her mind. 'She said she had a knife,' she recalled. 'She threatened to cut Hepzie's tail off with it. What if she'd already decided to kill Julian, the moment Yvette and Ron had gone?' Her heart began to thump. Then she forced a laugh. 'You've got me doing it now. We're both mad, suspecting a little old lady like her of such a dreadful crime. It's like a Grimm fairytale.'

'It's grim, anyway,' said Jessica, missing the reference.

'Grimm, as in Brothers Grimm,' Thea persisted. 'Dark forests and wicked witches.'

'Right,' nodded Jessica. 'Sounds pretty much like this place, then.'

'Very funny.'

They walked, with the dog, to the police Incident Room, only to be disconcerted by the distance between the High Street and the Hall. The lack of intensity in the investigations was highlighted by the eventual discovery of two officers and a laptop computer in one corner of the building. Jessica produced the knife, neatly confined in a plastic bag, and told the story of how it had been found. Glad beyond expression at having something concrete at last, both men seized on it voraciously. They produced forms to be filled in, and carefully recorded every word that Jessica uttered. Then one of them literally ran outside to his car and sped off to more familiar urban territory where forensics could be recruited to examine the find.

The remaining policeman almost clung to his visitors in his urgent need for company. 'Weird place, this,' he muttered. 'Nobody's been near us since yesterday morning. Where do they all *go?*'

'To work,' said Thea. 'Junction Nine on the

234

M5 is only about twenty minutes from here, and then the world's their oyster. Bristol, Birmingham, Manchester. They leave at seven and get home again twelve hours later, tireder and richer than they started. And far too preoccupied to think about the murder of a quiet old man they hardly knew.'

'Where are the farmers and the shepherds and all that sort of thing? I thought the country was all about that stuff.'

'Where are you from?' Thea asked, already having guessed from his accent.

'Solihull.'

'And you don't get out into the country-side much?'

'Days out with the kids,' he said defensively. 'Now and then.'

Thea gave up. Somehow it seemed unlikely that he would wander the hillsides with his bored offspring who would complain about smells and tired legs. At most, they might take the car for a spin to some small town with a castle or a newly opened theme park.

'It came as a shock to me, too,' said Jessica, in support of the man. 'There don't seem to be many proper farms left any more. So far, I haven't seen a single animal.'

'We'll go and look for some later on,' Thea promised her. 'There are still plenty of sheep around. Not many dairy cows, though. And you seldom see a pig.'

Both the others winced at this. Pigs were not a subject for ordinary conversation. Jessica hurriedly covered for her mother's lapse of protocol. 'I'm a probationer, actually,' she said. 'It was me who found the body on Sunday.'

The man nodded. 'Yes, I know. Your name's here on the screen, look.'

He swivelled the laptop for her to read, and with a sense of being permitted into a forbidden territory, Thea also looked over her daughter's shoulder. The font was too small to read properly, and the screen was divided into several boxes. It would take practice to interpret the information, and she found herself not sufficiently interested to pursue it.

'So I am,' said Jessica. 'It'll have linked to my personal file, I suppose.'

The man nodded. 'We've got everything about you right here at our fingertips,' he said proudly.

'But nothing on me, I hope,' said Thea, feeling queasy.

'Relationship with DS Hollis,' said the man carelessly. 'But that's not on the official database.'

It was too much for Thea. Frustrated rage threaded with fear threatened to loosen her tongue. This was not the place to deliver a lecture about human rights and personal privacy. It wasn't even the appropriate trigger to start such a rant. The man seemed to be saying it was little more than gossip anyway. Unbidden, the voice of Carl sounded in her ears. Carl, whose automatic position was on the side of liberty and minimal state intervention, was speaking now. 'This country is sliding into dictatorship, with the police as the main instrument of suppression.' And yet he had made no objection when his daughter expressed the first hint of a desire to enter the police force. 'Fight it from the inside, eh,' he'd smiled, never questioning that she would remain firmly of his opinion.

'Come on,' she said roughly. 'We can't stay away too long. What about Granny?'

'What about her indeed,' said Jessica darkly. 'I'm right behind you.'

Granny was visible through her window when they got back. She had pulled the curtains aside, and her face was almost pressed to the glass. She was obviously looking out for somebody or something. Thea waved to her, and pointed a jabbing finger at the street door, suggesting she be admitted.

The old woman leapt to comply and was at the door in seconds. Jessica hovered behind her mother, unsure what she ought to do. 'She can certainly move,' she muttered into Thea's ear.

'Have you seen Julian?' came the shrill

voice. 'He's *terribly* late. I'm waiting to do lunch for him and it's going to spoil at this rate.'

Thea made a soft moan, and Jessica went on muttering. 'Lunch at half past ten in the morning? That's a first.'

'Mrs Gardner, let me come in a talk to you for a minute,' said Thea. 'Let me help you remember what's happened in the last few days.'

'And where did Yvette go to? I want her. She's always going off, that hussy.'

Thea remembered the word *hussy* occurring before. 'And who's that? That isn't Frances, is it?' Granny squinted at Jessica with a convincing show of perplexity.

'No, that's my daughter, Jessica.'

'She looks like a nice girl. Kind. Friendly.' Mrs Gardner beamed suddenly, her sharp black eyes softening. 'Just like my Frances.'

'She's very nice,' Thea agreed.

'*She* can come in. And you might as well come too.' Granny pushed her door wider, and beckoned them inside.

'I forget things, you see,' she explained as she led the way into her main room. As before, it was clean and tidy. 'They melted parts of my brain with some dreadful drug. I'm suing them, but it won't bring my wits back. They're lost forever now.'

'But you have your health,' Thea observed. 'You seem wonderfully fit.'

'I keep busy. Up and down the stairs. Polishing, dusting.' She laughed, a sudden witchlike cackle. 'I was such a slut, you know. Filthy house, papers and books everywhere. I do remember that. People were very rude about it. Now I love to see it sparkling. Isn't that peculiar!'

Thea merely smiled. So much that Granny said left no room for a coherent response.

'We went for a walk – you and me,' the old woman suddenly remembered. 'I fell over and hurt my wrist.' She extended the affected arm, and twisted it dramatically. 'Seems all right now.'

'That's right. And can you remember what happened to Julian?' Jessica interrupted, staring intently into Granny's face. 'Your friend Julian was murdered at the weekend. Giles wrote it down for you, so you wouldn't forget. Have you still got the piece of paper?'

The old woman made a show of searching. 'Try your bureau,' Thea suggested, taking a step towards it.

'Keep out of it!' screeched Granny Gardner ferociously. 'It's private.'

'Here it is,' said Jessica calmly. 'Behind the sofa cushion.' She flourished a crumpled white sheet of A4. 'Not a very good place to keep it.'

Granny snatched it and peered closely at the large lettering. '"Julian is dead" it says here. Well, I knew that, didn't I?' She clamped her lips together and scowled at Thea. 'Fancy thinking you could go in my desk,' she reproached. 'Where were you brought up, I'd like to know?'

Thea adopted a submissive expression and mumbled, 'Sorry.'

The old woman consulted the notes again. 'It says I have to speak to the police. When will that be, I wonder? I can tell them who killed Julian, of course, if they ask me.' The air seemed to freeze, the only sound the loud clock on the mantelpiece. Jessica looked as if she couldn't risk taking a breath.

'Can you?' she whispered. 'Really?'

'Of course. It'll be Thomas's doing,' came the casual reply. 'Awful old queen, always jealous of Julian and me. We said he'd do one of us in, one of these days. Thomas is your man, you mark my words.' Granny's small dark eyes flitted from face to face, assessing the effect of her words. Then she cackled, a parody of a wicked old witch. 'You should see your faces,' she spluttered. 'What a hoot!'

Thea's mouth fell open, but no words came forth. The initial reasonableness of the accusation had silenced her, only for the following suggestion of malicious jokiness to utterly stun her. She looked to Jessica for rescue.

'You don't really believe Thomas could have killed Julian in cold blood, do you?' the

240

girl said gently. 'After all, he *loved* him. He's going to be lost without him.'

'Love, love,' tutted Granny dismissively. 'Stupid word. Doesn't mean a thing. Who wants love when they can have friendship?'

'Good question,' murmured Thea.

'It's going to rain,' came a sudden non sequitur. 'Lucky I didn't put the washing out.'

'Is there a washing line in your little garden?' Thea tried to recall whether she'd seen one.

'Just a string for a few things.'

'Would you show me?' Thea had no clear idea why she made such a request, apart from curiosity as to how Granny felt about her imprisonment at the rear of the house.

The old woman narrowed her eyes. 'You know I can't get out of there, don't you?' Again the sheer normality in the words and tone threw everything into doubt. 'They built a cage and put me in it.' She clasped her hands together. 'Not that you can blame them. Who knows what I might get up to if I was free to do what I like?'

Again there was no answer that Thea could think of, apart from a growing sense of agreement that Granny might be best kept confined, after all.

'Why are you here?' The question burst out like a gunshot. 'Why are you bothering me?' The old woman rustled the sheet of notes, crumpling it savagely. 'Are you the police?'

Jessica quickly shook her head. 'No, we're just friends. We'll go now, if there's nothing you need.'

'You must be one of those celebrity people,' Granny said with certainty. 'That'll be it.'

It was like trying to track the beam of a very erratic lighthouse. When it did flash onto you, all was clear and lucid for a few moments, before darkness fell again. She looked at Thea. 'Or have I got that wrong? It isn't Frances, is it?'

'Never mind,' said Thea, less gently than she knew she should. 'We'll leave you now. Unless you need something? What about some shopping?'

'The van comes,' said Granny. 'It's in my notebook. You can depend upon the van.'

'Well, then,' said Thea vaguely. 'That's all right, isn't it.'

'Mum,' came Jessica's voice, in a tone of alarm. 'Look!'

Thea's gaze wavered from edge to edge of the area to which her daughter pointed, without any firm result. 'What?' she demanded.

'That,' said Jessica, and Thea was suddenly inescapably focused on a pale-coloured raincoat, hanging over the back of an upright chair. There were streaks down the sleeve that was visible, as well as the lower portion. Streaks that had the grainy browny reddish appearance of dried blood.

CHAPTER THIRTEEN

'What happened here, Mrs Gardner?' Jessica asked, indicating the stains. 'Something made a nasty mess of your coat, didn't it?'

The old woman eyed the garment with surprise. 'Did it?' she said. 'That's my best mac.'

'It looks like blood,' Jessica suggested. 'All down the front and the sleeves.'

'How revolting,' said Granny, with no hint of emotion. 'Will it come off, do you think?'

'Would you like me to take it away and get it cleaned?' Thea winced at her own subterfuge, wondering if it was justified. Mrs Gardner nodded.

'If you like, dear. That would be kind of you. But I really shouldn't let you go to such trouble. Cleaners cost the earth, don't they.' Her eyes twinkled. 'And they might ask awkward questions.'

'Do you know how it happened?' Jessica spoke with stern authority, suddenly in role as a police officer almost for the first time since she arrived in Blockley.

'No idea,' Granny shook her head. 'Unless it was one of the lambs.'

'Lambs? What do you mean?'

'The sheep are lambing. I like to lend a hand if I can.'

'Where?' Jessica's eyes were prominent with amazed impatience.

Granny shrugged. 'Mostly at the Hugheses. They call for me if they're struggling. I'm First Reserve.'

'You help with delivering lambs? Wearing your mac?'

'Sometimes I do. Why not?'

Thea could hear the unspoken protests. *You're supposed to be ninety-two, damn it. How do you expect me to believe a word you say?*

'It does look a bit sort of *slimy*,' Thea noted, giving the stains a closer inspection. 'Hardly arterial bleeding, I'd say.'

'Well, let me take it, anyway.' Jessica sounded defeated by the complexities of life.

'Thank you, my dear. You're very kind,' said Mrs Gardner, with a complacent smile.

'It *could* be true,' said Thea for the third time. 'All sorts of people pitch in at lambing time. The woman I met in Cold Aston last year did it. It gets so busy at times. Twenty or thirty lambs born in a day, apparently.'

'So where are they? I haven't seen any sheep.'

'They keep them indoors these days,' Thea said, feeling very unsure of her facts. 'In any case, we haven't been anywhere much, have we? This whole area was founded on sheep and wool, after all.'

'OK.' Jessica flapped a hand to indicate she'd heard enough about sheep and lambs. 'The easiest thing is to take the coat for forensics to examine.'

Thea laughed. 'This is getting to be a habit. They'll start wondering whether we killed Julian, at this rate.'

Jessica didn't smile. 'It doesn't look good for the old lady – that's what they'll think. If this is human blood, and turns out to be Julian's, that's enough evidence to arrest and charge her. Especially if she's left traces on the knife as well.'

'They'd never get her to trial, though. There can't be many better cases of diminished responsibility in the history of murder investigations.'

'They'd send her to a special prison,' Jessica nodded. 'For the criminally insane.'

'How dreadful!' The implications struck Thea for the first time. 'We can't let that happen. Jess, we really can't.'

'We'll have to if it's proved that she killed him. She might do it again.'

'But what if she genuinely doesn't know she did it? What would she think about being sent to some gruesome institution? What about Yvette?'

'What about her?'

'The scandal,' Thea explained feebly.

'Listen,' said Jessica. 'There must be

something significant about the timing – the way it happened just as they went off to the back of beyond, where nobody can contact them. It can't possibly be a coincidence.'

'You think they had something to do with it? That they could even have *paid* someone to kill him and left the knife and the coat deliberately to incriminate Granny? Surely nobody would do a thing like that? They seemed really *nice*.'

Jessica snorted. 'Lots of people *seem* nice,' she said sourly.

It was a little after eleven, and Thea was already feeling it was to be another long day. 'What is it about time, when you're a house-sitter?' she demanded rhetorically. 'The days always seem endless, whether or not something's actually happening.'

Hepzie made no reply. Jessica had driven back to the Incident Room with Granny Gardner's mac, leaving her mother and the dog in the house. 'It doesn't need both of us,' she said.

Thea's head was full of visions of the arrest of a demented old lady, whose reaction was impossible to predict. She might laugh, or scream, or curse or weep. It would be intensely distressing whatever she did, and Thea had no wish to witness a development that was starting to feel inevitable. She was also tending to blame herself for the whole ghastly business. If she hadn't asked Jessica to join her, Julian's body would still be lying undiscovered next door. Not until the whiff of decomposition began to filter across the fence and through the kitchen window would anything be found. That, Thea judged, would have been a far preferable outcome. She would probably have gone by the time the stench began to be bothersome. Granny could have washed her mac, and probably nobody would ever have noticed the knife in the hallway drawer. Fiercely, she tried to rerun events, rewrite history, and make everything all right again.

Then Phil Hollis phoned her and told her there was no way he would be able to take her and Jessica for lunch that day.

'You sound a bit stressed,' she said.

'Pressures of work. There's something brewing and we're all on edge about it.'

'What sort of something?'

'You know I can't tell you. If our information is right, you'll be hearing it on the news tonight or tomorrow.'

'And if it's not?'

He snorted. 'You'll be hearing about it on the news with knobs on. "West Midlands cops blunder again."'

'Fingers crossed, then,' she said lightly, fighting to ignore the surges of anxiety afflicting her insides.

Jessica's return went some way towards

improving her fears about Granny, at least. 'They don't think it's human blood,' she said, slightly crestfallen.

'They can tell just by looking?'

'No, but you were right that there's a lot of mucus with it. The lambing story sounded fairly credible to them.'

Thea's eyebrows rose. 'What does a bloke from Solihull know about lambing?'

'Nothing, but there was a girl there as well, and her father's a farmer.'

'Right,' said Thea, trying to imagine the family dynamic whereby a self-employed free-thinking farmer managed to produce a daughter who opted to go into the police. Uncannily similar, of course, to the independent rebellious Carl and his increasingly institutionalised offspring.

'What about the knife?' she added.

'No word on that yet.'

Thea produced coffee, and broached the subject of lunch. 'Phil called to say he won't be lunching today. He's got a crisis or something.'

Jessica shrugged. 'I'm not sure I fancied being a gooseberry with you two, anyhow.'

'Don't be silly,' said Thea on a wave of irritation. 'I want you to get to know each other better.'

'Just don't force it, OK?'

'OK,' Thea sighed. 'Now, the next thing to do is give Hepzie a run. She hasn't been out at all today, except for the back garden.'

'I hope you're going to clean up after her before you go. The lawn's already a mine-field of doggie doo.'

Thea bit back the sharp reply she was tempted to give to that.

She took the dog along to the woodland, which was becoming increasingly familiar territory. The layout, which at first had seemed confusing, was now much clearer, thanks largely to the bird-watching exped-ition with Granny. It comprised a narrow band of trees forking in two directions at the end of the High Street, and then widening into the much larger Bourton Woods to the south. Tracing a path through them would take you to the small straggling town of Bourton-on-the-Hill, not in any way to be confused with Bourton-on-the-Water, several miles to the south.

She traced the same path as she had with Granny, to begin with, intending to turn back after five minutes or so. But the spaniel had more ambitious ideas. Following an interesting scent, she veered to the right and climbed the steep tree-covered escarpment to the fields above.

With some idea of testing her own fitness, Thea opted to follow, scrambling awkwardly over the slippery leaf mould, clinging to the lower trunks of the prevalent laurels, sometimes on all fours as the steepness increased. Looking back she realised it would be almost impossible to get down again the same way. At her call, the dog appeared, waggingly unconcerned at her mistress's breathlessness.

Emerging onto a broad field, she spotted the pretty farmhouse with its enormous barn some distance away, which confirmed her position. Again she had the sense of remoteness from civilisation, freedom from being overlooked and judged by spies in the sky. If she kept closely to the edge of the wood, she was surely invisible. Again, she slipped into a meditation on Upton and the Ditchfords.

The lost villages were, she admitted, much more interesting as fantasy than actuality. On the ground there was little to see. Almost nobody would recognise them as being the remnants of thriving settlements, with homes and stables and food stores and sheep pens. The echoes of human activity had long ago disappeared. But the knowing was everything. Looking north to the area of hilltop on which the unremarkable bumps and channels lay, Thea found it easy to imagine the bustle of daily life. She called to mind a conversation she had had with a visitor from Alaska, who had been in some Internet group with Carl. This woman had demanded to be taken to the most ancient sites in Britain – Avebury, Cadbury and

Tintagel, amongst others. She had worked hard at explaining to Thea how different it was in the two parts of the world. 'Here in England, there is no inch of land that has not been trodden a thousand times by human beings,' she had said. 'Where I come from, there are places which have never known a human foot. It makes one hell of a difference.'

Thea had failed to grasp the true import of this. She had looked down at the ground in front of her, a patch of featureless grass, and shaken her head. 'We can't hope to *know*, though, can we? Who has walked here, what they were feeling and thinking at the time. There could have been a violent death, right here, or a couple making love. It doesn't leave any trace.'

The Alaskan had smiled. 'Oh but it does,' she argued. 'It truly does. It changes the very air around us. You've gotta believe me here.'

But Thea could only see the grass, and could not feel the breath of a hundred ghosts on her neck. 'It would be paralysing to carry all that history around with us all the time,' she said.

'Right,' nodded the woman. 'But I'm not so sure you have a choice. They're here whether you admit it or not.'

And now, on the expanse of this open wold, Thea thought she could perhaps feel something of the weight of that long history, the Romans and the yeoman farmers and everybody else who had worked the land and scanned the variable sky.

And now there were only sheep. A dense flock of them picking feverishly at the new grass, with baby lambs at heel. The grey sky was brightening, she noted, and the air warming. Some of the lambs made exuberant little jumps, legs stiff, for no other reason than pleasure in being alive. Others burrowed under the dense fleece, tails wriggling crazily as they found the target.

Sheep! With young lambs. Barely a quarter of a mile from Blockley High Street! The discovery made Granny's claim to be involved in the lambing somehow much more credible. Calling to Hepzie, who was, Thea belatedly realised, in some danger from an irate shepherd as she trundled heedlessly across the field, she increased her speed, intent on finding an easier way down. 'Come on Heps,' she shrilled.

It took longer than she'd expected, but they eventually located the path down through the woods that they had used the previous afternoon. 'That's all the walk you get today,' she told the dog.

'I found some sheep,' she announced, as soon as she got inside. Jessica was sitting in one of the armchairs, her mobile in her hand.

'Well done,' muttered the girl. 'And I've

got a text message.'

'Oh? Who's it from?'

'Mike. My tutor constable. I have to report at five o'clock on Thursday for a disciplinary hearing.' She turned tragic eyes on her mother. 'Just when I'd managed to forget about it,' she wailed. 'What am I going to do? They'll dismiss me from the Force. I might have to go to court if the family press charges.'

Thea too had almost forgotten Jessica's trouble. The rapid return of the girl's confidence had seemed to suggest she had overstated the whole thing anyway.

'Oh, and Phil called again. Your mobile went off while you were out. I answered it and it was him. He seemed a bit upset not to speak to you. He doesn't like it when you go out without your phone.'

Thea felt unreasonably persecuted. 'Tough,' she said. 'I've just had half an hour of perfect solitude and freedom. A ringing phone would have wrecked the whole experience.'

'Tell him, not me,' shrugged Jessica.

'So what did he want? I only spoke to him less than an hour ago.'

'To warn you, I think. The media have got the scent of this big operation of his, and he thinks there might be something on the lunchtime news. Something about a bomb factory.'

'So I won't listen to the news,' Thea asserted. 'If he gets blown up, someone'll probably come and tell me.'

'Yeah. I expect they will.' Their eyes met, in a happy harmony, each knowing there was nothing more to be said.

'So let's go to that place on the corner and have something healthy for lunch,' Jessica suggested. 'They do wine, I notice.'

'What place?' Thea looked blank.

'It's called Murray's. By the church. You must have seen it.'

'Vaguely,' Thea lied. She had completely failed to observe any such place, even though she must have passed it two or three times.

The establishment turned out to be seriously surprising, much more suited to somewhere like Hay-on-Wye or Petworth or some other little town that attracted middle-class visitors eager to buy books or antiques. It was hard to imagine Blockley thronged with pilgrims keen to visit the church or the converted silk mills, pausing to take a slice of ciabatta and a glass of fine Riesling. But that was the Cotswolds – good living came before just about everything else.

The service was friendly, as they sat at a table at the back of the small dining area. They had salad and cake and wine and coffee and felt replete afterwards. Nobody else patronised the place while they were there.

'Quiet,' Thea commented to the man who

served them.

'Steady,' he corrected her. 'And we sell a lot of stuff from the deli. Best of all worlds, you see.'

She smiled encouragingly at him, and paid the modest bill.

As they left, a loud voice hailed them from a distance of about two yards. 'Hello! Fancy seeing you again. Remember me?'

It was Gussie, the woman Thea had driven to Paxford on Mother's Day, when she had the time wrong. Something about that mistake continued to rankle with her, colouring the whole of that day with a grey mist of confusion. But the woman looked strained, Thea noted, as if maintaining normal conversation was almost too big an effort. As if, perhaps, she was already regretting having drawn attention to herself.

'Oh, hello. Did you get your tyres mended?' Gussie nodded distractedly.

'And did they give you a good lunch?'

'Who?'

'Your son and his wife.'

With an eagerness that hinted at relief, Gussie launched into a lengthy reply. 'Oh – my God, I was in disgrace, I can tell you. The bloody clocks going forward, caught me out. Never usually get that sort of thing in a muddle, but I forgot the whole business. Arrived *really* late. They'd started without me. I got tepid chicken and lumpy gravy and you could see they thought it served me right. How d'you like Murrays, then?' She pointed her chin at the delicatessen.

'Fine,' Thea said. 'And what a surprise, to find something like this out here.'

'Tasteful place, Blockley,' grinned Gussie. 'Who's this?' She stared at Jessica.

'My daughter. She's here for a few days to keep me company while I'm at the Montgomerys.'

'Mum got the clocks wrong as well,' Jessica said, with a reassuring smile. 'They can't have announced it loudly enough on the media.'

'Media,' muttered Gussie as if the word offended her. 'Can't be doing with *media*, anyhow.'

Jessica's smile faded. Before she could think of a reply, Gussie was carrying on, 'Managed to do any more exploring, have you?'

'We went for a look at Upton, as you suggested,' Thea nodded. 'But we couldn't find anything at all.'

Jessica sniffed. 'If you ask me, we were in the wrong field completely. And it isn't a public footpath. I don't know what to make of these abandoned villages, to be honest.' She eyed Gussie closely. 'Are you an archaeologist as well?'

'Me? Of course not. I'm just a peasant farmer.'

She did look the part, to Thea's eyes. The red cheeks and network of lines around her eyes suggested a person seldom indoors. 'Sheep?' she asked.

'Some,' Gussie nodded. 'And a herd of Gloucester cattle. Very rare, very pretty. And a few pigs.'

'Gloucester Old Spots, I suppose?' Thea asked, feeling witty and sharp.

'Of course,' came the flattening answer. 'What other kind is there?'

With a sense of crossing a barrier that Gussie was fiercely trying to maintain, Thea changed the subject. 'You know about the trouble we've had, I expect?'

Gussie's face drooped, reminding Thea strongly of the same sagging features on Thomas Sewell's face the day before.

'Poor old Julian, you mean?' she whispered. 'Yes, I heard about that.'

'We found him actually,' said Jessica, glancing around for listening ears. 'On Sunday evening.'

'Did you indeed? And I suppose you think well of yourself as a result.'

Jessica gave a jerk of outraged surprise. 'I'm with the police,' she said, as if this explained everything.

'Bully for you,' muttered Gussie.

There was an awkward silence in which ruffled feathers slowly settled and Jessica eyed the church as if wishing she could go and explore it.

'I suppose I was out of order,' said Gussie stiffly. 'You can't be expected to understand, being strangers to the place. If anyone's to blame, it's Yvette and Ron for bringing you here.'

'Oh?' said Thea, meeting Jessica's eye. 'Do you mean it would have been better for Julian to lie rotting on the floor for a week?'

Gussie shifted her weight from one foot to the other, and sighed. 'Better for Gladys, if her daughter had been here to see she was all right. That's all I'm saying.'

'Is it?' Jessica challenged. 'Are you sure?'

Gussie seemed to give up some sort of inner struggle. 'You may as well know what the locals are saying,' she told them, shifting weight again. 'It might help put you in the picture, show you what you're up against.' She paused, her gaze directed along the High Street towards the Montgomery house. 'Most people believe Gladys killed him. They think the police know full well she did, and are just assembling their case against her. The trouble, of course–' her voice thickened, and a deep frown grooved her brow '–the trouble is, it would be shocking bad publicity to arrest a woman of her age for murder. Think of the headlines. In the *media*,' she added for Jessica's benefit.

'Do you think they'd let her get away with it, then?' Thea asked, with another nervous glance around the deserted street.

'How well do you know her?' Jessica asked.

'As well as anyone, you could say. She hasn't been out much in the past few years. Since her mind started to fail, they've kept her close to home. Not that you can blame them.' She glanced at Jessica sideways. 'You'll see the problem, I'm sure.'

Thea answered for her daughter. 'They couldn't keep her in gaol, could they? And they couldn't release her on bail if she was guilty of murder. What *would* happen?'

'If she's guilty, she'll have to be punished,' said Jessica.

Gussie took a deep breath. 'Don't be too sure about that. Cracked wits can cover a multitude of sins, I think you'll find.'

'But *why?*' Thea burst out. 'If she killed him – and I still don't see how she'd have the strength, or how she'd get in and out of his house unseen – what was her reason?'

'I've said enough.' Gussie squared her shoulders, and hefted the bulging shopping bag on her arm. 'There are still a few ewes to lamb, and they always get into trouble if I turn my back, stupid things.'

'Just a minute,' Jessica stopped her. 'Can I ask you something? Is it true that Mrs Gardner helps with the lambing, even now, at her age?'

Gussie snorted again. 'She'd like to, I know that. I can't understand the way some people find the messy business of birth so fascinating. But yes, if she can talk someone into letting her into the lambing shed, and if she can escape Yvette's eagle eye, she'll be there, even now. And she's good. You hear men talking about needing strength to haul the wretched creatures out – but that's rubbish. All you need is a feel for the right angle, and the nerve to follow it through. Men are much more likely to panic and gum up the whole works. I once saw Gladys deliver a perfectly *enormous* lamb, just using the tips of her fingers, pushing the skin back over its head, letting the mother do all the work. It was extraordinary. We couldn't believe it afterwards.'

'Yuk!' said Jessica faintly.

'Well, you did ask,' said Gussie, and trotted off down the hill towards the Post Office.

CHAPTER FOURTEEN

Thea and Jessica strolled the short distance along the High Street and past The Crown, in no rush to get back to the house. Hepzie had been left alone – something that Thea always hated doing. 'She yaps when I'm not there,' she said. 'Why is everywhere in this country so anti-dog? In a normal society, I could take her with me anywhere I went.'

'Hygiene, I guess,' said Jessica. 'Animals carry germs, or so everybody thinks.'

Thea sighed. 'Why does everything make me feel so *old?*'

'Not old, just middle-aged,' Jessica assured her. 'By Granny's standards, you're not even halfway yet.'

'Well I'm going to have to emigrate, rather than spend another fifty years in a country where I feel so alienated. All of a sudden I feel out of step with just about everybody.'

'It's probably only temporary,' Jessica comforted her. 'You need a fix of history, or nature study or something. We could go for a bit of a ramble this afternoon if you like.'

Thea frowned. 'I can't leave Granny for long,' she worried.

'Oh, forget her for a bit. She's obviously

managing perfectly well.'

'I'm not sure *managing* is quite the word. I'm beginning to think I'm being paid to make sure she doesn't kill anybody – and I failed in that on the first day.'

'Don't joke about it,' Jessica turned serious on an instant. 'That woman was right, you know. If the police think it was Granny who killed Julian, they'll be in a right old panic, wondering what to do about it. Not just because she's old, but because her mind doesn't work properly. It'd be a nightmare trying to figure out what to do with her. Worse than if it was a child who'd done it, and that's bad enough.'

'She didn't do it. Of course she didn't.' Thea became serious in her turn. 'The idea is ridiculous. I'd be more inclined to suspect that grandson, if I had to finger somebody.'

'What, nice Nick? Surely not.'

'Was he nice? I thought you didn't like him.'

'He was annoying, I admit. But we were both nasty to him.'

'We were in a state.'

Jessica nodded. 'That's true.'

'But I'm not sure he's nice. He didn't seem very upset about his grandad being slaughtered. And where is he now? Why isn't he arranging the funeral and all that stuff?'

'He probably is. He doesn't have to be here on the spot to do all that. And it's a bit soon to start clearing the house.'

'You're right, of course. Well, here we are then. And I forgot to set the burglar alarm again. It always seems such a nuisance.'

'Can you still remember the number?'

'Barely. They wouldn't let me write it down. What would Granny do if it went off, do you think?'

'Oh!' Jessica exclaimed suddenly. 'I wanted to look round the church. That woman made me forget all about it. Should I go back now, do you think?'

Thea shrugged. 'Why bother? Since when were you interested in churches?' She could hear the sudden escalation of yaps from her dog, who had heard them on the doorstep. 'I don't expect dogs are allowed in there, either,' she added. 'You go if you like, but I'm not coming. If there's anything amazing, let me know and I'll pop over later on.'

Jessica seemed to be in two minds about whether or not to go. 'I don't know why I think I'm interested,' she said. 'Why do people persist in looking around churches when they have no interest in religion?'

'Lots of reasons,' said Thea, inattentively. She was feeling agitated, impatient with her daughter's vacillations.

'Like what?'

Thea drew breath, and burst out with a list she would have thought was obvious. 'For one, it's likely to be the oldest building in town. For another, there's some sort of appeal about the atmosphere of a church. Makes you go quiet and thoughtful. For another, they sometimes have very beautiful artwork – carving, painting, glass, whatever. Aesthetically pleasing. Is that enough for you?'

'I'm not going,' Jessica decided.

'What a waste of breath, then,' Thea snapped.

The exchange had taken place through the opening of the front door, the delighted greeting from the dog, the automatic scanning of the hallway for anything unusual or disarrayed. All seemed undisturbed, and they went into the living room with little sense of purpose.

'Now what?' asked Jessica. 'I expect you to entertain me, you know.'

As a joke it misfired badly.

'Well, you're going to be disappointed, then. It's all I can do to entertain myself. I had hoped you'd provide me with some distraction.'

'What's the problem, Mum?' Jessica had plainly had enough. 'You're very bad tempered all of a sudden.'

Thea sighed, sinking into one of the big armchairs. 'Oh, I'm sorry. It must be that Gussie woman. Does everybody really think Granny killed Julian? Don't they see how bizarre that is? I'm convinced she wouldn't have had the strength, for one thing.'

'It does fit, though,' said Jessica gently.

'No better than the theory that he disturbed a burglar. Or that Fat Thomas did it in a final irresistible burst of jealousy. Or Nice Nick, wanting his inheritance. Granny was Julian's *friend*. Nobody's said anything to suggest she wanted him dead.'

Jessica seemed to grow in maturity as Thea watched. 'Perhaps it was a pact of some sort between them. Perhaps *he* wanted to die and she was the only person who'd do it for him.'

'You mean she just held the knife and he threw himself onto it, backwards?' Thea's brow wrinkled sceptically. 'I think even Granny would remember if that happened.'

'Who says she doesn't remember?' Jessica stared into the fireplace. 'We haven't done anything about psychology on the course, but I did it at A-level, remember. I've read all sorts of books about the way the mind works. People are incredibly good at burying nasty facts, denying them even to themselves. It's a defence mechanism.'

'Yes, yes.' Thea was impatient. 'I know all that. Even so – it flies in the face of reason and logic and ordinary common sense to accuse such an old woman of murder.'

Jessica sighed. 'That's the trouble, isn't it. Nobody's going to accuse her, unless there's overwhelming evidence. The police can be very sensitive to ridicule. You can see it now, can't you – the news footage. Even if they used WPCs, gently ushering her into the back of a car, it would still look bad.'

'Assuming she'd go gently. I bet she'd kick and scream and have to be carried.'

'See what I mean,' said Jessica.

The afternoon grew increasingly cloudy, with drizzle setting in by teatime. The view from the house shrank to that of the neighbouring houses and no further. Thea switched on the main light in the living room. 'Dear Diary,' she intoned, 'This is Day Four in Blockley and already it feels like home. Thea and Jessica have made friends with several local people and have solved the vicious murder of a harmless old man. Hepzibah grows fat on the sofa. In India, Yvette and Ron have enjoyed their first elephant ride, and Ron's stomach is expressing its outrage at the food.'

'You don't know that,' giggled Jessica.

'Yes I do. You haven't seen him. Besides, all English men react badly to foreign food. It's a universal truth.'

'And we haven't solved the murder, either,' Jessica pointed out.

'So we haven't. It was nothing but wishful thinking. Let's go and look at the silk mills.'

'Do we have to? We're sure to bump into one of your new friends.'

'That was rather the idea.'

'No need, look.' Jessica pointed to the window, where a man was peering in at them. 'I think we've got a visitor.'

It was James Osborne, Thea's brother-in-law and Jessica's uncle. He was dressed in a denim outfit that looked much too young for him. Thea still thought of him wearing police uniform, despite it being twelve years or more since he'd moved to CID and ceased to wear the crisp garments of his office.

James had a big heavy head, set squarely on wide shoulders. His colouring tended towards ginger, but he did not have the thin pale skin that often went with that. As he came in and enfolded Jessica in a hug, it was obvious that they were related. 'You two have got the same neck,' Thea said suddenly. 'I never noticed that before.'

Hepzie had once adored James, flinging herself unwelcomely at his legs whenever she saw him. But now she gave him a far more restrained greeting, which he barely even acknowledged. James was not a dog person.

Phil Hollis, however, was. Thea found herself almost resenting the arrival of the wrong detective. James was a poor substitute, as far as she was concerned. Hepzie's lukewarm response eerily echoed her own.

'And what can we do for you?' she asked primly.

'Cup of tea?' he said, with a smile she perceived as ingratiating. 'And some cake would be nice.'

'Sorry – cake's off today. There might be a packet of biscuits, though.'

As she went into the kitchen, Thea was in no doubt that she was not the main object of the visit. James had come to the aid of his suffering niece, having heard all about her difficulties the previous week. The killing of Julian Jolly was secondary to the need to assuage the girl's jangled confidence.

'I'll go and walk the dog for a bit,' she announced five minutes later. 'You two can have a good debriefing session without me. I'll stroll down to the shop and get some more provisions.'

'They sell cake at the place where we had lunch,' Jessica pointed out. 'You could bring some back with you.'

Thea nodded, thinking she had intended to stay out for an hour or so, in the hope that James would have gone by then.

She thought about this as she walked along the High Street with the spaniel pulling ahead. What was going on, that she felt so hostile towards the man who had been a pillar when her husband had died, a warm rock against which she had often beaten herself in her grief.

That, she suspected, might be part of the answer. James was forever associated with the first black weeks of her loss, and now she was recovering and attempting to construct a new relationship, he took her back to that dark place that she never wanted to experience again. Plus, he was Carl's brother. However much he might wish her well and approve of Phil, there were bound to be reservations. In any case, Thea wasn't sure that he *did* approve. She had never directly asked him, and he had been careful not to pass judgement, but she was not easy about it.

So she left him to her daughter. They were good for each other, and always had been. James and Rosie never had any children of their own, thanks to a defect in Rosie's back which was currently getting worse. The once brave and serene woman had grown taut with the pain in recent months, the fear for her own future clear in her eyes. It was tragic, everybody agreed. The condition did not respond to treatment, and was never going to. The increasing levels of analgesia were affecting her mind, and she was visibly retreating into her own tiny world. James carried this burden valiantly, as people carried their brain-damaged children or their impossible runs of bad fortune, but it was changing him, too. Jessica alone seemed immune to the aura around him. She remembered the loving laughing uncle of her childhood and could still find him beneath the distraction of his martyrdom.

There was no sense of resentment that Jessica was pouring out her professional problems to her uncle. Rather it came as a relief to Thea that there was someone who would know what to say. All she could think of was platitudes about being new to the work and Jessica probably over-reacting. Speaking from a position of ignorance, she was quite likely to make the whole thing worse. All she had been able to do was offer some diversion, and since that took the form of another police investigation – at least to a large extent – she wasn't confident that it was going to work.

The killing of Julian Jolly was a very peculiar business, she concluded, as she walked down through a curving row of modern houses towards the large converted silk mill at the bottom of the hill. Although the police presence was muted, most of the neighbouring residents must surely have been questioned, and yet there was no sense of a community stirred up by a crisis in their midst. No gatherings on street corners or inquisitive peerings through Julian's front window. Nobody had accosted Thea or Jessica to demand details of Julian's discovery. Perhaps the Gussie woman had got it right – that everyone believed Granny Gardner to be the killer, and were all too shocked or embarrassed or sensitive to make a major issue of it. Perhaps Julian had been universally disliked and the prevailing feeling was one of relief.

Or perhaps – and this seemed by far the most likely explanation to Thea – they were all too busy rushing off to their city jobs to worry about a dead old man. Even those who were retired seemed to have very full lives, to judge from the quantity of notices pinned to wooden doors all around the town. Clubs, talks, quizzes, outings – it would be a full-time job to keep up with it all. And then there were all the other obligations – to keep the garden tidy, and to monitor the intriguing details of the lives of celebrities such as Icarus Whatsisname. Both more compelling than a quiet little murder.

The silk mill that confronted Thea was an enormous edifice, rising to three storeys at the front, and four at the back. At least, the ground floor was invisible from the front. Rows and rows of identical windows looked out onto neat gardens, with spiral fire escapes attached to the façade, and she found herself wondering what kind of person would move into a sub-division of such a building. How many rooms did each resident have, and was there a waiting list to live there? Feeling like an intruder, she let the dog tow her down the road to the back of the building, where it was easier to imagine it as a working factory. In deep shadow from another large block beyond it, there was a row of doors, and not a flicker of life. She found herself thinking about the silk that had come from the place, earning fortunes for the mill owners and clothing the upper classes. And now, rather like the villages of Upton and Ditchford, it was all abandoned and forgotten.

The old ways were lost almost without trace. Only in the uncompromising hulk of the building's shell could the history be discerned, just as the lost villages were betrayed by the bumps and troughs in the land.

The connection with Julian was obvious. His death might not be making many ripples on the surface, but somebody somewhere had murdered him, and Thea knew quite well that any sudden death brought rifts and ructions that lasted down the decades, however hard everyone tried to forget.

But still she found it hard to care. A man she had never met, in a small town she might never visit again after next week – why should she bother about it when nobody else seemed to? Because Jessica was with her, came the answer. Jessica the police probationer who needed her principles reinforced, to judge by the things she had said during their walk to the Upton remains. Jessica had to know that every crime was important, that even a small matter of cheating undermined something vital about society. Carl's voice rang in Thea's ears, his rigorous ethics sometimes tedious or irritating, but always appreciated, deep down. Never particularly sociable herself, Thea nonetheless understood the fragility of human institutions and the disastrous consequences of social breakdown.

She began to walk back up the curving hill towards the centre of town. Hepzie still pulled ahead, as she always did when on the lead. Thea often found herself wishing she had a labrador, or some other obedient breed that hung back against your leg and would never dream of breaking the rhythm of your footsteps. But Hepzie was charming and endearing in most ways. What was one small defect set against all that, Thea thought fondly.

The sound of a throaty car engine caught her attention, as it came up the hill behind her in low gear. Cautiously, she pulled the dog closer, despite their being on a perfectly safe pavement. Where, she wondered, had it come from? Where, in fact, did the silk mill people keep their cars? Presumably a section of the building had been allocated to cars, but she had not noticed any garages.

The car drew level with her, and slowed to a standstill. 'Hiya, spaniel lady,' came a familiar voice. 'You doing OK? And the Granny? Still feisty and funny with her wits?'

He was almost shouting to compete with the rumble of the over-powerful engine. Thea just nodded and flapped her hand in a semi-wave. Then she noticed another familiar face in the passenger seat, as its owner leant towards Icarus Binns and said something to him.

Ick immediately turned off the ignition, and yanked up the handbrake, making the car rock slightly on the steep incline. 'Friend Nick wants to speak a word,' he said, leaning back to give a clear line of sight between the two.

Nick Jolly, however, seemed to prefer a more direct encounter. He unclasped his seatbelt and got out of the car, walking round the front of it to stand facing Thea on the pavement. He was about five feet ten, which made him eight or nine inches taller than her. Hepzie gave him a sociable greeting, jumping up at his legs and scrabbling at his jeans with sharp front claws. He set her down absently but firmly.

'You know each other?' Thea said foolishly, but unable to contain her surprise. She could think of no possible link between the celebrity from Essex and the gangling archaeologist from Dorset. Even the Blockley connection seemed very tenuous.

Nick smiled wanly. 'Not exactly. We met yesterday, as it happens. Ick was looking at a property in Paxford at the same time as me. It was a cock-up on the part of the agent, basically.'

Thea let her thoughts run riot. It felt as if

there was a whole raft of information in those few words. Icarus Binns and Nicholas Jolly were both planning to buy a house in the area. *Ick and Nick,* her agile mind repeated, with some relish. *Icarus and Nicholas.* How funny names could be, especially in conjunction with other names.

'And Cleo. Cleo is not to be forgot,' prompted Ick from the car.

'So you're thinking of moving here – both of you?' Thea said, looking from one to the other and thinking the speed with which Nick Jolly had moved was extraordinary.

Nick patted himself on the chest consideringly. 'You're thinking it's rather soon to be house-hunting,' he observed. 'I can see it must look that way. But the thing is, I have to do something while I wait for the funeral and all that. And I always wanted to live here. Because of Upton, you see,' he added, as if that made everything clear.

'Upton? The lost village?'

'Right. Except we call them *deserted,* not lost. You know it was excavated in the late sixties and early seventies, I suppose?'

Thea shook her head. 'Um – no, I don't think I knew that, did I?' She stared at him in confusion. Should she have known?

'Well, it was, and they found some very intriguing earlier remains. Pre-medieval. But they never managed to get a proper look. They didn't have the necessary skills or equipment to get beneath the medieval stuff, you see. Plus, there were severe time constraints. Putting in a new drain, or something, which meant they only had a few days.'

'Right,' she said slowly. 'Is this what you wanted to talk to me about?'

He gave the same strained smile as before. 'Oh, no. Sorry. No, no. I wanted to see if you were OK, that's all. Are the police bothering you much?'

She couldn't resist it. 'There's a Detective Superintendent talking to Jessica at this very moment,' she said, watching for his reaction.

He did not go pale or start to shake. He didn't bite his lip or hurry back to the car. But he did frown in puzzlement. 'Is there? Why's that, then?'

Thea relented. 'It isn't actually anything to do with your grandfather. As it happens, I'm surrounded by police officers. Two Detective Superintendents, would you believe? My brother-in-law, and my – um, boyfriend.' She looked away from his face, wary of saying too much after Jessica's warning the day before.

'I still can't really believe it,' Nick sighed. 'But you were right about my interview with the police. They obviously wanted to check my whereabouts before they would tell me anything about what happened. Can't blame them, I guess.' He repeated his familiar cheek-stroking mannerism. 'It feels so *strange,'* he burst out. 'Worrying about who might have killed him – it gets in the way of ... you know.'

'Grief,' Thea supplied succinctly. 'Yes, I know. It's another reason why murder is so horrifying.'

'Right. And now they won't let me into his house because they're still combing it for clues.'

'Clues!' came Icarus's rich tones from the car, where he was leaning out of the window following the whole conversation. 'Like a game, sounds to me. Follow the clues and get yo' killer – is that the thing?'

Thea felt herself turn into the same stiff humourless matron that she always became with Icarus. 'I don't think it's a game at all,' she said. 'And I doubt if that's how Nick sees it – losing his grandfather in such a terrible way.'

But Nick's eyes were shining with suppressed mirth, and his full lips were quivering ominously. 'Sorry,' he said, 'but it's the way he speaks.' He turned to the celebrity rapper. 'I *love* the way you speak,' he said with no hint of self-consciousness. 'You make everything sound like a poem.' He looked at Thea. 'He's taken me under his wing, so to speak, and I must say he's a tonic. Honestly, he's incredible with language, don't you think?'

Thea could find nothing to say to that which would not involve mendacity. 'Jessica says the same,' she managed, with a polite smile at Ick.

'Life's a poem,' said the celebrity easily, and then rapped his steering wheel with a knuckle. 'You coming now, or what is it?'

Nick took a few steps and then looked back at Thea. 'I meant to ask you about Gladys,' he remembered. 'How is she today?'

'Much the same, I think,' said Thea. 'It's rather hard to say – not knowing how she usually is. She finds it impossible to remember that your grandfather's dead, which makes it difficult.'

'Poor old girl.' He shook his head, his thick black hair sculpted to his skull. 'Must have scattered her last remaining wits, I should think. She must be devastated, seeing they were such good friends. Well – a bit more than friends, at one time, by all accounts.'

Thea resisted the urge to question him further on this point, merely smiling as he got back into the car. Only after they had disappeared did she realise she had no idea what the two were doing together, or where they were going.

It was after five when she got back to the house, half hoping that James would have gone. But not only was he still there, but there was a distinct atmosphere of impatience, suggesting they had been waiting for her to come back.

'At last!' Jessica exploded. 'We thought you'd only gone for some cake. What on earth have you been doing?'

'Cake!' Thea clapped a hand over her mouth. 'I forgot the cake. Hepzie and I went down to look at the silk mills. Then we got chatting with Nick and Ick.' She savoured the names again, a small secret pleasure.

'It doesn't matter,' said James tightly. 'We had a very nice chat.'

'Good. I hoped you would. Have you managed to persuade her she won't get the sack?'

James smiled and sent a conspiratorial glance at Jessica. 'There was never any question of that,' he said.

'You saw Nick,' Jessica prompted. 'What did he say?' Thea registered surprise that Nick had taken precedence over the famous Ick.

'He's looking for a house to buy and he hopes we weren't too upset. Something about Upton village as well. He and Ick met yesterday and now they seem to be bosom buddies.'

'What about Cleodie Mason?'

'No sign of her. Maybe she's gone back to work.'

'You know people here, do you?' James queried, trying to follow the thread.

'We met Icarus on Sunday evening, and

Nick yesterday,'

Jessica told him. 'Icarus Binns – you know. The rap singer. He's beautiful. Mum met him first on Saturday, actually, when Granny Gardner fell over.'

'Never heard of him,' James admitted proudly.

'Nor me,' said Thea. 'Thank goodness for that.'

Jessica scowled at them both. 'You're like that judge who didn't know who the Beatles were,' she accused. 'You, Uncle James – I'd have thought it was part of your job to keep abreast of popular culture.'

He grinned. 'Whatever gave you that idea?' he demanded.

Jessica ignored him, gathering up the cups from the tea they'd finished some time ago. James turned to Thea. 'Nick Jolly, do you mean? Grandson to the murder victim? He's already spending his inheritance, you reckon?'

Thea silently applauded his mental agility. 'The very man,' she confirmed. 'And if he's looking at the same properties as a famous rap star, he must think his expectations are substantial.'

'We're checking the old man's will today. Sounds as if it's something to take seriously.'

Thea gave him a sceptical look. 'If he'd killed his grandpa for the money, he wouldn't be likely to splurge the news that he was house-hunting already, would he? Isn't that a bit of a giveaway?'

James shrugged. 'His alibi seems sound. He was at a dig near Dorchester all day Sunday, with several colleagues. They'll all vouch for him, I assume.'

'Working on a Sunday?' Thea queried.

'Yep, they're at it seven days a week. One of those sites with a new road going over it at any moment. They were staying in a hall, on camp beds, all in together. He could never have driven up here, done the deed and got back without being seen.'

'Stranger things have happened,' said Thea.

James sidestepped that remark. 'We should get the full forensic report tomorrow morning,' he said. 'If there are traces of Dorset mud in Mr Jolly's house, we'll go over young Nick's story again. Meanwhile, my interest is a lot more local.'

'He thinks Granny did it,' said Jessica softly. 'He doesn't want to, but he does.'

'Oh?' Thea found her heart thumping alarmingly. 'But–'

'That knife you found is definitely the murder weapon,' James told her. 'It fits the wound exactly, and the blood is Mr Jolly's. So now we have to work out how it got into that drawer.'

'And when,' said Thea, her heart thundering so loudly it deafened her to her own thoughts.

'Mum,' Jessica said gently. 'It must have been while you were out on Sunday. Did you leave the back door unlocked?'

'Yes, it was unlocked all the time. Ron said ... he said it didn't matter. Nobody would get in.' She frowned. 'He seemed to *want* it left like that.'

James gave a small groan, and both women looked at him. 'Don't tell me that,' he pleaded. 'Do you realise what a sweat it would be to have to find them and bring them back for questioning?'

This was not a new idea for Thea. 'You'd be surprised,' she said, 'at how well I realise.'

'So we do what we can without them. Jess and I have gone over it in detail. Back door unlocked. Connecting door likewise. Key still on its hook. Key to back door in Julian's pocket.'

'Wait!' Thea held up a hand. 'I did lock the back on Saturday night. And I left the key in the lock. Doesn't that mean it would be impossible for anyone to open it from outside?'

'Not entirely. If they were determined, they could probably push it out.'

'But it would clatter onto the floor and wake me up.'

'You can't be sure of that.'

'You said you heard some odd thumps and bumps early on Sunday, anyway,' Jessica reminded her.

'Yes,' Thea agreed, thinking hard. 'But it

would work better if it had been opened from the inside, wouldn't it.' She fixed James with a penetrating stare. 'You're thinking Granny came through into this house, out of the back, over into Julian's, killed him, came home the same way, locking up after herself as she went. Then she washed the knife, came back and slipped it into that drawer. Then, for some reason she went out of the front, setting off the buzzer. But that doesn't work.'

'Why not?'

'Because I know the connecting door was locked when I went to bed on Saturday.'

'So? She must have a key to it.'

'So why leave it *unlocked* afterwards?'

'Plain forgetfulness.'

'Possible,' said Thea reluctantly. 'Perhaps she thought I'd heard her and panicked.'

'It's all guesswork at this stage, but it does fit the evidence,' James summarised, with no sign of satisfaction.

Thea's heart thundered even more powerfully. 'But surely she isn't clever enough. Besides...' But the thought had flown. In her imagination, she could see it all too clearly – the old woman flitting silently through the hall and into the back garden, knife in hand. It paralysed her tongue and made her dizzy.

CHAPTER FIFTEEN

Tuesday ended much as Monday had done, with the time change stretching the afternoon confusingly. 'I still can't get used to the new time,' Thea grumbled. 'I suppose it's because it came as such a surprise.'

'Are we eating out tonight?' Jessica looked hopeful, but Thea could summon no enthusiasm.

'We had lunch out,' she objected. 'We can't keep doing it.'

'Why not? This is my holiday, remember. What about that Churchill place in Paxford? We'll never get there at this rate. I've only got one more full day here.'

'Phil said he'd take us.'

'When?'

'When he can get some time. I suppose that business with the bombs is still taking all his attention.' They had watched the television news, to find nothing whatever about bomb factories.

'They must have managed to keep it blacked out for the time being,' said Jessica. 'Maybe there's a raid going on at this very moment.'

'Isn't it always four in the morning when

they do that?' Thea said.

'Usually,' Jessica conceded.

'So why doesn't he call and tell me what he's doing?' Thea embarrassed herself by wanting regular contact from the man. It was so *adolescent*, she chided herself. But they never ran out of things to say and she had to admit she looked forward to his calls. Even a text message – which she never thought she would manage – lifted her spirits. It felt like invading a territory that strictly belonged to the under-35s, and discovering all sorts of delights across the invisible border.

'I want to go somewhere tonight,' Jessica insisted. 'It's boring just staying here.'

'You sound about twelve,' Thea said, thinking that if her daughter was twelve, then she might easily be under thirty-five herself. Perhaps there'd been a time slip and they'd lost ten years, instead of one British Summer Time hour.

'Well, call Phil and see what he's doing. Then we'll decide.'

Unable to think of a good reason to refuse, Thea did as she was told. Phil answered his mobile on the first ring and sounded pleased that she'd called him. When she asked about his mysterious operation, he evaded the question with a careless, 'Oh, we think it's gone off the boil for the time being. Although...' He paused, and then began muttering to someone in the room with him.

'Ah, Thea, I can't talk for long.' He then asked earnestly after their welfare and whether they were obeying his orders and staying clear of the murder investigations.

'It's not difficult,' Thea assured him. 'As far as we can see, there aren't really any investigations going on. Nothing to affect us, anyway. James was here this afternoon. He's the SIO or whatever it's called. He thinks he knows who did it.'

'Good,' said Phil inattentively. She could hear a man's voice, apparently requiring Phil's response. 'Seems I've gotta go,' he said. 'Something else has just come up.'

'Poor you,' sighed Thea, thinking it all sounded quite good fun. Phil's voice was animated, even excited. 'Well make sure your men don't go shooting any innocent South Americans, OK.'

She knew it was the wrong thing to say, even as the words formed themselves. Obviously it was. It should have been such a self-evident taboo that it would never even cross her mind. But Thea maintained her principles and opinions, regardless of who she was speaking to, and there were aspects of the police that she didn't think she would ever quite accept.

'Don't worry about that.' His voice was abruptly clipped and distant, which was hardly surprising. 'Although I could point out that if you were in a bus with a suicide bomber, you might be quite glad if–'

'Yes, yes,' she cut him off hurriedly. 'I know all that. Sorry I spoke. So when are we going to see you?'

'I can't say. Honestly, darling, it wouldn't be fair to raise your hopes. You'll have to assume it won't be before the weekend. If it does settle down a bit, you know I'll be there like a shot. That's the best I can do.'

It was the first time he'd been so un-compromising about his availability – or the lack of it, even though they had been interrupted before by inconvenient crimes. On those occasions, Phil had been rueful, apologetic, sharing her sense of victimhood at the way things had worked out. Now he seemed to have gone over to a different side. Perhaps this was closer to the reality of how he felt about his work/life balance. Perhaps it was simply the romance fading, after eight short months. And if that was the case, then Thea might have to confront some uncom-fortable implications. Phil Hollis was forty-six; he probably had another ten years in the job. That was too long to tread water or live in a half-relationship where promises could never convincingly be made. She would be forced to create her own identity apart from him, maintain her own activities and inter-ests for the times when he was emotionally and physically separate from her. And how did a person manage that balance? Switching from independent self-sufficiency to welcoming partnership at a moment's notice? Was it actually possible, and even if it was, did she want to live like that?

'We're going to have to talk about this,' she said, as if Phil had been able to hear her thoughts.

'What? Talk about what?' She could hear another man's voice in the background, his tone urgent. 'Sorry, love. I'll have to go. Be careful, won't you?'

And he was gone. Thea felt as if he had left her with her face pressed up against a brick wall, her words thwarted, her feelings ignored.

Jessica had tactfully withdrawn to the kitchen during the phonecall. Now she ventured back, eyebrows raised. 'So?' she said. 'You look a bit stressy.'

Thea gazed at her daughter, slowly remembering that she too was in the police. 'Doesn't it ever worry you?' she asked. 'That your job is incompatible with having a proper relationship?'

Jessica's eyes widened further. 'Hang on a minute,' she protested. 'Don't bring *me* into it. I'm not a Detective Superintendent, and not likely to be. I get time off, like anybody else. Have you any idea how many hours the average plumber works in a week? Or systems analysts, or farmers, or AA men, or...' she ran out of jobs that removed people from their families, but the point was made.

'OK,' Thea put up a hand. 'Sorry. But that doesn't answer the point. It's all wrong. People should have time for each other.'

'Maybe they should just make better use of the time they have. It's probably *good* for a relationship to see each other only for short spells of time. Concentrates the mind. Maintains the mystery. All that sort of stuff.'

They both realised that it was new for the daughter to be counselling the mother. Jessica gave an embarrassed little laugh. 'But what do I know? If I don't get myself a proper boyfriend soon, there'll be rumours about me being a lesbian.'

Thea closed her eyes briefly. Not now, she prayed. Let's not get onto that now. 'So let's go to Paxford,' she said. 'It's obviously no good waiting for Phil to escort us.'

'And who needs men, anyway?' said Jessica, squaring her shoulders and raising a feminist fist.

The Churchill Arms was friendly, unassuming and in possession of a remarkably adventurous menu. The atmosphere was emphatically that of a pub, rather than a restaurant, which suited the Osborne women very well. They were uninterrupted by the arrival of anybody they knew, and by mutual consent they devoted most of their attention to the gourmet delights of grey mullet, creamed parsnips, braised pork and thoroughly luxurious sauces.

'This is the life,' sighed Jessica, scraping the last of the vegetables out of the dish and onto her plate. 'I do love food.'

Thea laughed. 'Maybe you should post a review of this place on that website? The one that had the rude piece about The Crown. Redress the balance, or something.'

'I just might do that,' the girl nodded, with her mouth full.

It was dark when they got back, and again the two women had to resist the encroaching nervousness. There was a reassuring light in Granny's front window, and no yapping from Hepzie as they let themselves in. 'You forgot to set the burglar alarm again,' Jessica said.

'And you never reminded me. It seems daft to me, especially with a ferocious spaniel guarding the place.'

The guard dog was squirming around their ankles, treating them both to her most lavish greetings, which included throwing herself onto her back and displaying a clean pink belly.

'We'd better watch the news,' said Jessica. 'There might be something about Phil's bomb by now.'

There was. A triumphalist report, second from the top, about the stalwart West

Midlands police foiling a desperate terrorist plot to cause maximum carnage in the centre of Birmingham. The top story concerned the resignation of a Government minister over a piece of rank incompetence in the management of the Health Service. 'Clever psychology,' Thea remarked. 'First the bad news, then the good. The hospitals might be collapsing, but we're safe in the hands of the vigilant boys in blue.'

Jessica seemed more than half inclined to take issue with her mother's tone, but she was distracted by the television. The third item featured a lavish premiere of a new film in Leicester Square. All the starring actors had turned out for it, their faces filling the screen as the cameras zoomed in on them.

'Oh!' squealed Jessica. 'That's Cleodie Mason. Look!' She leant forward eagerly, but the shot was barely two seconds long. Thea had missed it. 'I didn't know she was in a film. I thought she was a model.'

'Aren't they interchangeable? What about Liz Hurley? She's both, isn't she?'

To Thea's disappointment Jessica didn't reply with astonished approval at her mother's sudden celebrity awareness. The girl was still quivering with excitement. 'And we *saw* her, here, only two days ago. Isn't that amazing!'

Thea wanted to say something world-weary about it not being far from Blockley to

Leicester Square, and why the excitement, but she hadn't the heart. She had to accept that the celebrity culture was too strong for her. Few things were more thrilling, these days, than seeing someone you'd met in the flesh appearing on television. Some magical enhancement took place and the individual concerned acquired a new dimension in the process. Even more enchanting and marvellous, of course, when they appeared on the cinema screen. Cleodie Mason had instantly acquired major mythical status in the eyes of Jessica and probably most of the world's population.

The local news, when it followed with its patchy five-minute slot, was the familiar transition from super-stardom and world events to features about old ladies celebrating their centenary and quarrels about planning consent. Despite the foiled bomb plot being in the same region, the editors had clearly deemed it superfluous to do more than repeat the headlines already aired on the main news. Instead they showed a child with a rare bone disorder and its parents who were raising funds for a new treatment in America, and then a shot of a road accident on the A44.

'A serious accident took place late this afternoon, on the A44 near Blockley,' said the voiceover. 'A van was hit as it emerged from a field, and overturned. The driver of the Ford Focus, which collided with the van, was killed instantly. The contents of the van were strewn across the road, causing it to be closed for over an hour.' The film showed the mess spilt from the overturned van.

'It just looks like a lot of rubble,' said Jessica. 'Earth and stones and stuff.'

Thea tried to make sense of the scene. 'What a *lot* of it! The van must have been full to bursting. Why didn't they use a truck instead?'

'It's very weird. Why would anybody fill a van with soil?'

'Stealing it for their garden? Maybe those stones are from somebody's wall, and they didn't want to be noticed. It doesn't seem especially strange to me. They probably didn't have a truck handy.' Thea was slow to notice just how fascinated her daughter was with the story, already shrugging it off herself as something unworthy of her interest.

'Play it again,' Jessica instructed, nodding at the remote control next to Thea's elbow.

'What? It's not a video, Jess. It's ordinary news.'

'Yes, but you can run it again, on digital telly.'

Thea just stared at her. 'Are you sure?'

Jessica grabbed the gadget and with complete confidence pressed some of the keys. Sure enough, the same news item appeared again. The young police probationer gave it her full attention, freezing the picture every few seconds. 'That really is odd,' she repeated. 'And it must only be half a mile from here.'

'About that,' Thea nodded. 'You can hear the traffic from the woods at the end of the street.'

'Well, first thing tomorrow, we're going to have a look,' Jessica asserted. 'Apart from anything else, there shouldn't be a field gate opening onto a main A-road.'

'Is there a law against it?'

'Probably,' said Jessica. 'If there isn't, there ought to be.'

Thea was still unclear as to what was so interesting about the overturned van. As far as she could see, it looked slightly odd, but no more than that. 'I'd have thought the bit about Cleodie Whatnot would be much more exciting,' she said.

Jessica shrugged. 'It was, for about two minutes. Now I've got something else to think about.'

They went to bed just after eleven, Thea locking doors front and back, and leaving the kitchen immaculately clean, before treating herself to a long hot bath. It hadn't been a very productive day, she judged, looking back. Two meals out, a somewhat disturbing encounter with the Gussie woman and a lurking sense of imminent disappointment concerning Phil Hollis. Thoughts of him came packaged in a lumpy set of feelings that she knew she needed to disentangle as a matter of urgency. All along she had been prepared to construct a relationship that suited the real individuals they were, and not some pre-ordained pattern laid down by social expectations, such as they were. But awkward ideas like 'commitment' and 'ground rules' kept obtruding, much to her confusion. It was not going to be enough that they liked each other, had plenty of compatible interests and attitudes, and were irresistibly attracted physically. Listed like that, she wondered why these factors seemed to fall short of what was needed. What *else* was there, for heaven's sake?

It was impossible to answer, and she gave up. Phil Hollis floated away on the scented water, to be replaced by images of Granny Gardner next door, and the suggestion that she might have committed a murder.

Was there no rest, Thea's troubled spirit demanded? Even when Granny gave way to Jessica, there was just as much to worry about. At every turn, people were being troublesome. They all came bedecked with suspicion or anxiety or disappointment, as Thea revisited them one by one. Even her mother would be reproachful at the missed Mother's Day card.

She crept into bed, careful not to waken

the peacefully sleeping Jessica. Hepzie had made a warm place in the middle of the bed, and obligingly shifted over to let her mistress have the prepared spot. Here, Thea thought with a smile, was at last something – she almost said *somebody* to herself – that came unencumbered with worry. The dog had had her share of mishaps, but she was still as sweet and soft and devoted as ever. All she demanded was company, food and a few kind words. *Thank God for a dog*, Thea sighed, as she slipped into sleep.

This time when Granny's door buzzer went off, Thea knew right away what it was. But when she opened her eyes, sitting up quickly and dislodging the spaniel, everything was in darkness.

'What the hell's that?' came a muffled voice in the next bed.

'Granny's door. What time is it?' Thea's head felt heavy and thick. Hepzie was whining.

'Um ... let's see ... Jesus, it's one-fifteen in the morning. Surely she hasn't gone out at this time? What are we meant to do?'

'Go down and see, I suppose. She does get very confused about time – they told me that.'

'She must know it's *night*. It's pitch dark.'

'Well, the door's been opened for some reason. I'll have to check it out. That's what they're paying me for.'

'Come on, then. Leave the dog.' Jessica was abruptly businesslike. 'Let's get it over with.' She was out of bed and had switched on the main light.

Thea felt bleary and disoriented, blinking in the violence of the light. She had been deeply asleep, dreaming about a man that she recognised now, with some chagrin, as having been Ick, the rap singer. 'I was dreaming about Icarus Binns,' she said, fumbling for her dressing gown. 'Do we have to get dressed?'

'You're not allowed to dream about him. He's mine,' Jessica panted. 'Better put some trousers on. We might be out there for a while. She's getting quite a start on us at this rate.'

Less than two minutes later they were on the pavement, having deactivated the buzzer, and were scanning the dark street. There was a slight breeze, chilly on their skin. 'I can't see anything,' whispered Thea. 'Can you?'

The presence of sleeping strangers in all the surrounding houses was impossible to ignore. The consequences of waking them were too awful to contemplate. Thea quickly went to the cottage and pulled the door closed. Jessica was slowly scanning the street and beyond. 'Up there!' she pointed. 'There's some sort of light. It might be a torch.'

Thea took some seconds to locate it – a narrow beam of flickering light in what she supposed was a field behind the house across the street. 'That's where the sheep were,' she remembered. 'I expect it's a farmer, seeing if they're all right. I can hear one of them bleating.' The sound wafted across on the breeze, a plaintive cry, suggestive of distress.

'Unlikely to be a farmer at this time of night,' Jessica argued. 'If he wanted to inspect them at night he'd keep them indoors.'

Thea wondered fleetingly what Jessica knew about shepherding. She felt helpless, irritated and cold. 'What are we going to do, then?'

'I think that torch must be her. It's the only sign of life. How do we get there?'

The field was on a rising slope, to the south. Thea could not remember any sort of gate or path giving access to it. As far as she could recall, the only direct route led through somebody's garden. 'I have no idea,' she said. 'You're not suggesting we try to follow that light, are you?'

They were still whispering, standing on the pavement together. Blockley did not have street lights, but the breeze was shifting the clouds, and the moon was almost full. Every now and then, it found a gap and the pale light revealed more. 'We can try down there,' Jessica pointed at an open space beside a low stone wall, tipping invisibly downwards.

'There might be a way through.'

It was entirely surreal. Thea seriously asked herself whether she might still be dreaming, as they blundered down the narrow footway that meandered between small back gardens, bordered by stone walls. Jessica led, with Thea gripping her hand, held awkwardly behind her. They went in single file, stumbling frequently, and still terrified of awakening the slumbering neighbours.

It seemed a crazy quest. The bobbing light that they had been following disappeared from view. 'We'll never find her,' Thea breathed. 'Can't we go back?'

'There's a gate here,' Jessica announced. 'It goes into the field, look.' And again the moon obligingly cast pale rays onto the scene. There was indeed a gate. And beyond it, there appeared to be a sloping field containing dark shapes which could well be sheep. The sporadic bleating had stopped, but there did seem to be a certain restlessness in the flock.

Jessica didn't wait for a reply, but forged through the gate, stumbling on invisible stones and muttering crossly to herself. Thea followed, one hand held out in front of her. Although no longer pitch dark, it was still impossible to see very much.

'There she is,' the girl panted. 'Look!'

A dim beam of light shone on a complicated scene at the lower edge of the field.

The torch had been placed on the ground, propped against a stone, to illuminate the rear end of a prostrate sheep. Kneeling beside it was a human figure. Instinctively aware of a need for delicacy, the two crept closer.

Granny Gardner was deeply intent on her task, showing no awareness of the intruders. Not until they were only three feet away did she glance up at them. 'Nearly there now,' she panted. 'Would you point the torch here?'

Jessica picked up the light and shone it on a bulging grey patch that glistened wetly. The old woman was using her fingertips to nudge away the tightly stretched skin around the top of the bulge. There was no sign of undue effort or panic. The sheep groaned forlornly, its head outstretched on the cold ground. The bony fingers seemed to be working with an independent skill that was close to magic. 'Just a bit more,' Granny said evenly. 'What a big lambie it is. A terrible big lambie for a girl, isn't that so?'

The light wavered in Jessica's hands, and Thea simply stared helplessly at the minor miracle unfolding before her.

With a thin scream from the ewe, the wide head suddenly slid free, the elastic maternal tissue closing around its neck so it sagged grotesquely for a few seconds. 'Help me pull,' Granny ordered. 'The poor thing's too tired to do it on her own.'

Help was not quite the word. As Thea tried to grasp the slippery inert thing, the old woman slumped away, giving Thea complete responsibility. 'Just pull it,' Mrs Gardner instructed weakly.

So Thea pulled, and before she knew it, an entire lamb lay half on her feet, half on the short grass. Fluid gushed forth and the sheep gave a vigorous cry of relief.

'You did it!' Jessica cried, in disbelief. 'Is it alive?'

Granny crawled forward, and inserted a finger into the lamb's mouth, plucking away pieces of membrane. The ewe began to struggle to get up, ropes of grey tissue hanging out of her.

The lamb drunkenly shook its head and made a rattling sound, before sneezing. 'He's alive,' said Granny. 'Now we back off.'

The ewe turned to look at the thing that had caused her such trouble, and with a succession of throaty purring sounds, she greeted it. Then she nuzzled it comprehensively, cleaning up the yellow coating with which it had been born.

'Mission accomplished,' said Granny. 'We can go now. They'll be fine.'

'As simple as that?' Jessica was still unable to believe what had just happened. 'How do you know she'll feed him? Shouldn't we *tell* someone?'

'Sarah will find them in the morning.

She'll think it all happened on its own – so long as nobody tells her different,' she added with a fierce look.

Thea began to understand. 'You often do this, don't you?' she said.

'Now and then, when I hear one of them having difficulty. This poor girl was making quite a fuss. She's been put to a ram that was too big. She'd never have done it on her own. They'd both be dead by morning.'

'You saved them!' Jessica's tone was still lost in wonderment. 'That's so amazing. You're a real heroine.'

'It's just life,' Granny said, somewhat obscurely. 'I suppose that damned buzzer alerted you. I forgot to shut it off.' She stole a sideways glance at Thea, who took several seconds to grasp the import of the words.

'You mean you know how to stop it? But, it's so high up. How–?'

'I use a stick,' said the old woman calmly.

'And the door – isn't it always locked?'

'I unlock it. They never notice.' She chuckled. 'What they don't know won't worry them.'

Thea's emotions jostled painfully. Admiration, apprehension, confusion. And a sense of things reaching a climax, here in the chill of a dark March night.

Granny led the way back through the gate, followed by Jessica and then Thea, who was utterly lost in her bewildering thoughts.

Nobody spoke as they passed houses on both sides. Only when they got back into the High Street did Jessica whisper, 'The lamb's a boy, is it?'

'Dirty great ram lamb,' Granny confirmed. 'He'll be in somebody's freezer by October.'

Jessica gave a little yelp of distress. 'As soon as that? What a short life.'

'All the more precious then,' said Granny repressively. 'Now get back to bed, both of you, and I'll do the same.'

It took them a long time to get to sleep again. Jessica went over and over her first experience of birth, marvelling at the size of the lamb, the maternal instincts of the ewe. 'It was hurting her, wasn't it? Just like people.'

'Pretty much the same, yes,' Thea said. 'But instantly forgotten.'

'And she *loves* him. You could see.'

'Mmm.'

'And Granny – what an amazing woman!'

Thea let her prattle on, but she said little in reply. She was remembering that Granny Gardner did after all have a key to the connecting door, and that the old woman was suspected of bringing death as well as life, and thinking to herself that a person who could handle one with such calm confidence might well find little difficulty in inflicting the other.

CHAPTER SIXTEEN

'What time is it? What *day* is it?' Thea struggled to wake up. Jessica had pulled back her duvet and ousted the spaniel from her nest. She was holding a mug of tea in one hand.

'Nine fifteen on Wednesday, and a very fine morning it is too,' she said cheerfully. 'You're wasting it.'

'That *was* a dream, I suppose. About the lamb. It couldn't possibly have really happened.'

'I think it did. Either that or I had the same dream. And I haven't forgotten about going to look at the scene of that accident on the main road, either.'

'I still don't understand why you want to. They'll have cleaned it all up by now, anyway.'

'If they have, I'll tell you my idea. Otherwise it'll be obvious. I want you to have a fresh eye, without me planting thoughts in your head beforehand. Basic technique for getting a good witness statement. No leading questions.'

'Uurghh,' mumbled Thea, still only half awake.

'There's eggs and bacon downstairs, if that helps to get you moving. And I might even do some proper coffee.'

'Oh, to be young again,' mourned Thea. 'And not need sleep.'

For the second time they walked through the woods and across the fields in the direction of the A44, this time carrying on straight instead of trespassing down the private track past the Dutch barn. They had left the dog behind. 'She won't be safe on that road,' they agreed. Having consulted the map, it became clear that all they had to do was to follow the Diamond Way footpath, which crossed the A44 at a spot which Jessica thought would be perfect. They were quickly out of the trees and climbing up steep fields to where the road was shielded by a narrow band of trees. The noise of traffic grew louder as they approached.

'These are fresh tyre tracks,' Jessica observed.

'Spoken like a true detective,' teased Thea. 'So what? We know a van drove along here. The news said so.'

'Yes, but *why?* What was it doing up here?'

'It could be anything. Bringing new fencing materials. Delivering something to the farm, and taking a short cut back onto the road. I don't see why you think it's important.'

'Intuition,' said Jessica unhelpfully.

They marched on, the path quite dry beneath their feet, and were suddenly confronted by the road. 'There!' said Jessica, pointing to a pile of muddy soil some yards along the road. 'That must be where it happened.'

She had been right about the dangerous access onto the main road. The point where the van on the news report must have joined the road was not an official gateway at all, but a gap in the hedge that had evidently been recently enlarged. 'Asking for trouble,' said Thea. 'How stupid to come out there in daylight. It might be OK at night, when you could see what was coming from the headlights.'

There was a narrow grass verge on the opposite side of the road, backed by trees, where the spillage from the overturned van had obviously been swept into a relatively tidy heap. In a gap between the fast-flowing vehicles, Jessica darted across, leaving Thea to follow at her own pace. Watching her daughter running ahead, she was gripped by the age-old visceral terror of a mother in the face of traffic. Jessica was six again, heedless and vulnerable, and impossibly precious.

'That was scary,' she panted, as she reached the other side. 'Thank goodness we didn't bring Hepzie.'

Jessica did not reply, but moved to the side of the heap furthest from the road, pushing between the trees to do so. She dug at it gently with the toe of her shoe. 'Why?' she demanded. 'Why cart this totally ordinary soil away in a closed van which was not designed to carry it?'

Thea continued to feel vulnerable to the traffic, cowering as far as she could from the road. There was no pavement. She tried to concentrate on the heap of soil. 'Was it loose, do you think?'

Jessica's eyes widened, as she considered the question. 'Maybe it wasn't.' She scanned the road back to where they'd emerged from the footpath. 'Aha!' she cried, and trotted a short way along the verge to where something black was sitting. She dragged at it, revealing a black bin liner heavy enough to be containing something. Thea went to join her, stepping awkwardly in her effort to stay off the road. Before reaching the girl's side, she had found a similar bag in a dip beneath a clump of newly grown cow parsley.

'It was bagged!' Jessica announced. 'And the bags all got broken and jumbled when the accident happened.'

'Which confirms my theory that they were taking it for a garden somewhere. A lot of nice topsoil, nicked from one of those fields.'

'Have you ever heard of anybody doing that? Why would they come all out here for it? What's special about this soil?'

Thea felt she was being tested. 'I have no

idea,' she said impatiently.

'What did we pass on the way here?'

'Fields,' snapped Thea. 'That's all.'

'And a deserted village,' Jessica reminded her. 'A very interesting deserted village at that. You told me yourself it was excavated back in the seventies, and a lot of questions were raised about it.'

'So?'

'So I think somebody's been doing some more unofficial digging, trying to find out more about it, while keeping the whole thing secret. And...' she gave her mother an unsmiling stare 'and we know Julian Jolly was involved. Isn't it reasonable to think his murder might have some connection with this pile of dirt?'

Thea gave her head a clarifying shake, hoping something would click into place. It didn't. 'Spell it out for me,' she pleaded. 'Just a bit more.'

Jessica emitted a jagged sigh. 'I already did,' she said. 'You're supposed to be the historian. I thought you'd be ahead of me by now.'

'I'm sleep deprived, remember.'

Jessica feigned patience. 'What if Julian had discovered something important about the ruins of Upton village? He only had to stroll along the Diamond Way any time he wanted to and rootle about in a corner, somewhere discreet. He could have unearthed – oh, I don't know – old pots or statuettes or something. Bones, even. Maybe he found evidence of a druid temple or neolithic grave or something. And then some rival archaeologist found out about it, got jealous and murdered him. Possible, don't you think? So what we need to do next is see who was driving that van.'

Thea stared at the soil strewn along the roadside. 'Inventive,' she acknowledged. 'Do you mind telling me again what the van person was doing with all this earth.'

'That's obvious. The rival person has been trying to find the same evidence that Julian did. They needed to dispose of the earth they'd removed, otherwise it would be a giveaway that they'd been digging there.'

'Jess, darling, I don't think archaeologists work like that. What would be the point? They don't need to be so secretive. And how would the rival have found out what Julian was doing? Assuming he was doing *anything*.'

'They write reports, don't they? He'd be bound to want to tell people once he was sure he'd found something special.'

'But why would somebody kill him for it?'

Jessica scowled. 'That's where I thought you'd come up with some suggestions. You're the historian, not me.'

'Don't keep *saying* that. I know practically nothing about the medieval period and even less about the neolithic.'

'Well, never mind that now. We'll have to go back to the site of the village and have a good look round.'

Thea followed submissively, torn between admiration for her daughter's mental and physical energy, and a growing concern that the one-woman murder investigation was descending into farce. *Two*-women, she corrected herself. Like it or not, she seemed to be cast in the role of sidekick.

This time, as they marched down the track past the Dutch barn, Jessica had thrown aside her worries about private property. 'This is important,' she said. 'We need to see for ourselves.'

The remains of poor abandoned Upton were much the same as those of the Ditchfords. Barely visible furrows, ridges, grassy mounds were all that could be detected. It covered an area of some size, with a farmhouse at one corner. Thea was convinced the occupant must be watching them from a window as they trespassed on his field. Jessica took a few steps in random directions, plainly frustrated. 'There's nothing to see,' she complained. 'How do they know a village was here, anyway?'

'Trained eye,' said Thea. 'And local tradition. Old records. Place names. It was excavated in the sixties, I think, and again briefly in the seventies. We'll have to look it up.'

Then Jessica yelped. 'See there!' she pointed eastwards. 'There's been some digging, look.'

Thea looked, and had to concede that an area had been recently disturbed. 'But they'd have been perfectly visible from that house,' she objected.

'So maybe they've got permission. Or are pretending to be doing something else. Digging drainage ditches or something.'

'Then why smuggle out the spoil in a van?'

'Spoil? Don't you mean *soil?*'

'I believe it's a technical term,' said Thea with dignity. 'Now, come on. We're not getting anywhere, and I'm starting to worry about Granny. We haven't seen her yet today.'

Jessica cast another look around the field and sighed with frustration. 'We'll have to remember the exact location of this digging,' she said. 'But I don't know where we ought to go from here. I mean – look at it.' She swept an arm in a broad half-circle. 'It's all just fields. What's been going on? I *know* it has something to do with Julian. I can just feel it.'

'Come and find some websites about it,' Thea urged. 'That'll help.'

They retraced their steps, down to the sheltered concavity that contained Blockley. They could see much of the town from the footpath, pausing to admire the shapes and colours that looked as if they'd occurred naturally, rather than being constructed by mankind. Thea glanced back at where Upton had once been, trying to imagine the peaceful pre-traffic atmosphere of the place.

Eager to learn more from the Internet, Jessica's pace was brisk. At the gate from the Warren into the High Street, she paused and turned to wait for Thea. Birds were singing overhead, and sheep bleated.

'I wonder how the lamb is this morning,' Thea said, hearing the bleats. 'We might be able to see it in a minute.'

Through the generous gaps between houses, the field containing the sheep was quite easy to see. Several animals dotted the hillside, including three or four lambs. 'It all looks quite calm and contented,' Jessica observed. 'We might not recognise ours again now.'

'It was wonderful, though, wasn't it? A little miracle at midnight.'

'It was half past one,' Jessica corrected her. 'But yes, it was pretty amazing.'

'Uh-oh,' said Thea, a few moments later. 'Something's happening.'

A small group of people stood on the pavement close to Thea's car. As they approached, mother and daughter became aware of increasing noise. Granny's door buzzer, the furious barking of the spaniel and raised voices all combined to disturb the Blockley peace.

'That bloody buzzer,' said Jessica. 'It's enough to drive anybody mad. Besides, I thought you left it off during the day.'

'I do usually,' said Thea. 'But with things as they are, I just thought ... well, I switched it on before we went out. I don't really know why.'

Thea examined the tableau assembled before her. Granny Gardner was there, looking very subdued, her shoulders slumped. Thomas of the bulging midriff stood facing her like an enraged headmaster. Giles, the shambling hack, leant over her protectively and a woman Thea had never seen before was speaking loudly, wagging a forefinger to mark the import of her words.

'What's going on?' Thea asked, only to be comprehensively ignored. Jessica had gone into the main house, returning with Hepzie under one arm, the hindquarters and long tail dangling inelegantly. The buzzer had stopped.

'That's better,' said the girl. 'Now if you people will just stop shouting, we can all relax.'

The effect was magical. The whole group fell silent and gazed at her in stunned surprise.

Then Granny said, 'Hello, dear. How's your little dog today?' She reached out to fondle Hepzie's soft head. The old woman was unrecognisable from the competent sheep-midwife of the early hours. She breathed heavily and her eyes looked damp.

The spaniel struggled to escape. 'Put her down,' said Thea. 'She'll be all right.'

Jessica obeyed, and the dog began to sniff the legs of stout Thomas, before moving to the strange woman.

'What's all this about?' Thea tried again. 'Has something happened?'

'Not your business, madam,' said Thomas softly. The tone gave the words a sinister edge that was more startling than if he had shouted. She groped for a reply that would put him in his place, but could think of nothing that sounded sufficiently dignified. She looked to her daughter for rescue.

'That's rather uncalled for,' said Jessica. Belatedly Thea realised that this was Police Probationer Osborne in professional mode. Chin up, bland expression, confidence in her authority – it was magnificent.

'True though,' said Thomas unrepentantly.

'It was her sheep,' said Granny suddenly. 'In the night.'

Thea leapt in. 'But you should be *grateful* to her!' she burst out. 'She saved your animals, both of them. They'd have been dead otherwise.'

The woman bowed her head in grave agreement. 'I'm aware of that,' she said. 'Unfortunately, she failed to fasten the gate properly afterwards and the sheep have eaten several prize plants in Thomas's garden.'

Thea felt a relief of tension not unlike air escaping from an overfilled tyre. She laughed. 'Is that all?' she gasped. 'As if that matters!'

For a moment she thought Thomas was going to hit her. 'All the buds from my young horse chestnut, every leaf from the eucalyptus, the climbing hydrangea *ruined*, and countless lilies stopped in their tracks,' he enumerated, his eyes bulging more with each item.

Thea stood her ground. 'They'll grow again,' she said. 'The eucalyptus especially will come back better than ever. Believe me – I know. The same thing happened at my house, a few years ago.'

'Mum,' came Jessica's warning voice. 'I think...'

Thea looked round in time to see Granny Gardner slowly passing out in Jessica's grasp. Giles, who might have been expected to take the main burden, appeared to be far too distracted by Thomas's rage to even notice what was happening. The sheep woman squawked and tried to help, but the men were in her way.

'She's *fainted*,' the woman yelped unnecessarily.

'Get her indoors,' said Thea. 'Better go

into the main house – there's more space there.' She led the way, hoping one of the men would come to his senses and give Jessica some assistance. 'One of you should probably call an ambulance,' she added.

Nobody seemed to hear her. The whole party shuffled into the house, followed by the puzzled dog. Granny was laid carefully on the sofa and Jessica knelt beside her.

'Her colour's quite good,' she said. 'And she's got a strong pulse.'

The girl's air of authority was, if anything, even greater in the face of a genuine crisis. Thea was about to repeat her instruction about the ambulance, when she remembered what had happened on Saturday afternoon. Then, while she and Icarus Binns had been discussing the best course of action, Granny had staged a dramatic recovery. Something about the flickering eyelids gave rise to a suspicion that the same thing could well be about to happen again.

'Space!' she said. 'We must give her more space. Could you three go away, do you think? Jessica's trained for this sort of thing. We'll be perfectly all right on our own.'

Giles was the first to sidle towards the door. 'Come on,' he said to the others. 'I think these ladies have got things under control now.'

'Don't think I've forgotten about my garden,' blustered Thomas, addressing the comatose Gladys. 'I'll be back when your daughter's home again, wanting recompense.'

The sheep woman was last to leave. She hovered in the doorway, a smile flickering on her lips. 'She'll be all right, won't she?' she said, with no sign of concern.

'I think she will,' said Thea, returning the smile. 'She worked a miracle on your sheep, you know.'

'How would *you* know?'

'We were there,' said Thea simply. 'We followed her and held the torch. Actually,' she confided, 'it was me who finally pulled it out.'

From the sofa came a splutter and an indignant, 'Only because I'd done the important part.'

'Hello,' said Thea, with a wink at Jessica. 'Feeling better?'

'A bit,' whispered Granny. 'Thank you, dear.'

'I'm afraid I don't know your names,' the woman said, looking from Thea to Jessica. 'I'm Sarah Livingstone Graham. A bit of a mouthful, I know. I've got a little property between here and Batsford. The sheep field is rather an outpost. I'm afraid I neglect them a bit. I have to admit I thought they'd finished lambing. Gladys pulled a fast one on me, silly girl.'

Thea introduced herself and Jessica, and

317

all three stood gazing at Granny, who was clearly enjoying the attention.

'Works every time,' she chuckled. 'Sometimes it's wonderful to be old. Everyone's so afraid you'll die on them, that's what it is. Thomas deserved a shock, silly old buffer.'

'You'd better not try it too often,' said Jessica severely. 'Crying wolf, and all that.'

'Oh, no. I'm very discriminating. Besides, it was *you* I was thinking of. *You* left the gate open, not me.'

Thea tried to recall the sequence of events, and was forced to concede that this might be true. She pulled an embarrassed face at Sarah Livingstone Graham. 'Sorry,' she said.

Sarah laughed. 'I won't say anything. You were right, anyway, about the garden. Probably the best thing that could happen to it, in the long run.'

The two older women moved out onto the pavement, leaving Jessica to wrestle with her conflicting impressions of Granny Gardner. 'How well do you know her?' Thea asked softly.

'Gladys? Well enough to know she's an old fraud.'

'Really? You mean all this forgetfulness is an act?'

'Not quite. But she milks it shamelessly. Poor Yvette must be a saint to put up with it. What a mother to get yourself landed with, eh? Right from the word go, too.'

Thea let her confusion show. 'Sorry?' she said.

'Oh, you won't have heard. Yvette manages to keep it very quiet. She's a friend of mine, you see.'

Thea waited, scarcely caring whether or not Sarah chose to tell her anything more.

'The fact is, Yvette was born in prison. Quite a thing, eh!'

'You mean – Granny was serving a prison sentence at the time?'

'Precisely. Yvette was brought up by her father for the first eight years. Then Gladys was released and took over.'

'Eight years! My God – what did she do?'

'Manslaughter,' said Sarah. 'She was thirty, and pregnant and – well, I ought not to have told you. Don't say a word to anybody locally, will you? It's always been a deep dark secret. But, well, with things as they are, I expect it'll come out before long. I just don't want it to be through me.'

She doesn't know Jessica's a police officer, Thea realised.

'Why tell me, then?' she demanded. 'I'm a total stranger. Why splurge it now?'

Sarah Livingstone Graham gave a bitter little smile. 'Because it suddenly got too heavy for me to carry any longer. And surely you know a stranger is always the best person to tell a secret to?'

Thea suddenly felt the weight on her own shoulders, the leaden implications, the unsavoury questions. 'Well, thank you very much,' she said angrily.

Sarah took a step towards the road. 'I must go,' she said. 'It was nice to meet you, and I'm sorry. But you can walk away any time you like – which is more than can be said for the rest of us.'

Thea stumbled back into the cottage, where Jessica was impatiently watching the street from the front window. 'At last!' she said crossly.

'How is she?' Thea said softly, looking at the small figure on the sofa.

'She seems OK.'

'Mrs Gardner?' Thea began. 'Can you hear me?'

The old eyes flew open, the thin lips twitched in a half-smile. 'I'm not deaf,' she said.

'Well, I need to know you're really all right, otherwise I'll have to call a doctor,' Thea said firmly. 'Everybody thought you'd died on us, half an hour ago.'

The old woman chortled contentedly. 'Such fun,' she said. 'Aren't I a bad old thing!' In the light of Sarah's revelation, Thea wanted to agree, loudly and reproachfully. Instead, she merely nodded.

'So let's see you upright, then,' she said. 'Just to be sure.' Obligingly, Granny swung her legs off the sofa, and sat up straight. Even a much younger person might have turned giddy at the sudden change of position, but there was no sign of any such thing.

'Better get you home then,' said Thea. Without even thinking about it, they used the connecting door to the cottage, and Granny was settled comfortably in her living room.

'I'll do my tapestry for a bit, shall I?' she said. 'It's coming along nicely.'

Thea fetched it from the table, opening it out to show Jessica. From what she remembered, considerable progress had been made since Saturday. 'Goodness, you've done a lot since I saw it last,' she said. 'You must sit up with it half the night.'

The old woman made no reply to that, watching Jessica's stunned assessment of the wild colours in the picture. She smiled as she took it from Thea, and laid it out tidily on her lap.

'We'll leave you for a bit, then,' said Thea. 'And if you need anything, just...' She floundered, unsure of the best instruction to give.

'Shout,' said Granny. 'If I need you, I'll shout.'

'Right,' said Thea weakly.

Thea left Jessica searching the Internet for information on Upton, while she rustled up an early lunch. 'Take the laptop into the study,' Thea suggested. 'There's a nice empty desk to work on in there. You can make notes.'

'Are we allowed? People don't usually like strangers going into their study.'

'Just do it. I'll call you when the food's ready.'

She had said nothing about the dramatic revelation about Gladys Gardner as gaol-bird. Time enough for that, she judged, when she'd formed some conclusions for herself as to whether or not it was significant. Sixty years was a very long time. Simply because a person had brought about another person's death in their younger days it could not possibly be taken as evidence that they could do the same again in extreme old age. Could it?

Without knowing the full story, it was impossible to decide. And the only way to discover the story was to hunt through old newspapers – or ask the woman herself. At least, she supposed, the police had not made the connection. The record of Mrs Gardner's conviction and imprisonment in the 1940s had failed to show up on their computer files. It was quite probable that she had changed her name upon release, recreated herself, perhaps more than once. In sixty years, just about anything could happen.

She heard Jessica calling from the study and went to join her. 'There's a whole article here about the Upton excavations,' she reported. 'I wish I could print it out.'

'Why not use Ron's printer. He'll never know.'

'Mother!' The girl was horrified. 'That's a terrible idea.'

'Why? All you have to do is switch the cable from his machine to mine.'

'And use his paper. And – oh, what the hell.'

Thea disappeared into the kitchen, leaving Jessica to sort out her own ethics as best she might. It seemed that the use of the desk was considered permissible, since a series of mutterings emerged from the study. 'Well, well' and 'No, that's not what I wanted' and other hums and clicks from the girl and the machinery.

The meal was on the table before Jessica emerged with a page of jotted notes. She read from it as she ate.

'Upton Deserted Medieval Village was first excavated between 1959 and 1968, revealing a densely occupied site. Twelve thousand sherds of pottery were found. Then in 1973 the people at that house we saw decided to run a water pipe through it, and a team of archaeologists from Birmingham University were allowed to record what was dug up in the process. Lots of boring diagrams of trenches, dum de dum. But they did find signs of much older settlement under the medieval stuff. I lost count, but there seem to have been about thirty buildings *at least* in that one field.' She looked up, eyes sparkling. 'That's practically a *town*. Isn't it exciting!'

Thea smiled. 'History *is* exciting,' she agreed. 'I've been telling you that for years.'

'Yes, I know. But imagine it, all bustling and busy, with people having babies and building houses and getting water from a well, and going to church and keeping sheep. Spinning, weaving, making all those pots...' she paused briefly for breath. 'Suddenly it's all come alive for me.'

'Good,' Thea approved. 'But does it tell us anything about the death of Julian?'

'Not that I can see,' Jessica admitted. 'But I bet there's something, if we could just work it out.'

Thea took a breath. 'Why don't you try searching for Julian, and Granny – and Joanna Southcott? While you're at it, you might as well see if there's anything that jumps out. It's amazing what you can find on some of these obscure websites.'

'OK,' Jessica shrugged. 'But I can't see old Granny Gardner showing up in any of them.'

'You might be surprised,' said Thea, with an inward shudder.

'She was bonkers,' Jessica announced, emerging from the study nearly an hour

324

later. 'A complete nutcase.'

'Who?' Thea had managed to resist the temptation to read the screen over Jessica's shoulder, and was instead watching *Reservoir Dogs* on DVD. Somehow it seemed to capture the mood she was in.

'Joanna Southcott.'

'OK,' said Thea, with a surge of relief. 'Justify.'

'You name it. When she was living here in Blockley, she was visited by God at four every morning and given loads of prophecies which she wrote down. She was constantly hiding them in boxes and opening them again. The last box somehow acquired mystical significance. One story has it that it was opened in 1927 and contained nothing but rubbish. There's a prophecy that says the year 2004 will be one of huge crisis and the box must be opened in order to avert catastrophe. The Day of Judgement itself, according to some. It just goes on. There's plenty of websites run by her followers, who think she really was the "woman clothed with the sun" which is a line from the Book of Revelation apparently. A second Messiah, or possibly the mother of the second Messiah. Shiloh is his name. He was going to be born here in Blockley.'

Jessica was reading from a printed page. Evidently, thought Thea, there were no more scruples about using Ron's equipment. 'It's all stark raving mad,' the girl went on. 'How can anybody be clothed with the sun, anyway? It doesn't make sense.'

'Plenty to go on, though, if you're into that sort of thing,' Thea said. 'She must be due for a big revival, by the sound of it.'

'Except she was wrong about 2004. That must have been a bit of a downer for the followers. They're called the Panacea Society, by the way. Isn't that a wonderful name!'

'Splendid,' said Thea coolly. 'So – nothing about Granny or Julian?'

'Not so far. Gladys Gardner is a much more common name than you might expect. He's got a few mentions in archaeology circles.'

'Nothing to link him with Joanna South-cott?' Thea was thinking slowly, half her mind still on the film she'd been watching.

'Not that I can find.' Jessica sighed. 'It feels as if we're wasting time,' she complained. 'Where's Uncle James? What are the police doing? Everything's gone so *quiet*.'

'Don't knock it,' said Thea. 'I don't think it's going to last.'

A sense of urgency was growing, with Jessica due to depart next day. 'I can't leave without knowing who killed Julian,' she wailed.

'You might have to. Besides, you've got

plenty waiting for you back in Manchester. You'll soon forget all this.'

'Not with you here for another week. I'll be terrified someone's going to murder you next.'

'Well, don't be. You're as bad as James and Phil. I hate people worrying about me. Your father never did it.'

'You never went off to strange places on your own when he was alive. He didn't have anything to worry *about*, did he?'

They exchanged the special gentle smile they reserved for talk about Carl. Then they went back to the business in hand.

Jessica went back for a final trawl of the Internet, and Thea was left to scour her conscience about whether or not to divulge the secret about Granny Gardner's shady past. Before long, Jessica was back, with little to report. 'I can't see anything to connect Julian with *anything*,' she said. 'Not even Upton. But how could he *resist*, when it's right here on his doorstep? He must have been itching to have a proper look at what was there.'

'Not necessarily. This country is riddled with sites like that. They're everywhere you go. Burial chambers, Roman villas, abandoned villages – most of it lost without trace. Gone and forgotten, for ever.'

'I never thought of it before. It makes you scared of where you put your feet, doesn't it.

Whose bones you might be walking on.'

Thea laughed. 'Bones don't mind what you do to them. So where does this leave us, do you think? Any theories?'

Jessica hesitated. 'Well, I was looking at those photos in the study just now. Come and see. You can tell me I'm crazy if you like.' Thea followed her into the small room, where Jessica stood back, waving a finger at one of the pictures.

'Don't you think that might be Upton? There's the little farmhouse, look.'

Thea followed the pointing finger. 'Is it? Are you sure?'

'That mound, see? It's where we saw signs of digging this morning. It looks just like that, from the south, where we were.' She clicked the computer's mouse a few times, and up came a diagram of the whole site. 'That's it,' she pointed. 'Two mounds close together, then another a little way away. And that photo,' she indicated the one next to the first, 'is these furrows here. It all fits.'

Thea was unconvinced. 'You're reading too much into this,' she demurred. But then she made a closer comparison and changed her mind. 'Well, there is a trench running there and *there*,' she noted, 'just like in the photo.'

'Right!'

'But why does it matter? I mean, so what?'

'I have no idea,' said Jessica. 'But it's

beginning to amount to something that looks like a motive.'

'Is it? Whose motive? What do you mean?'

Jessica shook herself briskly. 'First we need to find out who that van belongs to. And who was driving it. And whether that digging at the site is recent, and matches the soil from the van. And whether Ron Thingummy is some kind of archaeologist.'

'Heavens! And how are you going to do all that?'

'Phone Uncle James, of course.'

Thea's feelings were mixed concerning her daughter's sudden intense involvement in the killing of Julian Jolly. There was certainly something admirable in the way she tackled her own hypothesis, but to Thea it still seemed hopelessly fragile, from a logical point of view. In the light of what she now knew, it seemed even further offbeam than before. But she also found that she was glad to have the spotlight off Granny. It gave her time to work out her own line of action.

'Guess what!' Jessica crowed, having finished the phonecall to James.

'What?'

'The van belongs to Nick Jolly. Nice Nick, grandson of the victim. And he was driving it when the accident took place. He's been kept in hospital overnight, but isn't badly hurt.'

'The other driver died,' Thea remembered. 'Was it anybody local?'

'A girl from Moreton, apparently. Twenty-five, single.' Jessica spoke unemotionally, but Thea was not deceived. Carl, their husband and father, had been killed in a road accident which had been none of his own fault.

'He must be feeling dreadful,' she said. 'What a ghastly thing to happen.'

'He might be prosecuted for dangerous driving. Serve him right if he is.'

'That won't bring the girl back, though, will it?'

Jessica shook her head dumbly.

James had also confided several more details from the investigation, which Jessica shared with her mother. 'There are four witnesses who saw Julian at the Little Village Hall on Saturday afternoon, where there's a photographic exhibition on this week.'

'Little Village Hall? Where's that?'

Jessica sighed exaggeratedly. 'Mother, you are hopeless! Haven't you seen the sign to it, on the corner opposite the deli? It's perfectly clear.'

Thea shook her head apologetically.

'Well, it's up a steep little street that runs parallel to this one, more or less. We can go for a look, if you like.'

'Not now. Stick to the point. What else did James say?'

'They've been looking into Granny's background.'

Thea froze, awaiting the blow. Then she realised that if it was the blow she anticipated, Jessica would not have left it until third in her list of findings. She looked up cautiously. 'Oh yes?'

'She worked with Julian from the early seventies, so she's known him for more than thirty years – maybe a lot more. Before that she had her own business, restoring ancient artefacts. It did very well and she sold it and moved here.'

'No husband?'

'It seems not.'

'And what about the other daughter? Frances?'

'Don't know,' Jessica shrugged. 'He didn't say.'

Thea knew she couldn't stay silent any longer. If Jessica found out later that the secret had been kept from her, she would be rightfully angry. 'Um ... Jess... That woman this morning. The owner of the sheep. She told me something when I went outside with her.'

'When you left me with Granny, with no idea what to say to her,' Jessica nodded. 'Go on.'

'Well, she said Granny had a record. She was in prison in the 1940s. For manslaughter.'

'No!' Jessica's eyes protruded with amazement. 'But – it would be on file. They would have found it.'

'Well, they haven't, have they? Or if they have, they're not saying.'

Jessica was thinking feverishly. 'They can't know. If they did, they'd have arrested her by now.'

'Really? It was sixty years ago. It doesn't prove anything.'

'We'll have to tell them.'

'Yes,' said Thea miserably.

They reran the events of Sunday morning, compulsively fitting and refitting the known facts about keys and doors and unexplained noises. 'Oh, and Uncle James said there were no fingerprints on the knife, just the blood residue. The handle had been cleaned more thoroughly than the rest of it,' Jessica remembered. 'And the blood on the mac is definitely sheep, not human.'

'It's all horribly simple, isn't it,' Thea sighed. 'Granny gets up at six, goes out through the back gardens, into next door, does the deed and comes back. Just as James said yesterday.'

'Did she say last night that she can turn off the buzzer?' Jessica asked. 'I wasn't sure I heard her properly.'

Thea nodded. 'I think that just proves she's much more cunning than she seems. It turns out she's had the key to the connecting door all along. She just pretended to lose it. After last night and this morning, I'm afraid nothing would really surprise me. She's incredibly cunning.' She cast a look of anguish at her daughter. 'But she's such a nice old thing. I really *like* her. I don't want to be the one to get her carted off to prison.'

'But if you don't, you'd be perverting the course of justice,' Jessica said sternly. 'Concealing evidence and obstructing the police. You could go to prison with her.'

'At least I might be able to look after her then,' said Thea. 'Like I'm supposed to.'

'It suddenly seems dreadfully straight-forward,' said Jessica, ignoring the moment of melodrama. 'I think we ought to call Uncle James back and tell him, right away.'

Thea panicked. 'No, not yet,' she pleaded. 'Granny isn't going anywhere. She'll be asleep, anyway, after the disturbed night. Let her have a bit more time.' She stopped, wondering at herself. What difference could another few hours make? 'Sorry,' she ended lamely. 'I just feel we needn't be in too much rush.'

'You've got too attached to her,' Jessica accused.

'Maybe I have.' Thea rubbed both hands down her cheeks. 'I can't bear to think of how it'll be. Can't we just try – I mean, there *might* be another explanation. What about this Joanna Southcott business?

Thomas – he was working on it with Julian. And Nick ... the car ... Icarus. There is *something* going on there. Can't we – that is – I think we could just have one last try. Let's leave it till tomorrow, Jess. Please. Then if they take Granny away, I can lock up the house and leave at the same time as you. I won't need to be here then.' She was begging, despising the note in her own voice. But the more she carried on, the more vital it seemed.

'All right,' said Jessica reluctantly. 'Although you realise we'll be in trouble if they ever find out what we've done. We'll need to say we didn't know, or didn't see the significance.'

'That's easy,' said Thea. 'We'll call them tomorrow. After breakfast. When she's got her strength back.'

CHAPTER SEVENTEEN

In the protracted daylight, before turning their minds to an evening meal, Thea insisted they took the dog out for another walk in The Warren. 'But I'm *tired,*' Jessica complained. 'I wanted to just chill out on the sofa for a bit. Why do we have to go for walks all the time?'

'It's nice for the dog, and it'll give us something else to think about. We'll go mad if we just sit here doing nothing till bedtime. We can pretend everything's normal, once we're outside. We can listen to the birdsong and admire the spring flowers. Some of these gardens are really something.'

'Except the ones the sheep have destroyed, thanks to us.'

Thea ignored that remark and chivvied daughter and dog along to the woods.

The Warren seemed gloomier than before, the laurels rising tall to their right, and the ground rather muddy underfoot. Hepzie disappeared ahead of them, and Jessica complained about the state of her shoes. 'Why are we going this way?' she demanded.

'For variety, mainly. There's quite a big wood down here. I was interested to see it.

When I came here this morning, I didn't manage to get very far.'

But they didn't get far this time, either. Jessica quickly baulked at going any further. 'I don't like these woods,' she said. 'They're dark and boring. And I haven't got the right boots for all this mud.'

Thea was reminded of a similar walk near Cold Aston with her sister Jocelyn. The memory was not a happy one, and she was easily persuaded to turn back. She called the dog, which was slow to respond. 'I suppose she's had enough exercise for now. Maybe we should have taken the car and gone somewhere more interesting.'

Jessica shook her head. 'I'm not in the mood for a walk, wherever it might be,' she insisted. 'There's too much else going on. This feels like avoidance behaviour to me. We ought to be talking to people, even if it's only Granny.'

'Granny's probably fast asleep,' said Thea.

'Lucky her, if she is.' Jessica determinedly began to retrace her steps, ostentatiously jumping across the worst of the mud in the rutted pathway.

'All that energy drained away, then?' Thea tried not to sound sarcastic, but the painful memory of that morning, being dragged out of bed and across the fields to stare at a pile of soil was still rankling somewhat. When it was her turn to lead an expedition, things were rather different, it seemed.

But Jessica hadn't heard her. She was already several yards ahead, and had apparently spotted something on the steeply rising bank that ran alongside, where Thea had scrambled after the dog the previous day. 'Hello!' she called. 'How did you get up there?'

There was no reply, but a figure came crashing down through the undergrowth at breakneck speed, very much out of control. It made a noise rather like 'Wheeee!'

Thea stood back, but Jessica positioned herself with outspread arms, intending to arrest the headlong descent. 'Careful!' Thea called.

It was all accomplished untidily, breathlessly, but with no injury. Laughing heartily, hair flying in all directions, Icarus Binns hung with his arms round Jessica's neck. She wrapped her own arms around him, and they stood in close conjunction for a long thirty seconds.

'Put him down,' Thea ordered crossly. 'He can stand up by himself.'

Gradually the two disentangled. Jessica's eyes were sparkling with the thrill of being so close to a world-famous star. Icarus gave Thea a boyish grin, and started brushing at himself. 'Dangerous, these woods, isn't that the truth,' he panted. 'Once started, there was no stopping the tumbling Ick. Clever girl person saved the day.'

It was the longest speech Jessica had heard him utter and the strange use of English instantly captivated her. 'Clever girl person,' she repeated with a giggle. 'That's me, all right.'

'You should be more careful,' said Thea, hating herself.

'Hey!' Jessica reached a hand to touch him again, as if helplessly magnetised. 'We saw your girlfriend on telly last night. Why weren't you with her?'

He spread his hands. 'Not my taste, that film scene thing,' he said. 'Speaking other man's words, showing your face like a piece of artwork with all your bad bits taken out. No, no, not for Ick. Nobody's words but mine pass these flawed teeth.' He grimaced at them, displaying a set of incisors that had clearly never known a dentist's braces. Over-lapping, uneven, with long sharp canines and disconcerting grey crevices, his point was comprehensively made. Mother and daughter both laughed.

'So why are you here in the woods?' Jessica continued, more in order to keep the conversation going than any real curiosity.

'Getting myself lost,' came the disarming reply. 'New friend Nick tells me – just an easy straight walk from Upton, oh, yes. Not easy, far from straight. Then when I catch a sight of the pretty dog, hope is born again.

These woods is *dangerous*, man.' His voice rose to a high note of outrage.

'Upton? The lost village?' Jessica queried. 'Is that where you've been?'

He rolled his eyes for comic effect. 'That very place.' His voice turned quiet and low. 'We is searching for the Box – though I should not be saying anything to you. Nick says it needs to be secret till it's found. But...' he sighed '...it's gone past the moment now. Nick has mega trouble, killing that tragical girl the way he did. No more box-quest for him or me. Back to the seething city in the morning light, with Cleo to soothe and silence after my failings, how she sees it.'

'Er – what box?' asked Thea, thinking she had used the word herself quite recently, but unable to pinpoint the context.

'Authentic box of prophecies, planted by the Southcott lady,' he said, as if it was obvious. 'Like holy grail, Nick says. Sell the story for big buck money, and giving me the subject for a hundred songs. Big coincidental thing, him and me bumping together at that manor house for sale. Both we two hunting down the magical treasure.'

'What's supposed to be in the box, then?' In spite of herself, Thea was intrigued. But scepticism lingered, especially over the apparently lucky encounter between Nick and Ick.

'A cure for the ills of the world,' said Ick,

clearly quoting. 'The whole reason I brings myself to Blockley Town, when I heard it was that lady's place.'

'You knew about her before?' asked Thea.

He nodded. 'Book of Revelation foretold her, so she said.' His face registered something rueful. 'My mother lady, she has a thing for old Joanna. All the books and sayings are on her tongue, all day long. She gave me this liking for the secret stuff.' He shrugged. 'Maybe we write the Southcott Code, with all the world reading us.'

'I wouldn't rely on it,' said Thea. 'The world's probably had enough of Codes for a while.'

Icarus laughed, but Jessica threw her a furious look. 'Don't mock,' she hissed.

Thea met Ick's eyes, confident that he wouldn't recognise mockery if it stamped on his foot. 'It sounds very interesting,' she said. 'Do many people in Blockley know about all this?'

He wriggled his shoulders. 'Some,' he said. 'Blockley Town and Joanna Southcott goes together in the history books.'

'I've just been reading about the Box on the Internet,' Jessica told him. 'Something about all the bishops having to witness it being opened. Is that right?'

'Visions and revelations, prophecies and warnings,' Icarus intoned. 'All in the lady's box.'

'And Nick Jolly thinks it might be buried in the ruins of Upton?' Thea paused to get the chronology straight. 'In her day, there'd have been even less visible evidence of a deserted village than there is now. At least, there'd have been less awareness of what the mounds actually were. Do the records suggest she placed the box there deliberately because she knew it was an abandoned village?'

Ick put up his hands defensively. 'Whoa! I is no student, reading dusty old records and such. Nick's the professor here, not Ick.'

'And he's been digging around, trying to find it,' Jessica summarised. 'So what about Julian?'

The question fell weightily, spreading ripples of sobriety. Icarus let his face go blank, the gold accessories somehow dulled. Thea felt her heart begin to thump. They seemed to be on the edge of something.

Jessica spoke again. 'Did he know about the box, and the idea that it might be at Upton?'

Ick nodded slowly. 'He *began* it,' he said. 'With his Thomas comrade-friend. Or so I think and believe. Nick's old grandpa, he found some wormy documentations and the idea got itself born inside him.'

'And he told Nick? Who else knows about this? How did *you* get to hear of it?'

'Young Cleo girl,' he muttered. 'Listening too much to my demented mamma, getting

341

herself excited. Speaking to film maker man, with story ideas. Get the whole business for us alone, making mega money.'

Thea wanted to scream at his verbal convolutions. 'For heaven's sake!' she exploded. 'Can't you speak more normally?'

Jessica went white with rage at this. 'Mother, how *could* you? Icarus is an *artist*. He's famous for speaking like this. He's a rap poet. This is his own unique way of communicating. What's your problem? It's easy enough to understand what he's saying. It's wonderful, in fact. He's the modern Shakespeare.'

Icarus put a calming hand on her back. 'Easy, daughter lady, easy,' he soothed. 'Not any problem. It's good you understand, but your momma don't have such a fine ear, that's all it is.' He gave Thea a forgiving smile.

And against her better judgement, Thea did find herself repeating *wormy documentations* to herself, forced to admit that it had a certain ring to it. 'Sorry,' she murmured. 'I'm just not used to it, I suppose.' Icarus's forgiving smile broadened, and he reached out to pat her shoulder.

Jessica, however, was still ruffled. 'You interrupted something really important,' she accused her mother. She gave Icarus a straight look. 'What you said just now sounded dangerously close to a motive for murder,' she said unemotionally. 'You and Nick and Cleodie in a gang, searching for the box and keeping Julian out of the picture. If he found out about it, you might well want him dead.'

Ick smiled broadly, the jumbled fangs giving him a wolfish look. Thea found herself wondering how he got away with such a deviation from the stereotype of bright white teeth in a dark-skinned face. She also found herself wishing she had some of the background information on him that Jessica had. It was like never having heard of Paul McCartney or Elvis Presley. When had she got so dull and middle-aged and out of the loop?

'Ick's no killer,' he said gently. 'And that is my solemn promise.'

Jessica manifested some internal conflict, twisting her mouth and taking in a deep breath. 'You did know I'm in the police?' she asked him. 'I can't just leave it here.'

He nodded. 'Nick man spoke about it. Pretty young police girl, his words about you were. New and full of ideals, but off duty for some days with mamma.'

'OK. So why would he be interested? I mean, what did it matter to him?'

'He likes you,' said Ick simply. 'Talks about you being so nice and friendly when he arrives to thank for finding the dead body.'

'Hmm,' said Jessica doubtfully. 'I see.'

And that seemed to be it. Together they began to walk towards the High Street, Hepzie relieved that the people were moving at last, circling them in wagging approval. By mutual consent, the conversation lapsed into idle comments about the weather, with Thea still ruffled by her failure to appreciate the celebrated star and his poetry.

Before parting at the Montgomery door, Jessica checked that Ick was still staying at The Crown and would notify her if he planned to leave within the next day. With complete dignity he bowed to her request.

'If he's a murderer, I'm the new Messiah,' Jessica muttered to Thea as they went into the house.

'I'm ruling nothing out,' Thea said.

The atmosphere continued prickly, for which Thea blamed herself. Jessica was not going to forgive her rudeness to Ick for a while, she realised. It was akin to blasphemy, and the chilly treatment was only to be expected.

But it was not the first time the two had hit rough patches. Friction between mother and daughter was surely an inescapable fact of life. The difference this time was that Jessica had somehow gained a superiority both moral and professional. She knew more than her mother did about police procedure. She also knew more about popular culture and the status of renowned performers. The previous sullen teenage despair at the general ignorance and obstructiveness of parents had matured into a genuine assertion of equality. Thea had been judged as an equal and found wanting. It was the fate, she supposed, of mothers everywhere – edged to the outer boundaries of society, decade by decade, taken less and less seriously as looks faded and memory grew less reliable. *But not at forty-two!* Thea wailed to herself. Surely I've got twenty or thirty more years in which I might expect to be taken seriously?

And with her habitual good humour and optimism, she answered her own cry. Obviously she was over-reacting. All that was happening was a minor adjustment in the balance of power between her and Jessica.

Through it all, they were both impatient to get back to the computer and check out the story of Joanna Southcott in more detail. At least, she congratulated herself, she had – albeit faintly – heard of that particular luminary, even if she was ignorant about Icarus Binns.

Jessica naturally assumed that it was for her to operate the keyboard, and when Thea began to hover behind her, she turned impatiently. 'Maybe you should go and see if Granny's OK,' she said.

Thea choked back the resentment at being ordered around by her daughter, and went to listen at the connecting door. The reassuring murmur of the television was audible from the other side. 'She's fine,' she reported, when she got back. 'I suppose I'd better go and cook something now.'

'Mum.' Jessica stopped her. 'I *really* think we should call Uncle James tonight, now we've got all this stuff about Ick as well.'

'Surely it can wait,' Thea said, trying not to let the note of pleading return. 'He won't thank us, if he's had a hard day.'

'Maybe you're right. But I know I won't sleep a wink, for thinking about it all.'

'And if you don't, I suppose that means I won't either.'

'Well, one of us should listen out for Granny – in case she tries to run away in the night.'

Thea tried to laugh. 'I wouldn't put it past her.'

'What you mean is, you'd be quite glad if she did.'

The evening was only made tolerable by a determined pact to avoid the subject of Granny and Julian completely. They played a marathon tournament of Scrabble, with Jessica increasingly outraged by her mother's use of words nobody had heard of. 'What the hell is an auklet?' she demanded. 'I'm definitely challenging that.'

'It's a baby auk, of course,' Thea defended. They had found an impressively substantial dictionary in Ron's study and were using it to settle disagreements. Thea's definition proved almost right. 'Any variety of small auk,' they discovered.

'Duh!' said Thea as if it had been obvious from the start. 'That gives me forty-seven, if my calculations are correct.' She had placed the K on a triple letter score in two directions, turning the word *thin* into *think*.

'You're much too good at this,' grumbled Jessica.

'I've had a lot of practice. I was hooked on internet Scrabble this time last year. It ruins a person for the real thing. I ought to give you some sort of advantage, I suppose. Like making sure you always get the Z and the Q.'

'That wouldn't help,' said Jessica glumly. 'I don't have the right sort of mind.'

'You're doing very well,' patronised Thea. 'And it's a great distraction.'

It had been, until she said that. They were abruptly plunged back into anguished hypothesising about how Granny Gardner would react to being arrested and possibly charged with the unlawful killing of Julian Jolly and their pact evaporated.

'I suppose they'll do that awful trick of bashing on the door at six in the morning,' said Thea.

'They won't. Of course they won't. They know she isn't going anywhere. I've told you already, they'll be extremely sensitive.'

'She still won't understand what's happening. If she genuinely can't remember anything about it, she'll be terrified. Can you imagine it?' Thea shuddered.

Jessica sighed. 'I thought we weren't going to talk about it.'

'I can't help it. It's just so *awful*.'

'I think it might be less awful than you think. She's a tough old thing, and don't forget we're not sure how much of her forgetfulness is just an act. She could be playing games with us all. Being old in itself isn't any reason to give a person special treatment.'

Thea considered this clumsy statement with as much objectivity as she could muster. A jumble of conflicting impressions of the old woman collided in her head, crystallised by the strange walk they'd undertaken on Saturday afternoon. One moment Granny had been surging ahead, firmly grasping Hepzie's lead and very much in control of herself. The next she was a helpless heap of old bones on the pavement. And then she'd got up again and walked home only slightly the worse for the experience. It had gone on like that ever since. Bewildered and frail one moment, deftly delivering a stuck lamb the next. She was like two people in one body. Maybe more than two. And at least one of those personae was capable of driving a knife into an old man's back. An old man she knew well and could manipulate just as she manipulated everybody around her. Thea recalled the contradictory instructions left by Ron and Yvette. What they had actually been saying was along the same lines – if Granny A manifests, you have to do *this*. But if she wakes up as Granny B – then *this* would be better.

Thea struggled to assure herself that whatever happened would be for the best. If nothing else, the murder of Julian Jolly had provided a powerful distraction from Jessica's trouble in Manchester, but for all that it was only a distraction. Jessica would have to go back the next day, face a reprimand, learn how to avoid such calamities in future and make herself vulnerable once more to whatever the criminal urban classes might elect to throw at her. James's undoubted generosity in allowing the girl access to the Blockley investigations ought to earn Thea's gratitude, she knew. But it had also deprived her of the lazy little holiday she had envisaged. She had been drawn in to the horrid little murder, against her will, and now found herself forced to face the imminent arrest of an old lady she had come to admire and respect.

The idea that somehow Icarus Binns and Nick Jolly had been involved in murder was tempting, if only because it exonerated

Granny. But in her heart, Thea couldn't believe it. The complications of the locked doors, the closed access through the gardens, the timing, all worked against it being a viable explanation.

Before turning out the light and trying to sleep, Jessica said, 'Granny mentioned Julian and Thomas writing about the box – do you remember?'

'When the police asked her what she knew about Julian,' Thea confirmed. 'Yes. It didn't make much sense at the time.'

'It means she knew about it. It links everything up, in a way.'

'You mean they *all* killed him? One held him, another kept lookout, and a third stabbed him. You think one of those was Granny?'

Jessica pushed her face into the pillow and moaned.

Thea switched off the light.

They woke with the dawn light, with most of the same emotions of the night before still active. *Jessica's last day*, Thea remembered, with a stab of unease. Outside it was raining.

'I'll phone Uncle James at nine,' said Jessica. The portentousness swelled around them, as if they'd named a moment for an execution.

Somehow nine o'clock arrived without Thea rushing into the cottage to warn

Granny and help her to hide inside a hollow tree in The Warren. She sat listening, gesturing occasionally and screwing up her face. From Jessica's end of the lengthy conversation, it seemed that it was not running to the expected script. Almost, Thea thought, there could be room for optimism.

'Well? What did he say?' Thea demanded, a quarter-second after the call was finished.

'He knew about her record already.'

'And?'

'It isn't evidence. It can't be revealed in court. It means nothing to this investigation.'

'Oh. That's good, isn't it?'

'Is it?'

'Well, it means they're not charging round here with battering rams to arrest the poor old thing.'

'After what he just told me, I think they probably should.'

Thea leant back gingerly in the chair. 'Go on, then – tell me,' she invited.

'Gladys Fielding, as she was then, had a baby boy. He was two when he contracted meningitis. He died in hospital. She killed the doctor who tried to save him.'

'My God! How?'

'Stabbed him with a pair of sharp scissors. In the back.'

'And they called it manslaughter?'

'She was out of her mind with grief for the child. The doctor was insensitive. A nurse testified to say she thought anybody might have done it, under the circumstances.'

'And she was pregnant.'

'Pardon?'

'I might have forgotten to tell you that bit. She was expecting Yvette, and had her while she was in prison. Yvette's father brought her up for the first eight years.'

'Blimey!' said Jessica.

They sat quietly contemplating the tragic story for a few minutes. Then Thea said, 'So they don't see it as an indication that she stabbed Julian in the back with a kitchen knife?'

'They do. Of course they do. But it isn't evidence. And they're still hoping it turns out to have been somebody else.'

'What about Nick, then?'

'Nick?'

'Yes – Nick. The grandson who's suddenly best buddies with Icarus, owner of the van carrying soil from diggings in a restricted site, while searching for a mythical object.'

'Ah. That Nick. Yes. Uncle James actually thinks he could possibly be the perp.'

'Perp? Do English police officers say *perp*?'

Jessica giggled. 'Not very often. It's rather good, though, don't you think? Better than *killer* or *murderer*.'

'No it isn't. It's a nasty American euphemism, like *passed on* and a thousand other silly phrases.'

'Mum, please, not now. I can feel us about to start on political correctness and I don't think I can face it. Did you hear what I said about Nick?'

'James thinks he could be the person who killed Julian – his own grandfather.'

'Right. But it's no more than a hunch, because of the road accident and his suspicious behaviour. There's no evidence against him, either.'

'So how is he?'

'Recovering. They think he can be discharged tomorrow or Saturday.'

Thea could think of nothing to say. Suddenly the whole process felt as if it had nothing to do with her at all. She merely had to keep an eye on Granny, the wonderful nonagenarian who delivered lambs in the middle of the night and aroused complicated feelings amongst the people of Blockley, and savagely killed insensitive doctors. Had the sympathetic nurses applauded her, she wondered? Had she done them all a favour by removing a tyrant from their midst?

Perhaps it was because the old woman was so independent and stoical that Thea felt such a desire to protect her. The life spark or spirit or whatever you called it was simultaneously strong and fragile, arousing admiration and concern in equal measure. Granny Gardner was like silk, Thea concluded, in her flurry of poetic musings.

Slender filaments spun together to form a cord as tough as steel – that was Gladys Gardner, formerly Fielding.

'You're not saying much,' Jessica noted crossly. 'Tell me what you're thinking.'

'I'm thinking about Blockley, I suppose, and how much more there is to it than appears at first glance. Not just the history going back to the Dark Ages and beyond, but the silk mills and Joanna Southcott and the sheep – and there's bound to be more. I bet if we went to the church we'd find a whole new load of stories. I'm feeling a bit overwhelmed by it all, I suppose – but in a nice way. There's no possibility of being bored – you only have to walk fifty yards in any direction and there's some amazing new thing to find out.'

'Yeah.' Jessica was doubtful, but Thea suspected she was getting some of the same feeling in spite of herself – thanks to Google as much as Blockley itself, admittedly. 'I'm with you on the Southcott woman. That really is something you could get your teeth into.'

'Pity you're going back this afternoon.'

'Yeah,' said Jessica again, with a shudder. 'Don't remind me.'

'It's going to be fine. Didn't James manage to persuade you it would?'

'Sort of. But it still feels like being summoned to the Year Head at school. You remember Mr Mattingley.' She shuddered

354

again. 'Terrifying man.'

'Last of his kind,' Thea recalled. 'Not afraid to enforce discipline. I thought you'd approve of that now.'

'I do, in a way. But he still makes me tremble, just thinking about him.' She was visibly struck by a thought. 'And you wouldn't believe the number of times I fantasised about killing him. I *yearned* to stick a compass between his ribs, or push him out of the art room window. And there's Granny, who really did it. Maybe twice. Makes you think, doesn't it.'

They lapsed into silence. An unsettling mixture of urgency and paralysis seemed to have gripped them. The weather became less and less inviting, but to remain indoors with nothing to do but bicker between themselves until lunchtime did not feel like a valid option.

'We still haven't been to look at the church,' Jessica said without enthusiasm.

'Perhaps we should. It might have some link with Joanna Southcott.'

'Will it be open, do you think?'

'We could go and see. It's practically next door, after all. And maybe we'll meet some-body who'll invite us back to theirs and tell us some good stories.'

'Nobody's going to be out in this weather,' said Jessica. 'But we might as well give it a try.'

Shrugging into waterproof jackets and shoes, they left the dog behind and headed along the street. Before reaching the church, Jessica drew her mother's attention to the small brown sign indicating 'The Little Village Hall'.

'Pooh!' scorned Thea. 'That's tiny. No wonder I didn't notice it.'

'Tell you what,' Jessica said. 'Let's see if that art exhibition's still on. The one Julian went to on Saturday.'

The Little Village Hall, as it was officially designated, was very close by. 'It's photographs, not art,' Jessica corrected, tapping the publicity poster on the door.

A woman sitting just inside gave them a fierce look as they entered. 'And what makes you think photography isn't art?' she demanded angrily.

Jessica's jaw dropped, and Thea felt the disproportionate sense of alarm and outrage that comes from unexpected aggression in a stranger.

'Well,' stammered Jessica, 'I suppose it can be sometimes. I didn't mean to...' she trailed away, wondering why she felt the need to defend herself.

'Just you look at the pictures before you pass judgement,' the woman told her. 'That's all we ask.'

'Do we have to pay to come in?' Thea wondered.

'No, but we'd like you to sign the book.'
The tone had softened. Perhaps it had been
a long boring week for the woman, sitting
waiting for visitors who never materialised.
Thea and Jessica had the whole place to
themselves on this drizzly Thursday morning. It seemed unwise, however, to attack
them when they did show up. They signed
the book and started towards the right-hand
wall and the first of the display.

'No, you're meant to start on the left,' said
the woman tiredly. 'It goes in a clockwise
direction.'

Thea could sense her daughter's growing
impatience with the ill-tempered custodian,
but they both changed course as instructed.
They had not reached the first picture when
the woman said, 'You're the people who
found Julian, aren't you? On Sunday? I've
seen you in the village once or twice.'

Jessica turned to answer her. 'Yes, that's
right. I understand he was here on Saturday.'

'He was. Not surprisingly, considering
there are several of his photographs on display. We missed him when he didn't come in
on Sunday as well. He liked to explain his
work to people.'

A thought struck Thea. 'Are there some of
Ron Montgomery's as well?'

'A few. The sepia group over there, and
another pair on that wall.' She pointed to

the wall on the right.

The space was unimaginatively arranged, with two of the walls covered quite densely with pictures, and a row of freestanding boards at the far end, made necessary by a small stage. Two short rows of similar boards were positioned in the middle of the hall, facing each other with a fairly narrow walkway between them.

'What a lot!' Jessica said. 'Are these all by local people?'

'Definitely. We have a very active Photographic Society, and with the new technology – well, some people have become very prolific.'

Thea had begun her inspection. The level of experimentation surprised her, with montages and superimposings regularly to be found. The church tower had a large tree growing out of it in one, and the children's playground was thickly strewn with imported sheep and cows in another. 'Clever!' she breathed, hoping to appease the woman on the door. Privately, she found them merely silly.

Jessica had skated past the early displays, apparently attracted by something at the further end of the left hand wall. A suppressed yelp alerted Thea, who hurried to join her, glad to find that they were hidden from view by one of the display boards in the middle of the room.

'What?' she said.

'Look!'

The picture was A3 size and very eye-catching. In the centre was a carved wooden chest, painted with gold and scarlet markings. At each corner was a view in sepia, of open countryside, showing the familiar patterns of furrows and ridges that could be found at Upton and the Ditchfords. Beneath the chest was a copied image of the face of Joanna Southcott, which had appeared on more than one of the websites Jessica had located.

'That clinches it,' said Thea. 'Just as Icarus said.'

'So it can't be very secret,' muttered Jessica. She pointed to the caption beside the picture. 'The Blockley Box' she read. 'By Julian Jolly'.

'Not particularly good as art,' said Thea critically. 'Quite poor composition, and the mixture of colour and sepia doesn't work at all for me.' She spoke audibly, unable to resist winding up the woman by the door.

Jessica snorted her amusement. 'I think it has a certain boldness,' she argued. 'It caught my eye from quite a distance.'

'Well, perhaps. It does seem to be trying to *say* something.'

This was certainly true. Thea stared at the picture, legacy of a murdered man, and tried to understand its message. Had the police not discovered it already? Would they regard it with a new interest now that Jessica had recounted the meeting with Icarus and the whole business about the Southcott Box and Upton's ruins?

They forced themselves to give due attention to the other work on display. One group of simple images of leaves and grasses appealed to Thea. The name beside them was familiar, but for a moment she couldn't place it. 'Sarah Livingstone Graham.' Of course – the sheep woman! The delicacy of the photographs seemed at odds with the rather hearty person she'd spoken to the day before. If asked to predict, she would have said there'd be photos of animals, perhaps in attitudes of distress, and farmyards with old tractors and pools of stagnant mud. She gave herself time to absorb the subtle shots of single instances of transient life, taken at very close quarters, the scars and holes made by insects or harsh weather suggesting a real fragility.

'I could live with these,' she murmured. 'They're wonderful.'

Jessica drifted closer and cast an unimpressed look at the pictures. 'Can't say they do much for me,' she said. 'But I have found some I like.'

They spent half an hour in the hall, during which time no other visitors appeared. As they left, Thea faced the woman. 'We were wrong,' she said with a smile. 'They definitely are art, after all. Or some of them, anyway.'

'I'm glad to hear it,' said the woman, barely managing a returning smile. 'But you're wrong about the Blockley Box. It's a masterpiece. You probably don't appreciate the context, but I can assure you it's going to become a very special part of Blockley's heritage, now that Julian...'

With shocking suddenness, the woman burst into noisy uninhibited sobs, which echoed round the hall. Thea had the impression that the tears had been gathering force and pressure ever since the woman had heard about Julian's death. It was like the bursting of a dam, and she half expected to see a small river of salty fluid flowing across the table on which the weeping head was buried. The shoulders heaved and the noise did not abate. Thea and Jessica exchanged appalled glances, knowing they could not leave the woman like this.

'Er... Is there anybody...? I mean, you shouldn't stay here...' Thea's voice was almost drowned by the sobbing.

And then rescue arrived, as Thea remembered it had done at least once before. The tall figure of Giles Stevenson materialised, looking rather damp about the shoulders. 'Hey, hey,' he sang in a voice of infinite gentleness. 'Carola, my dear. We can't have this, can we? I could hear you from ten yards away.' He glanced at Thea and Jessica. 'Have you gone and upset her?' he accused them.

'I suppose we have,' said Thea. 'Without meaning to.'

The sobs subsided into choking breaths, and she raised her blotchy face to his, where he leant protectively over her. 'Oh, Giles,' she gasped. 'It just hit me, without warning. I was *fine* until now. Oh dear.'

'I know,' he said. 'It goes like that. I *did* wonder...'

'It's not Julian I'm crying for, you see,' she spluttered, her chest still heaving spasmodically. 'I didn't like him any more than the rest of you. No, I was crying for poor Gladys. Poor old Gladys Gardner.'

CHAPTER EIGHTEEN

'Maybe she didn't mean what it sounded like,' said Thea. 'We probably heard it all wrong. She was just upset because Granny was so fond of Julian and will be lost without him.'

'Except she also said that *nobody* liked the man.'

Thea made a sceptical rumble. 'Well, we know *that* isn't true. Granny kept on about him all day on Saturday. You didn't hear her – she made him sound like her best friend in the whole world. And Thomas loved him, remember.'

'But we haven't heard anybody actually say he was a nice person. Nick called him a curmudgeon.'

Thea could only agree. The composite picture building up was of a man who had managed to make himself comprehensively unpopular on all sides.

'Time's running out,' Jessica remarked, checking her watch. 'It's ten forty-five.'

'This is ridiculous!' Thea exploded. 'Don't the police have any firm pieces of evidence, for heaven's sake? What have they been *doing* all week? What am I meant to do once you've gone?'

Jessica grimaced. 'They're doing what they always do, as you know perfectly well. But they've had to withdraw a lot of officers because of the Birmingham bomb factory. The media are screaming for a result on that. The general public are far more concerned with a nice exciting terrorist threat than the death of a solitary old man. And the police do have to obey the public, when all's said and done.'

'Do they? Even when the public are being their usual stupid selves? If they had any sense at all they'd be more alarmed by a murder in a quiet High Street than some gang of lunatics mixing up their Semtex in a homemade bunsen burner, or whatever it was. The chances are they'd only blow themselves up, anyway.'

'You're wrong,' Jessica told her calmly. 'In just about every detail. Ask Phil – he'll tell you.'

The reference to Phil came at the same instant as Thea was already wishing he was with them. She had increasingly found herself craving his touch and his smiling eyes looking down at her, as the day had progressed. Several times she had mentally spoken to him, wanting his reactions and reassurances. When Jessica uttered his name, the impact on Thea was great enough to half convince her that he was at that moment sitting outside the house in his car, waiting for them to return, Hepzie jumping at the window, having seen him.

But he wasn't. As they turned into the High Street again, there were no other vehicles than their two small cars on the pavement outside the Montgomery house and its cottage. The anticipated image faded and Thea felt acute disappointment.

'I'm going to phone him,' she decided to herself. 'And tell him I'm feeling neglected.'

Half an hour later, washing up their coffee mugs, Thea wondered aloud about the fate of Nick Jolly. 'They'll have to prosecute him for dangerous driving, won't they? How does that affect his being a murder suspect? Can they manage both at the same time? Or what?'

Jessica considered this technical issue, looking worried. 'I ought to know this,' she said. 'I think the more serious charge takes precedence. It must do, I'm sure. Then the lesser ones are asked to be taken into consideration. But it's useful to have something to hold him on, for the time being.'

'Except he's in hospital. How does that work?'

'There'll be an officer guarding him. One of the most tedious of all the jobs, according to Mike. They can't formally interview him until a doctor judges him fit.'

'It would be very convenient if he did turn

out to be the killer. Neat.'

Jessica gave her mother a warning look. 'Convenience doesn't come into it,' she said sternly. 'You know it doesn't.'

Thea sighed. 'But think how terribly *in*convenient it would be if they found firm evidence pointing to Granny.' Ever since the call to James, her hopes had been rising that Granny would walk free, to live out her limited days in peace. But every few minutes, the fragility of these hopes made itself felt. The police would find a way to convict her, and she, Thea, did not want to be part of whatever might happen then.

Jessica seemed to read her thoughts. 'I didn't tell you everything he said,' she confessed. 'They can't just let it all slide. Uncle James is arranging for a team to search her cottage sometime today. There has to be a special geriatric worker present, and there's a protocol. They'll do their best not to upset her.'

Thea felt a chilly current flowing through her, a dread combined with a sense of injustice. 'I ought to warn her,' she agonised. 'But I know it wouldn't do any good.'

'They really don't want to have to do it. It'll make them feel terrible.'

'It sounds as if it's all sewn up. They've actually decided she killed Julian. So what about the Southcott Box business, and Upton and Nick and all that? What about those pictures in that exhibition?'

'They investigate everything,' Jessica said tiredly. 'And all we have to do is to let them get on with it.'

'I'm going to talk to her, one last time,' Thea announced, at eleven-thirty, as they were sitting nervously awaiting developments. 'I won't say anything about the police. I just want to be with her for a bit. After all, I am being paid to watch over her. You could say I've failed in my mission – letting her commit a murder. It must have happened while I was here.'

'Mmm,' said Jessica non-committally.

Seeing no further point in abiding by the rule about the connecting door, Thea gently opened it and let herself into the small hallway on the other side. 'Hello?' she called. 'Mrs Gardner?'

'Who is it?' came a querulous voice from the upper floor. 'Is that you, Yvette?'

'No, it's Thea Osborne. Can I come up?'

'I'm poorly today,' the voice floated down. It sounded thin, with a wobble in the word *poorly*.

Thea hurried to the bedroom, where she was buffeted by a powerful smell on the threshold of the room. Something strong and sour and disgusting.

'I was sick,' said the little voice. 'All over myself.'

She spoke accurately. Vomit spread copiously across the bedclothes, as well as down the front of Granny's brushed cotton nightie. It looked as if she must have eaten at least a five-course meal.

'Oh, Lord, so you were,' said Thea. 'When did this happen?'

'Don't know. I was a greedy girl. I had too much.'

Thea couldn't avoid a sudden suspicion that there was something deliberate going on. 'What would you have done if I hadn't turned up?' she demanded.

'Don't know.' The same whining little girl voice as before rendered Thea helpless. There was obviously nothing to be done but a wholesale cleaning-up operation, which was not going to be any fun at all. Through gritted teeth, she pulled all the bedclothes free and bundled them up. There were two blankets and a sheet, all badly affected. She carried them into the bathroom and hurled everything into the bath. That, she realised, would make it impossible to give the old woman the thorough clean she needed. She went back, thinking about the task ahead.

'We'll have to get you washed,' she said. 'Take that nightie off.'

Granny Gardner was marooned on the naked bed, huddled into herself with her knees drawn up. She whimpered and made no move to obey Thea's order.

'Come on. You can't stay like that.'

'I can do it for myself,' came a much stronger voice. 'I'm not an invalid.'

'Thank goodness for that,' snapped Thea. 'Off you go, then. Take some clothes with you, and get changed in the bathroom. You'll have to wash your hair as well.'

Slowly, stiffly, Granny rolled off the bed and took a collection of clothes from a chair. 'Clean pants,' she muttered and went across the room to a chest of drawers. Thea watched her, thinking about old age and dignity and the basic procedures necessary for survival. How did anyone cope with the moment when it became inescapable that some of those procedures were no longer within one's capabilities? When you couldn't get your own socks on, or climb in and out of a bath, or get the tops off jars of jam? Wouldn't the terror of the next phase drive some individuals into the haven of senility? Was it not acknowledged that senility was generally quite pleasant for the person afflicted with it? Was this the point at which Gladys Gardner had arrived?

'Do you feel poorly?' she asked. 'How's your tummy?'

'Empty. Sore. And my throat hurts. I couldn't get to the lavatory in time,' she added plaintively. 'It was so sudden.'

For a moment Thea thought this was an admission of incontinence, until she understood that Granny meant she'd wanted to throw up into the loo. 'It happens like that sometimes,' she said, with sympathy. 'Especially if you've been asleep.'

'Thank you, dear,' came the stately reply. 'You're being very understanding.'

Twenty minutes later, Thea had helped the old woman downstairs and made her some dry toast and weak tea. 'I must just pop next door and tell my daughter what's happening,' she excused herself.

'Daughter? I had a daughter,' came the fuddled reply. 'Two of them, in a manner of speaking. Do you know Frances? She's gone away, you know. She won't know what's happened to her father.'

Father? Before she could elicit anything more, Granny had slipped away into the bathroom, and closed the door firmly behind her.

Which left Thea ample time to think. Had she heard correctly? Had Granny just revealed that Julian Jolly was the father of Frances, her second daughter? And if so, what difference might that make?

Could Frances have taken the opportunity presented by her sister's absence to pay a clandestine visit to Blockley and attack the old man while the coast was clear? Might her aged mother have assisted her in some way? Thea felt an urgent desire to go and tell

Jessica what she had just heard, and perhaps make another call to James at the same time. Instead, she knew she had to stay with Mrs Gardner and see that she was all right. But there was no reason why she shouldn't try a few questions at the same time.

'When did you last see Frances?' she asked, when a refreshed and fragrant Granny was finally installed on the sofa downstairs.

'Yvette refuses to have her here. I never see her any more.'

Encouraged, Thea continued. 'She was a late baby, is that right?'

It was much easier than she could ever have imagined. Granny Gardner met her eye and smiled sadly. 'I thought I was too old for child-bearing. I thought I didn't need to worry about it any more.'

'Did Yvette help you bring her up?'

'Oh, no.' The old woman frowned at the plate in front of her. 'Oh, no. Yvette was long gone by then. Twenty-five, at least, she must have been.'

'So you brought her up? You must miss her now.'

'Who? I don't miss Yvette. She doesn't have any feeling for me, you know. Pushing me out of my own home into this cottage, where the servants used to be.'

It was slipping away, and Thea made no attempt to get it back. The police were coming – very probably to arrest Gladys Gardner for the killing of Julian Jolly and nothing was going to stop them.

Or so she believed. Gradually, as if in slow motion, Granny began to slump sideways, one hand raised to her head. 'Oh-h-h-h,' she moaned. 'It hurts.'

At first Thea simply thought it was a head-ache, probably exaggerated by the drama queen she was learning to mistrust so completely. 'What's the matter?' she asked.

There was no reply. Granny's left leg began to jitter weirdly of its own accord, and her left hand opened and closed convulsively.

Not waiting to witness any further display of symptoms, Thea rushed through to the main house, calling for Jessica. 'Phone for an ambulance!' she shouted. 'Granny's having a stroke.'

Jessica was on the sofa with the dog, a book in one hand. She looked up sharply, but didn't move. 'A stroke? Are you sure? She's not play-acting again?'

'No, I'm not sure of anything – but that's what it looks like. Her head hurts and her left side is acting strangely. Christ, Jess, this is an emergency.'

'You've been in there for ages. Why the sudden panic?'

Thea forced herself to calm down. 'It's only just happened. She was sick earlier on, and she's been cleaning herself up.' She felt sick herself, all of a sudden. 'That might have been part of it,' she realised. 'We need an ambulance right away.'

Jessica screwed up her face, trying to judge the urgency. 'All right. You do it. Just dial 999 and give them this address. If you're sure, that is. You do understand the implications, don't you?' She scrutinised her mother closely. 'It's not some clever trick to evade arrest?'

Thea took a deep breath. 'Absolutely not. I'm scared to go back in there, in case she's gone and died. I shouldn't leave her alone. I want you to phone, and I'll go back and stay with her.'

When she went back to the cottage, Granny was sitting exactly as Thea had left her. Before she could say or do anything there was a knock on the door, which was briefly confusing. She thought at first it was the connecting door she should open. When the knock came again, she remembered with a hollow thud that it was the police, come as promised to search the cottage, and perhaps arrest the old woman. Fumbling with the lock, she was burdened by a sense of treachery. Could she deflect them, she wondered. Would they go away if she told them Granny had had a stroke?

But when she finally got the door open, there was no group of authority figures confronting her. Instead there was a familiar woman in a headscarf. 'Gussie!' she cried, almost throwing her arms around the woman.

'Hello,' said Gussie calmly. 'What's the matter?'

'Granny's poorly. I think it might even be a stroke. She was sick earlier on, and now she's … well, come and see for yourself.'

Turning back into the house, followed by the newcomer, Thea met Jessica clutching her mobile phone. 'Have you called an ambulance?' Thea demanded.

Jessica shook her head. 'I thought I ought to see her for myself first. They'll want to know the symptoms.'

'What's all this then, Gladys?' they heard Gussie loudly asking Granny in the living room. 'Trying one of your old tricks on these good ladies, I shouldn't wonder.'

The room felt uncomfortably crowded with all four of them in it. Thea wanted to explain the imminent arrival of the police to Gussie, but couldn't bring herself to do it in front of Granny, who although appearing decidedly droopy, could probably hear quite well.

'Come into the kitchen for a minute,' she urged. 'I've got something to tell you.'

'What about the ambulance?' Jessica asked. 'Is she bad enough for that?'

Granny Gardner's head jerked at these words, and her lopsided mouth made urgent gargling sounds. Thea's suspicions that she could hear and understand what was being said were confirmed, at the same time as her diagnosis of a stroke seemed more and more probable.

Gussie seemed to grow taller and more authoritative. 'Hold your horses,' she ordered. 'No need to do anything rash. I suggest we calm down and have a little chat together. Gladys should hear it all. I don't believe in secrets.'

The realisation that Mrs Gardner could not make coherent statements was slow to hit Thea. When it did, she felt a powerful sense of frustration and disappointment. She had wanted to hear the whole story directly from the old woman. If she had killed Julian, Thea wanted to know why, and precisely how it had been achieved.

'But she needs a doctor,' insisted Jessica. 'We can't just sit around chatting when she's like this.'

'We'll get a doctor in a little while,' Gussie soothed her. 'Someone who'll come to the house and keep the disturbance to a minimum. Not an ambulance and those great clumping medics in their dreadful yellow jackets.'

'I think it's more important to postpone the arrival of the police,' said Thea. 'Can you call James and tell him what's happened? He might be able to head them off.'

Gussie had settled herself on a chair

pushed up close to Granny's, and the old woman was clutching her hand tightly. 'Don't worry, my old love,' she crooned. 'We'll have you straight in no time. I seem to remember this has happened before a time or two, hasn't it?'

Granny nodded, and to Thea's unmedical eye, it seemed as if there was slightly more control in the movement. 'Has it?' she asked. 'And she recovered completely afterwards?'

'That's right. They call it a TIA – transient ischaemic accident. Doesn't that sound marvellous? It's like a mini-stroke, and Gladys knows it's a sign that there will be a big one sooner or later. It's like the rumblings of a volcano before the eventual eruption. We've talked about it, haven't we lovey? There's one of those living will things tucked in her desk, saying she doesn't want to be rushed to hospital and resurrected when the time comes.'

Thea began to realise that Gussie was a closer friend to Granny than had first appeared.

Jessica still hovered with her phone. 'I'll try to get hold of Uncle James then,' she said. 'If it isn't too late. I'd have thought they'd be here by now.'

'Are you talking about the police?' Gussie asked her.

Thea and Jessica both nodded. Gussie laughed. 'You'll be lucky. Haven't you heard the news?'

Blank looks answered the question. 'There's been a bomb in the middle of Birmingham, at nine-thirty this morning. Every available cop from six counties is going to be fully tied up for days to come. Arresting one old lady, even for an unlawful killing, isn't going to feature on their to-do list for quite some time. No sense in trying to phone anybody, either,' she added to Jessica. 'You'd never get through.'

'Good God!' Thea conducted the automatic mental trawl through all those she most loved, checking whether any of them could have been in central Birmingham in the morning rush hour. The person at the top of the list was the most likely to be a victim. 'Phil!' she gasped. 'Phil could have been there.'

Jessica gave her a look. 'Why would he? He doesn't live or work in Birmingham. Don't be paranoid, Mum.'

'Yes, but...'

Gussie looked from one to the other. 'If he's OK, he'll call you,' she said. 'Meanwhile, we've got work to do.' She looked at her hand, gripped like a lifeline by old Granny Gardner, and flourished the other one towards the oak bureau. 'Look in there for instructions. If we go against her wishes, she's sure to come back to haunt us.'

Cautiously, Thea peered into the row of cubbyholes, pulling out bank books, chequebook stubs, insurance documents. 'I can't see anything,' she reported.

'Keep looking,' Gussie ordered.

In the final section, there was the leather-bound notebook she had seen before. 'There's this,' she said, producing it for Gussie to see.

'That won't be it,' said Gussie.

But Thea opened it anyway. The first page had a list of names and dates. 'Birthdays, I think,' she said.

The second page was blank, and on the third, in large print, were the words, *Letter for Frances*.

Thea took it to the sofa, showing it to Gussie and the recumbent Gladys. 'What does this mean?' she asked. Both looked at her blankly.

'Whatever it is, it isn't important now,' said Gussie. 'Keep looking for her will, there's a good woman.'

Thea placed the notebook on the table, and returned to her quest.

Behind her, Granny spoke thickly. 'Can I please have a drink?' she said.

Then her head seemed to slump sideways, causing even the stalwart Gussie to panic.

'Can you go to the bathroom and find her pills?' she said tightly. 'There's something she's supposed to take when this happens.'

Jessica followed the order with a look that said *Don't blame me if she goes and dies on us,* returning with an orange plastic canister of tablets. 'These?' she said.

'I don't expect there was much of a choice,' said Gussie. 'Gladys hasn't been one for medication in recent years.'

Jessica nodded and Granny was given two of the pills with a glass of water, her mouth working spasmodically as she swallowed them.

Gussie organised everything for the next half hour with the efficiency of a practised nurse. Granny was propped semi-upright on several soft cushions. Thea, having failed in her search for the living will, but willing to believe Gussie's insistence that the last thing they wanted was an ambulance, turned on the television, with the sound low, watching the scenes of spectacular destruction in England's second city. The death toll was, however, smaller than first feared. Twelve people killed and fifty injured. Jessica's insistence that Phil Hollis was unlikely to be amongst them finally persuaded her. The news quickly turned to speculation and punditry, infuriatingly repetitive and insubstantial. After ten minutes, she turned it off again.

'OK,' said Gussie. 'This is what we're going to do. Gladys is no worse, is she? You can see that for yourselves. Right?'

Her assistants both nodded cautiously.

'I happen to know that there's a doctor due at a gathering here in the High Street, which has probably started by now.' She glanced at her watch. 'It's sure to involve lunch. It's some women's group meeting – I've no idea what it's about, but they were talking about it in the Post Office on Tuesday. A woman called Suzy Collins was mentioned, and she's qualified as a GP. She's not working at the moment, because she's got two young children and has opted to stay at home with them.'

Thea made a winding-up motion with her hand, suggesting that Gussie get to the point.

'So, I suggest one of us nips along to the house and asks her to come and have a look at Gladys.'

'But why so unofficial?' Jessica asked. 'What's wrong with just calling her regular doctor to come and check her over?'

'Because her regular doctor struck her off his list when she started proceedings against him five years ago, and no one else will touch her. It's Suzy or an ambulance, basically. I know Suzy slightly. She'll do as she's asked.'

'She'll get into trouble,' Jessica warned. 'This is not the way to do things at all.'

'We'll face that when we come to it,' said Gussie. 'Now, for reasons I needn't explain, I think it would be best if one of you went, rather than me.'

Thea found herself all too clearly imagining reasons why Gussie might not be welcome in certain Blockley homes. The woman exuded an aura of trouble and conflict and outspokenness, despite her gentle treatment of Granny Gardner. 'I'll go,' she said. 'Which house is it?'

Gussie gave directions, and Thea set out, muttering 'Suzy Collins' to herself as she went. She turned up the broad driveway of one of the houses in the quieter stretch of the High Street, before it disappeared into The Warren. She could hear loud female voices as she approached the house, pierced with sudden laughter. The meeting was clearly a lively one. The front door stood very slightly ajar, and she pushed it open.

There was a wide hallway, with a door off to the left, where the gathering was in full swing. A single voice was dominating the others: 'When Frank sees this, he'll think he's died and gone to heaven. And if he doesn't, then what the hell! I'll be OK on my own with one of these, won't I.'

'But how does it *work?*' came a different voice. 'I never thought I was naïve, but I really don't...'

'Just *feel* this silk,' sighed another.

Thea stood close to the open door, listening with growing alarm. She almost retreated without showing herself, until she remembered Granny's plight. The next ten seconds were spent reminding herself that she was as broad minded and sexually active

381

as any woman might expect to be at her age.

And then she walked straight into the Ann Summers Party.

CHAPTER NINETEEN

Nobody noticed her at first, and Thea had time to take in the scene before her. On one table an array of underwear was displayed – scarlet and black seemed to be the dominant colours. But much more compelling was the selection of objects laid out on the floor in the centre of a circle of women rather awkwardly kneeling, crouching, sitting and handling the things with little sign of inhibition.

Thea reminded herself again that there was no reason to disapprove of anything she was seeing. A healthy sex life was a highly desirable part of anyone's existence, and if some sensuality helped to keep it going, then so be it. The fact that the gadgets mostly appeared to be designed to bring pleasure to women whether or not a man was involved gave rise to social and moral questions that Thea was not tempted to go into at that point.

'Excuse me,' she said, quite loudly. 'Is Suzy Collins here?'

Even the discovery of a stranger in their midst did not appear to disconcert the gathering. 'Suzy?' said a woman close to Thea. 'Yes – that's her. Suzy! Somebody wants you.'

Suzy looked up and smiled. 'Oh?' she said. She was holding a device that included straps and a switch, which she had just activated. The women either side of her were screeching their amusement at the result. At the sight of Thea's face, Suzy got to her feet and went towards her, still holding the gadget.

The room fell silent as Thea embarked on her rehearsed speech. 'Could you please come and look at a friend of mine? I think she might have had a small stroke?'

It sounded both idiotic and impertinent as the words echoed in her own ears. Why bother a young woman at a party when there were proper services available at the end of a phone?

'A friend of yours? Who are you? How did you know I was here?' asked Suzy. She was very young, with curly black hair and a curvaceous body.

'It's only just down the street a few doors,' Thea urged her. 'I know it's a terrible imposition, but we thought it would be the quickest and easiest thing to do.'

'I haven't got anything with me. All I could do would be to look at her. And I'm not practising at the moment. I couldn't...'

Thea had managed to draw her out into the hall. In the doorway, Suzy had turned and lobbed the dildo at the nearest woman, who caught it deftly.

'We'd just like your advice, that's all. It's all a bit complicated, you see.' Thea was floundering. Whatever she had planned to say had deserted her.

'It sounds like something in the French Resistance,' Suzy smiled. 'Is your friend a spy, or a runaway criminal?'

'Well,' Thea began, habitually literal and wanting to be an honest as possible. 'Not really.'

'An illegal immigrant? An asylum seeker? Here in Blockley? Surely not!'

It was proving easier than Thea had feared to lead the young doctor to Granny's cottage. Something about the instinctive need to tend the sick, she supposed. Or perhaps it was sheer unadulterated curiosity.

'Good God, it's not Gladys Gardner, is it?' Suzy stared at the building as if it might be about to burst into flames. 'I might have known. You must be the Montgomerys' house-sitter. Bloody hell, I can't attend to her. I'd never hear the end of it.'

'Oh, please,' Thea begged. 'She really isn't very well. And she doesn't want to go to hospital. We didn't think we'd got much choice.'

'But how did you know about me? Who told you?'

The question was answered by Gussie's appearance at the door. 'Oh-oh,' said Suzy. 'Now I get it.' She seemed to have already accepted defeat and stepped into the cottage with a sigh.

The first difference Thea noticed was the absence of Jessica. 'She said she has to leave by two,' said Gussie. 'She has to be in Manchester at five.'

'Oh God, so she does,' Thea remembered. 'The last thing she needs is to get into more trouble.' She looked at her watch. 'That gives her ten minutes,' she realised with alarm.

The next change was Granny herself. Although her mouth was still crooked and her left arm dangled awkwardly over the edge of the sofa, the look in her eyes was a lot brighter. 'Feeling better?' Thea asked her.

The old woman nodded, and attempted a grin. 'Yerrth,' she mumbled.

Thea sat down on one of the armchairs, leaving plenty of space for the doctor to perform her examination. The avalanche of events, impressions, connections and worries accumulated over the past twenty-four hours or so was weighing her down. There was so much to think about, so many threads to keep hold of, so much still waiting to be faced. A multitude of unanswered questions thronged her mind. What about Upton and Icarus and Nick, for a start? Thea still hoped and believed that Julian's murder was associated with that muddled story, despite the stack of evidence against Gladys Gardner. The confirmatory exhibits at the photographic show needed to be properly processed, too. Had Jessica managed to explain what they'd seen to James? Was the entire police investigation now suspended because of some infuriating terrorism in Birmingham?

After two minutes of distracted thinking along such lines, Thea gave up and concentrated on the present moment. Suzy Collins was taking Granny's pulse, peering into her eyes, testing the muscle tone of the limbs on the left side. She seemed frustrated and unsure. 'I can't even listen to her heart without any equipment,' she complained. 'She's going to have to have a proper check-up.'

With some energy, the old woman shook her head on the cushion, in an emphatic rejection. 'Nononono,' she blathered. 'Talk, mutht talk. Hoollan. Killed Hoollan.'

But the old woman never got a chance to make what promised to be a deathbed confession. Jessica called hurried goodbyes, and as Thea stood at the front door waving to her departing daughter, she was approached by a pale thin woman in her late forties.

'Hello,' she said shyly. 'Are you the house-sitter? I'm afraid I don't know your name. Nick Jolly phoned me.'

Thea guessed instantly who she was. 'Yes, I'm the house-sitter,' she said. 'Thea Osborne. And you must be Frances, come to see your mother?'

The woman gave a curiously reluctant little nod. 'How is she?' she asked. 'It's a long time since I've seen her.'

Thea escorted the woman into the hallway of the Montgomerys' house, and detained her for a few moments. 'She isn't at all well,' she said. 'There's a doctor with her now. Why did Nick phone you? What did he say?'

'Um ... quite a lot, actually. I'm afraid he's very upset.'

Thea's head was throbbing with impressions, remembered remarks, suspicions, all jostling for urgent examination. 'I hope you don't mind, but I really need to ask you something,' she said. 'The police are likely to be here any time now–'

'They'll arrest her for murder, won't they?' Frances had a hand to her throat, her voice a breathy whisper.

'Did Nick tell you that?'

'In a way. They've read the will, you see. I didn't expect them to do it so soon ... but of course they'd need to find out what kind of funeral he wanted. I thought there might be more time.'

'Sorry,' said Thea. 'I have no idea what you're talking about.'

Frances gave her a confused look, which rapidly mutated into something sterner. 'No, of course you don't. But then, it isn't really your business, is it? I'm sure you've done a great job with the old lady, but really you needn't know all our family business, need you? I'd like to see her now, if it's all right with you.'

'But–' Thea wanted to know so much more, while accepting the reprimand for her curiosity.

With a hesitancy she could barely understand herself, she stood aside as Frances went through the connecting door. Instantly the newcomer was kneeling beside the old woman on the sofa, clutching her hand and repeating, 'Mum! Mum – it's me, Frances. Open your eyes and look at me.'

Thea and the doctor exchanged glances and by mutual consent withdrew to the side of the room, taking Gussie with them. Slowly, Mrs Gardner responded to the voice in her ear.

'Frances!' she sighed, when recognition dawned. A tear trickled down a lined old cheek. 'You're not to be here. Go, lovely, go away and hide.'

'Too late, Mum. I can't let them do it. It isn't right. And do you know – he's left it all to me, after all. I never thought he would. All but that stupid car. Nick can have that, and welcome.'

Granny Gardner gave a feeble smile and nodded. 'He loved you. I always said so.'

Frances looked at Suzy. 'Is she seriously ill? She looks as if she ought to be in hospital.'

Before the doctor could reply, Granny

gave a strange sighing gasp, and stretched her arms out stiffly along her body for a few seconds. Then she went limp, and the half-open eyes lost all focus.

The doctor rallied first and grabbed the limp left wrist. She put her ear close to the bony old chest. She raised the head and blew gently onto an open eye.

'My God, she's gone,' she said.

Nobody moved for half a minute, each waiting for one of the others to break the spell. Then Gussie stepped in front of Frances. 'Remember me?' she said. 'I knew you twenty years ago.'

But Frances was in no state for social exchanges. She knelt limply on the floor, clinging to her mother's frail hand. 'She can't be dead,' she pleaded, looking from the doctor to Thea and back. 'Tell me she isn't dead.'

Thea tightened her jaw with resolve. 'I'm dreadfully sorry,' she said. 'But really we need to clear a few things up before the police get here. And you...' she addressed Suzy '...you'll be in trouble if you don't contact someone right away, won't you?'

'I'm in trouble as it is,' said the doctor calmly. 'But yes, I need to make some calls. I'll go outside and do it.'

Gussie seemed at a loss. 'Poor old Glad,' she murmured. 'What a way to go.' Then she looked at Frances. 'Made it at the last minute, didn't you. She thought she'd never see you again.'

'She saw me on Sunday,' said Frances in a flat tone. 'When we killed Julian.'

That afternoon consisted of a medley of telephone calls, questions, people in and out, more questions. Both mobiles and the Montgomerys' landline were in constant use. Thea could almost feel the air crackling with all the words, real and electronic, flying to and fro. The police were summoned, the doctor quizzed, Gussie and Frances treated with bemused courtesy. Granny was taken away by two respectful men in dark suits, and Thea wept to see her go. But at the front of her mind, insisting and clamouring, was a string of questions for Frances. Why? How? But the more urgent necessity of dealing with Granny Gardner's death required that she hold her tongue for the time being.

Giles Stevenson put in an appearance, his shoulders sagging. 'Poor old love,' he sighed. 'But perhaps it was for the best. I did think, you know ... when she banged on my door on Sunday morning. So *manic*, you see. Not like herself at all...'

Thomas Sewell loitered self-effacingly on the pavement outside the house, until Thea went out to speak to him.

'Gladys dead? As well as Julian? Well, well, it's how he would have wanted it.'

Even Icarus Binns, his hair in disarray,

flitted back and forth past the front window. Thea went out to speak to him. 'The Granny lady breathed her last, is that the fact?'

Thea nodded.

'Ick has been a foolish boy,' he simpered. 'Got himself in shit with the trespassing rules. And bad boy Nick mobiled to say no more Box hunting. Whole thing a magical madness, he says.'

'So he didn't find anything – the day he dug up all that soil and drove it away in his van?'

Ick shrugged, and Thea pressed him. 'So why did he do that? Take away the soil?'

'Keeping the secret,' Ick hazarded. 'Not to give house-people the knowing about the digging work. Not so easy to hide.'

Still she couldn't let it go. 'He could have just put it back in the hole he'd dug,' she persisted.

Ick frowned doubtfully, but said nothing. Thea gave him a pitying look. 'If you ask me, he was going to keep on digging without you, but the accident made him think again. In any case,' she added, 'you can be sure there never was a box buried at Upton. The idea is ridiculous.'

Ick eyed her severely. Then his face relaxed and he heaved a sigh. 'Sad to think of the Granny lady departing this life so sudden.'

'I know. Anyway – it was good to meet you, and my daughter was thrilled. You were the bright spot in a difficult time.'

'Pretty policeman girl,' he sighed. 'Nice, sensible friend to Ick. Listen for her featuring in some songs, little while from now. And maybe mamma lady can understand more word relations.'

She gave him a grateful smile. 'Perhaps,' she nodded.

He reached out with a calloused finger and lightly touched her cheek. 'Living in a different world, world of pain and serious doing,' he half-sang. 'World where Ick can't manage, with the richness of its badness. Ick's a spirit can't breathe the air of worldy shit.'

She laughed at him. 'I believe you,' she said. 'Fly free, then and give my regards to Cleodie.'

He spun away, hair flying, fingers shaping an imaginary revolver shooting himself in the temple.

At last the opportunity came to speak privately to Frances. The police attention thus far had been restricted to the reappearance of Sergeant Tom and Ginger Eddie, who sighed and sympathised, and seemed genuinely sorry about the old woman's death.

'I want to make a statement about the killing of Julian Jolly,' Frances told them formally.

Suppressing his surprise, Tom nodded. 'I'll notify the plain clothes people,' he said.

'But do you mind if we give them another hour or so? It's total chaos across the whole region just at the moment, as you can imagine. You were lucky we managed to get here. It's only because we said we'd put in some overtime.'

Thea cocked an eyebrow at this, knowing that in time of such crisis, all personnel would be required to work extra hours in any case.

But it gave her some time with Frances, for which she was grateful.

'I know I have no right to ask – but do you mind just telling me a bit more of the story?' she pleaded.

Unemotionally, Frances gave the bare facts that Julian was her father. She had been born to Gladys Gardner in the early nineteen-sixties, when her mother was forty-seven and Julian in his early thirties. 'She bewitched him, according to the story, with her wicked past and sense of mischief. He was always a bit dry. And he was a useless father to me. I didn't even know about him until I was twenty-five.'

Thea murmured encouragement, eager to know more.

Julian had, it seemed, been prevented from openly acknowledging his daughter by his outraged wife. All his paternal attentions were devoted to his son Malcolm, father of Nick. Although they never lived together,

Frances's parents remained close, and by the time she was twelve, they were actually working in harness, while maintaining the secret of Frances's parentage. Hilda, Julian's wife, pretended to be unaware of the continuing relationship, sliding slowly into ill health and self-obsession.

'But why *kill* him?' Thea demanded. 'What did he do to deserve that?'

'Money, mainly,' came the calm reply. 'He told Yvette, quite casually last month, that he was changing his will and leaving everything to Nick. She wasted no time in gloating to me about it, I can tell you. Said I didn't deserve a penny, anyhow, the way I never came to see Mum. So I did come to see her, the moment my damned sister was out of the way. I didn't realise, you know, how much I hated him, until the moment was upon me. But he knew. He barely struggled after the first surprise in the living room.' Her eyes remained fixed on a patch of late sunlight slanting through the window. 'You know – I think he was worried about upsetting my mum by putting up any resistance. I think he loved her that much.'

'So – I mean, did she know what she was doing?' Thea was still having serious difficulty in imagining the scene.

Frances frowned helplessly. 'I don't know whether she did, right at the end. But when I turned up, it was as if she'd already known

I was coming, and had everything planned. She was fantastic with the buzzer and the door keys and all that. Mind you, she was always very sharp about locks and that sort of thing. I used to tease her that it was because of her time in prison.'

'But did she want Julian dead?' Thea was still lost.

'She thought it was what *he* wanted – and I think she might have been right there. He was ill and felt that most of his work had been a waste of time. And he missed his stupid wife more than Mum or I liked to admit.'

'I can't believe it,' argued Thea. 'I just can't.'

'Because you can't see beyond the sweet old lady, all pink and smiling and innocent,' Frances accused. 'She was never like that in the least. She was forgetful and confused at times, but she was always the same person. The woman who stabbed that doctor, who never flinched from getting her hands dirty or telling people the stark truth about themselves.'

'Yes,' said Thea slowly. 'I had started to realise that.'

Frances met her eyes. 'You knew she'd killed him?'

'My daughter was fairly convinced. But did she? I mean – which of you...?'

Frances seemed to shrink slightly, as if the

full import of her situation was beginning to dawn on her. 'Nobody will believe me, will they? And it doesn't much matter anyway. I've burnt all my bridges by coming back here so soon. But, for the record, since you seem to care so much – it was Mum. I held him down, and she did it. Then I dragged him into the kitchen, so nobody could see him from the street.'

'And the plan was to let her take the blame. To let you go scot free. So why come back today and blow it? She died knowing you'd ruined the whole plan.' Thea was accusing.

Frances sighed.

'I couldn't go through with it – couldn't see her in some ghastly prison. Somehow I thought they'd never really charge her. But Nick said – well, he persuaded me they would.'

'But you hadn't said anything before she died,' Thea remembered. 'You could just have kept quiet. You'd already told me to mind my own business. What changed?'

Frances wiped away a tear. 'The flowers,' she said. 'I saw the Mother's Day flowers on the table, with the card saying they were from me. I don't know who gave them to her, but it certainly wasn't me. It would never have crossed my mind.'

'So?' Thea was still painfully lost in the convolutions of the other woman's life.

'So, even though it was far too late to matter, I decided to be a decent daughter for once in my life, and face up to what I've done.'

'Oh.' Thea paused. 'But you got the money anyway. Julian hadn't changed his will. Wasn't it all for nothing?'

Frances gave an unbearable smile. 'That's right,' she said. 'But who's to say he wouldn't have got around to it in another day or two?'

'You won't be allowed to keep it now. Will you?'

'I won't be wanting it where I'm going. Will I?' said Frances.

The publishers hope that this book has given you enjoyable reading. Large Print Books are especially designed to be as easy to see and hold as possible. If you wish a complete list of our books please ask at your local library or write directly to:

Magna Large Print Books
Magna House, Long Preston,
Skipton, North Yorkshire.
BD23 4ND

This Large Print Book, for people
who cannot read normal print,
is published under the auspices of

THE ULVERSCROFT FOUNDATION

... we hope you have enjoyed this book.
Please think for a moment about those
who have worse eyesight than you ...
and are unable to even read or enjoy
Large Print without great difficulty.

You can help them by sending a
donation, large or small, to:

**The Ulverscroft Foundation,
1, The Green, Bradgate Road,
Anstey, Leicestershire, LE7 7FU,
England.**
or request a copy of our brochure for
more details.

The Foundation will use all donations
to assist those people who are visually
impaired and need special attention
with medical research, diagnosis
and treatment.

Thank you very much for your help.